W9-BBL-268

"BLACK MOUNTAIN BREAKDOWN
has a jaunty charm that is entirely infectious . . .
Reading it is a genuine pleasure!"

The Washington Star

**"OH LORD WHAT A FUNNY, SWEET,
DREAMY, PRECISE, SCARY BOOK . . .**
The closest thing to reading this would be reading
MADAME BOVARY while listening to Loretta Lynn
and watching 'Guiding Light.' The reason I bring up
'Guiding Light' is that I wish BLACK MOUNTAIN
BREAKDOWN came on every afternoon. But it's
going to come along only once."

Roy Blount, Jr.

"BLACK MOUNTAIN BREAKDOWN
is like a country song. It is true and real; it is loving
and sad; it has a country song's vividness, humor,
sorrow, and real-life power."

Annie Dillard

Black Mountain Breakdown

Lee Smith

BALLANTINE BOOKS • NEW YORK

"I'm Thinking Tonight of My Blue Eyes," by A. P. Carter Copyright 1929 and 1930 by Peer International Corporation. Copyrights renewed by Peer International Corportaion. Used by permission. All rights reserved.

Copyright © 1980 by Lee Smith

All rights reserved. This book, or parts thereof, must not be reproduced in any form without permission. Published in the United States by Ballantine Books, a division of Random House, Inc., New York, and simultaneously in Canada by Random House of Canada, Limited, Toronto, Canada

Library of Congress Catalog Card Number: 80-17993

ISBN 0-345-30125-0

This edition published by arrangement with
G. P. Putnam's Sons

Manufactured in the United States of America

First Ballantine Books Edition: January 1982

I have used the old family names, the actual place names, and some of the legends and history of Buchanan County, Virginia, in this novel. For much of this information, I am indebted to Nancy Virginia Baker's book, *Bountiful and Beautiful: A Bicentennial History of Buchanan County, Virginia, 1776–1976*, printed at the Buchanan County Vocational School; and to many items which have appeared over the years in *The Virginia Mountaineer*, especially the weekly "Lore and Legend" column by Sam Varney, Jr. In the latter portion of the novel, I use some direct quotations from the unpublished memoirs of my ancestor Charlotte Field, born in 1842 on the Eastern Shore of Virginia. All characters in this novel are entirely fictitious.

This novel is loosely based upon my story "Paralyzed: A True Story," which appeared in the Southern women's issue of *Southern Exposure*, spring 1977. Another portion of the novel appeared in the winter issue of the *Carolina Quarterly*.

I am indebted to Margaret Ketchum for her editing skills and constant encouragement.

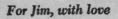

For Jim, with love

I

Now THE LIGHTNING BUGS come up from the mossy ground along the river bank, first one, then two together, more, hesitant at first, from the darkness gathered there already in the brush beneath the trees. Crystal sits and watches, holds her breath, the Mason jar beside her knee; if she looks down, she can't even see it now. She touches it with her finger and feels the glass with the letters raised and indecipherable in the dimness so that they could be anything, any words at all. They could be French. Suddenly out of the scrub grass at her knees comes rising a small pale flickering light, sickly unearthly yellowish green, fairy light. It is so close she can breathe on it and see the whirring, tiny wings. Crystal doesn't move. She could catch it, but she doesn't. Only her eyes move to follow the flight, erratic at first as if blown by wind although there is no wind in the hot still damp of early June on the river bank, then up into the dark branches, away and gone. Crystal can barely see the river on down the bank, barely hear it. She looks across the river bed now to the railroad track cut into the mountain which goes straight up on the other side, almost perpendicular, impenetrable, too steep for houses or even trails: Black Mountain. Its rocky top makes a jagged black hump across the sky and it is surprisingly light that far up in the sky, but the river bottom lies deep in the mountain's shadow and even in Crystal's yard now and in Agnes's yard next door and on Highway 460 in front of the house it is dark. Cars have got their lights on.

"You get any yet?"

Crystal jumps, even though she knows it's only Agnes, and, standing up, she knocks over her jar and has to bend down to get it.

3

"Come on," Agnes says. "I've been waiting for you over at the house. I thought that was what we said, after supper at my house. What are you doing out here anyway?" Even now, at twelve, Agnes has a flat and nasal, curious voice.

"I'm coming," Crystal says, pulling beggar-lice off the back of her shorts. She hates to leave the river. Beside it in the dark, she can think it is like her daddy told her it used to be, not flat and dried out and little, but big and wide and full of water. The Levisa River. With huge log rafts on it floating down through the mountains in spring and early summer to the sawmills in Catlettsburg, Kentucky. Sometimes men rode those logs all the way, Daddy said. In the 1920s. Just sitting and floating, it would take days, watching the land coming at you on either side like a dream, the green trees hanging into the water, not ever knowing what would be around a bend. Seeing animals, too. Daddy said these hills were full of animals then, all kinds. Maybe see a panther. And the water would be clear with fish in it. You could see straight to the bottom. Now the water is black because they wash coal in it upriver, at the Island Creek tipple at Vansant. And the coal dust sinks to the bottom and covers the rocks so they are black, too. The *real* black rock, the one Daddy said they named the town for, doesn't even exist anymore. It used to hang way out over a swimming hole near Hoot Owl and everybody jumped from it and two people drowned in that hole. But when the Norfolk and Western came through in the thirties and built the railroad, they blasted the rock into little bitty pieces and it fell into the river and was gone. Probably you could find a piece of it now, in the river by Hoot Owl, if you knew where to look.

"I'm going on." Agnes is mad. "I don't like it out here."

"Why not?" Crystal asks. She turns her head toward the yard, and Agnes, and sees that Agnes has already got a bunch of lightning bugs in her jar. Captive and pulsing, they cast a soft irregular glow like the twinkle lights last winter on her aunts' Christmas tree.

"Booger man might get us," Agnes says scornfully. She is not scared of any booger man herself, but she knows Crystal is or anyway she used to be. "I've got better things to do than stand out here in some old trees and get a cold." Agnes sounds like Lorene, Crystal's mother.

4

Agnes goes up the bank and Crystal follows, still picking off beggar-lice because she knows how mad her mother will get if she comes in with them still all over her shorts.

At the edge of the back yards Crystal can see their neighborhood all stretched out along the road. Lights shine at the back of every house, in the kitchens where the women are finishing up. Sometimes the black shadow of a woman's head crosses a kitchen window for a minute and then vanishes. Agnes's mama's shadow stays firmly there in her lighted square. That's where their sink is, by the window. In the front rooms, the televisions are on and the men are watching TV or reading the paper, tired. But not at her house. Crystal knows what's happening there. And sometimes she wishes she lived in one of these other houses, where probably some of the men have gone to sleep already, stretched out in reclining chairs. The Varney boys, Horn and Daris, who are older, have got a big light on in their driveway and they are out there working on a car. That's what they do all the time. Their yard is full of parts of cars. Still they are good boys: Horn was the quarterback last year at Black Rock High, and they are Eagle Scouts. Crystal would like to have the Varney boys for brothers, grease-stained and open and grinning all the time. Not like her own: Jules, who is so old she doesn't even know him, he's just thin and furious when he's home which is almost never now, off teaching in a college; or Sykes, plain ornery, her mother says, always up to something, so they sent him off to military school at Union Springs and that didn't do any good at all except to make him more secretive about what he's up to. Tomorrow he's going to summer school at VPI. Idly, Crystal wonders where he is now. His window is dark. But she doesn't really care. The way he treats her daddy, she will be glad when he's gone for good.

"Get that one," Agnes says. "Go on."

Crystal catches it and puts it into her jar and screws the top back on. It looks lonesome in there by itself and so she catches another one and then another and some more, and by then they are in Agnes's back yard by the clothesline, close enough to hear Jubal Thacker's daddy picking his guitar on his back porch beyond the Thackers' garden. He's doing "Wildwood Flower," Crystal realizes as she goes up the steps, doing it slow, with the music floating out soft and a little bit sad in the green June night across all the back yards.

I will laugh, I will sing, and my heart will be gay.

A light bulb hangs down low over Agnes's kitchen table and it makes Crystal blink. With her finger she traces a pattern on the red oilcloth and looks in the open door through the dining room which is almost never used and into the living room where the television is on and Agnes's family is sitting around.

Agnes's father, Hassell McClanahan, a fat red-faced man, is shining shoes. He runs the hardware store downtown and he has his shoes all spread out on newspaper on the floor. He bends down from the sofa over his belly to shine them. "Hello there, Crystal," he calls. He has a big smile and a big rough friendly voice, his customer smile and voice which he has used so much in the hardware store that they come natural now. Agnes's mama is fat, too. She is sewing something all the time. It is through her that Crystal is somehow related to Agnes, because Agnes's mama was a Hibbitts, but Crystal isn't sure how it works.

"You sure you don't want some?" Agnes says. "This is real good buttermilk."

"We just had supper before I came out," Crystal says.

"That was a long time ago. That was *hours*," Agnes says. As usual she is right.

Agnes puts a blue bowl on the table with a thick square of cornbread in it, then pours buttermilk over the cornbread and into the bowl. She gets a spoon and sits down to eat. Crystal is looking through a *Life* magazine that she got from a pile of magazines on one end of the big table. She stops at some pictures of Mexico.

"I'd like to go there," she says, pointing.

"Not me," declares Agnes. "You can't drink the water. Give you diarrhea all the time."

"Well," Crystal says.

"I want to go to Lookout Mountain, Tennessee," says Agnes's little sister Pauletta, who has recently changed her name to Babe, dancing in on the plastic runner which goes from the living room through the dining room to protect the beige wall-to-wall carpet. Babe, at ten, is a showoff and old for her age. But Crystal likes her. Babe is plump, too, but she has curly red hair and giggles a lot.

6

"What are you all fixed up for?" Agnes says, wiping her mouth.

"Mama doesn't care," says Babe. She is wearing dark-red lipstick and has used it on her cheeks too, for rouge, and over her T-shirt she has a long double strand of imitation pearls, one pink, one blue. "Watch this," she says. She does a tap dance step that she has seen on TV, which ends by Babe slapping her foot behind her back with her hand.

"That's pretty good," Crystal says.

"I know it," says Babe.

"Huh," Agnes says.

Babe gets a Coke from the refrigerator and shakes it up to make it fizz, then opens it and sticks the whole top into her mouth, so that some of the fizz runs down her chin and gets on the pearls.

"You all want to watch *The Dating Game?*" Babe asks.

"I don't think so," Crystal says. Now she is looking at pictures of California. "I've got to go home in a minute."

"You know who I'd like to have a date with?" Babe says. "Frankie AV-a-lon, that's who. See you around, clowns." She shakes up the Coke some more on her way back to the living room. Agnes's mama's head is bent and she sews.

Crystal laughs.

"What's so funny?" Agnes says.

"Pauletta. I mean Babe."

"If you had to live with her twenty-four hours every day you wouldn't think she's so funny," Agnes says, licking the back of her spoon. She takes the blue bowl over and puts it into the sink.

"Well, maybe," Crystal says.

Crystal and Agnes are almost exactly the same age, one month apart. Agnes was born at home, in the room upstairs which is her room still, but Crystal was born in the Clinch Valley Hospital in Richlands, Virginia, because her mother had to have a Caesarean. Crystal is blond and fair, with features so fine they don't look real sometimes; she looks like an old-fashioned painting of a girl, but the color comes and goes in her cheeks. Now, at twelve, she is thin and awkward, all bones and angles, but sometimes already people will stop and stare at her downtown. Crystal is not beautiful yet, but it is clear that she will be. The reason they stare is that already she looks so different. Her face is unusual here. She doesn't look like a Spangler, her father's people, or a Sykes, either one. She doesn't look like anybody else in Black Rock, and her eyes in particular are strange, a dark intense blue, dreaming and distant as she walks holding hands with her girl friends after school, always in a gaggle of girls, always somehow clearly separate among them. Agnes is there, too, these days, wherever Crystal is. Agnes is heavy and red-haired like any McClanahan, but her hair is curly and light-colored, sandy, and she has a broad flat nose ("nigger nose," Chester Lester taunts, although he has never seen a Negro in his life) and a small, pursed mouth. She is always elected treasurer of her class. Agnes can take care of herself, but she is not sure that Crystal can. Crystal seems to lack something, some hard thing inside her that Agnes and Babe were born with. Agnes watches out for Crystal, and they are best friends, of course. They do everything together. (Once Crystal got her foot stuck in the old cattle guard at the end of Agnes's driveway when they were walking up to the Esso station for a Milky Way, and Agnes put her own foot in and got it stuck there, too, until Mr. Thacker came out with a crowbar and pried them loose.)

Now Agnes and Crystal go out into the front yard and catch lightning bugs until they are tired of it and the jars are full, and then they sit together on the porch swing and put the jars on the little table before them, fantastic lanterns, while beyond the climbing clematis vine on the porch posts and beyond the little yard the traffic goes by on the road. They rock the swing. They sit out here a lot, because of the way things are over at Crystal's house.

If they want to talk they have to talk loud, over the noise of the traffic, because the road is not far from the front of these houses although the back yards are sizable, big enough for gardens, vast for children. And there is a lot of traffic: 460 is the only real road that runs through these mountains, going from Richlands, Virginia, up into the Black Rock area, following first the Dismal River and then the Levisa, winding and climbing up and then back down into Pikeville, Kentucky. There are other roads going up the hollers, some paved and some not, depending on how many people live up them. Houses everywhere are close to the roads because anything resembling flat land is so hard to come by, must be bulldozed out and created.

Crystal sees the map of this county in her mind; she has studied it in school. A ragged diamond shape. Heavily inhabited where it is inhabited, with people piled up all along the creeks while whole mountains and mountain-sides go empty and wild. Crystal rocks and thinks about the wild places, how it would be there. They say that the first man who ever settled in this county was a trapper named Stigner who lived in a big hollow tree up near the bend of Slate Creek. Of course it would not have been Slate Creek *then,* Crystal reminds herself. There was no coal and so there would have been no slate either, just a big creek without a name and a hollow tree there, cut out by lightning perhaps.

Crystal wonders who the people are in all these cars and trucks and where in the world they are going. The traffic puts her in a kind of a trance. She watches it sometimes for hours. Sometimes the same cars go up and down, up and down, until she wonders what they're looking for. Sometimes she sees a car from out of state. Now all she can see is their lights, flashing out into the night when they come around the curve by the Esso station, then beamed again on the road through their neighborhood, headed downtown. A lot of times cars rattle when they hit the hole in the road in front of Agnes's house. Now something clanks on the side of the road.

"What's that?" Crystal says.

"Beer can," says Agnes.

Crystal stretches. She was almost asleep in the swing. Summer rolls out in front of her as far as that road goes; fall, and junior high school, seem far, far away. Already this summer Crystal has read *Scaramouche.* Right now she is reading *Quo Vadis.*

"Who's that?" Agnes asks. Agnes can't see very well in the dark, but Crystal has cat eyes. A couple walks up the side of the road toward the Esso station, holding hands.

"Pearl Deskins," Crystal whispers, "and some boy."

"Who is it?"

"I don't know," Crystal whispers back. "I can't see him

9

real good, but I probably wouldn't know him anyway. He looks a whole lot older to me."

The traffic has slacked off now, and for a minute no car comes. Pearl Deskins and the boy are like shadows without bodies, walking. They stop to light cigarettes and when the match flares up, Crystal sees momentarily Pearl's thin, feral face, black eyes, her red mouth.

"I wish you'd look at that!" Agnes says. *"Smoking!"*

Pearl Deskins lives in a trailer up by the Esso station. She is only two years older than Agnes and Crystal, but it seems like ten years to them. Pearl is thin, but her breasts poke out like hard little rocks through the tight little sweaters she wears, and she was on the Absentee Hot List last year for skipping school so much. Crystal is sure that Pearl doesn't even know their names. Pearl is wild and mysterious; Crystal wonders where she goes and what she does with boys.

"She's got an awful reputation," Agnes says.

"I know it," Crystal answers. A thrill shoots through her and makes her tremble inside; to hide it, she stretches again.

"You remember what we said," says Agnes, "in the club."

"I know it," Crystal says again, and thinks how they cut their fingers and mixed their blood and said they would be best friends always and have nothing ever to do with boys.

Pearl giggles and the sound floats back at them over the neighborhood. Crystal shivers. Jubal Thacker's daddy has quit picking and gone to bed. Fluorescent arc lights go on up at the Esso station, past the Presbyterian church. They think you're born saved or damned already, Presbyterians do. Chester Lester's house is all dark, too, although Crystal can't imagine he's gone to bed yet. He's too mean to sleep. Chester Lester has got something wrong with him, she knows. Once he threw lighted matches at her and Agnes and another time he had a kitchen knife and made them pull down their pants for him to see. Still another time, Chester Lester tied Crystal up to a sycamore tree in the Raineses' yard and put frogs on her. That's why she hates them so much now. The Varney boys have gone off in one of their cars making a racket as usual. Nancy Shortridge, who is visiting her grandmother several houses down, has gone to Bristol today to get her braces adjusted and she won't be back until tomorrow. Crystal is jealous of Nancy for getting to stay in a motel. Agnes is jealous of Nancy for existing, for ever coming to stay with her grandmother at all. Crystal always wants to ask Nancy to be in their games.

"Where's Jubal?" Crystal asks. Sometimes he plays with them, too. Jubal is skinny and tousle-headed and small; Agnes can beat him at any game. He has a wide sweet smile and sometimes he gets so tickled that he will roll over and over laughing.

"Don't you remember?" Agnes sits up and jerks the swing. Sometimes she gets so exasperated with Crystal.

"Remember what?" Crystal says.

"He's gone to Bible camp."

"Oh yeah," says Crystal. "Well. He can have it," she says after a minute. "You couldn't pay me to go there."

"You don't have to be so ugly about it if you never have been there yourself," Agnes says. She is very righteous. "It might be fun."

"Not *Baptist*," Crystal says.

"You'll be sorry," Agnes warns her. She is quite serious. Agnes is a Baptist, too, but of course her daddy is a businessman and so they are not hard-shell Baptists like the Thackers are. Crystal's mother is a Methodist, but Crystal is not anything; her daddy is not anything, either. Crystal is surprisingly firm on this point, which worries Agnes a lot. What kind of a heaven will it be, if Crystal can't even get one foot inside the gate?

"Ag-*nes?*" Agnes's mama calls her from inside the screen door, going up on the last syllable like she always does. Agnes's mama has a tired, pretty voice.

"I'm coming in a minute, Mama. I'm going to walk Crystal home."

Crystal picks up her jar and they go down the concrete front steps and across the grass to Crystal's house, not more than thirty yards away.

"Why don't you come in for a minute?" Crystal says.

By habit they walk around back, knowing without even thinking about it that the front door will be locked, and go into the kitchen-dinette area, as Crystal's mother calls it.

"Don't slam the door," Lorene says when they open it.

11

"Hi, Agnes, come on in," she adds. Lorene looks at the lightning bug jar in Crystal's hands. "Not more of *those!*" she says.

Lorene can't understand how her own daughter could enjoy staying out in the dark night fooling with bugs. Or how she could have a best friend like Agnes. Why, Crystal is almost big enough to start dating! And Lorene can't even get her to roll up her hair. Lorene's own hair is rolled up right now, in pink plastic curlers with snap-on tops. Neva, her sister who is a beautician, came over and did it right after supper and told Lorene all the news she heard that day at the beauty shop.

"Is Daddy still up?" Crystal says.

"How should I know?" snaps Lorene. "I've got better things to do than sit around in there in the dark."

"Crystal honey?" He has heard her voice; he is calling her from the front room.

"Come on," Crystal says. Agnes gets a saltine from the box on the table, cuts herself a slice of Velveeta from the foil-wrapped brick of it lying there, and follows Crystal through the house.

Lorene shakes her head. Then she spreads her hands out on the table and looks at them. Neva gave her a manicure too, while she was over here, and they are trying out a new shade: Florida Rose. It looks good. Lorene wishes she had some lipstick the same color, to match; probably Neva could order her some. Lorene fixes herself another cup of coffee and turns back to the TV, where Perry Mason is trying to solve a mystery about a rich beautiful heiress who is receiving murder threats. Lorene thinks she has solved it already; she thinks the heiress is doing it to herself, to get attention. Lorene smiles after the commercial, when Perry begins to realize this, too. She would have made a good detective, she thinks, or a psychiatrist. She can always tell what makes somebody tick. Nearing fifty now, Lorene is still a blond, strong woman, running to fat maybe, but she keeps herself up, wears heels when she goes to town. "I may not be a lady," she says, "but by God I'll dress like one." Although she has been married to Grant Spangler for nearly thirty years, she's still more Sykes than Spangler. She has never lost that hustle which brought him to her in the first place like a pale summer moth to a porch light, that same hustle all the Sykeses

12

have, which enabled old man Sykes, for instance— Lorene's father—to turn a junk business into a car dealership and invent a rivet that would give every one of them a guaranteed income for the rest of their lives. And the rivet money is in Lorene's name, not Grant's. She thinks about her rivet money downtown in the bank, accumulating interest. Lorene has a passbook savings account and a part interest in Neva's Clip-N-Curl. She's no fool, which is a good thing, since she is married to one.

Of course it irritates her the way things have turned out, and it especially gets her the way Grant just lies there in her front room with the Venetian blinds drawn so that he doesn't know sometimes if it's night or day and she can't even get in there to vacuum. But this has come about slowly, over a period of years, so she is accustomed to it now. His removal to the front room was so gradual as to be almost imperceptible, a slow receding from life, and her own move to the back of the house was just as gradual. Lorene does not complain. She may have married Grant because he was a Spangler, but even now that his father's Little Emma mine has failed, even if she could have seen ahead somehow through all the years to this time and this year, Lorene is not sure she would have done anything different. She takes pride in the fact that she has never said a word against him to anyone, has never mentioned his drinking to anybody, not even to her brother Garnett when he has come around hinting at it.

At least Lorene ~~she has~~ the child of her old age, the joy of her heart. When Crystal was born, she quit hollering at Grant and trying to change things, fixed up her kitchen and grew philosophical, centering herself firmly in the child. Maybe it was because Crystal was a Caesarean baby and didn't get all pushed and pulled and wrinkled coming through the tubes, but Lorene thought when she first saw her that she had never, never seen a more beautiful child. Lorene named her the prettiest name she could think of, Crystal Renée. Lorene thinks of the little dresses she used to dress Crystal in, and the little white shoes with straps. Crystal will grow up to be somebody; Lorene will see to that. Crystal will go to a fine school on that rivet money. She will marry a doctor. But whatever she does, she will be somebody special, because Lorene is raising her that way. Of course Grant has a

13

bad influence on Crystal, but Lorene ignores it, as she ignores everything she can't change. Lorene deals with her problems by rising above them. Now she stares at the closed door and drums her rosy nails for a minute on the tabletop. Then she switches the channels to see what else might be on TV.

Behind the door is another room, another world almost. Here where Grant stays, even the air seems denser and different somehow. It smells like old smoke, like liquor, like Grant himself, yet the combination is not unpleasant really and Crystal loves it. The room is shadowy now, the only light coming from a floor lamp in the corner by the armchair, but even this light must have been too bright and so a blue shirt, or a piece of a shirt, has been thrown carelessly over the shade. This creates an irregular spread of light and a jagged shadow in the far corner of the room. Clearly this was Lorene's best room once, her parlor. There is a gold sunburst clock above the mantel, no longer running. The artificial logs in the fireplace have fallen off their wrought-iron stand. The furniture is mostly a French Provincial living-room set, with shiny off-white brocaded upholstery: a sofa and three matching chairs. Now the brocade is dirty and some stuffing sticks out from the arm of the chair by the door. A squatty coffee table sprawls at a rakish angle before the sofa, only its gold claw feet protruding from the papers and books jumbled high on its top and spilling over ▮▮▮▮▮▮▮▮▮▮ Other books are stacked about the room, ▮▮▮▮▮▮▮▮ piles of clothing in the corners. The fancy gold drapes hang limp and open, but the Venetian blinds behind them are shut tight, a flat gray dusty expanse on the wall by the locked front door.

Grant is reading poetry to the girls. He half sits, half lies in the armchair so that the light falls on his thin dog-eared book, *One Hundred and One Famous Poems*. Crystal sits close to him on the floor, holding on to his knee under the old blue silk robe he always wears. She is careful not to knock over the glass on the floor by his chair. Agnes is stretched out full length facing them with her chin on her fists, her plump bottom sticking straight up.

    " 'Abou Ben Adhem (may his tribe increase!)
    Awoke one night from a deep dream of peace . . .' "

Grant begins, his voice gaining strength as he goes on, until it is as rich and full again as it used to be back when people said he ought to make a preacher—how he laughed at them—or a courtroom lawyer at least.

> " 'And saw within the moonlight in the room,
> Making it rich and like a lily in bloom,
> An angel writing in a book of gold . . .' "

Now Grant is into it fully, the cadenced rhythms, the rise and dip and fall of the lines, and his voice drops nearly to a whisper and then comes out strong and loud and resonant as he gestures grandly with the book and waves it in the air, going mostly from memory and rising to his fullest power on *"Lo!* Ben Adhem's name led all the rest!" The final word of the poem echoes in the room and the giant shadow of the book and Grant's arm on the opposite wall disappears as his arm drops back to his lap and he sinks again, spent, into the battered chair. Grant laughs to break the silence.

"Oh, I love that one," Crystal says. Her face is turned up to her father and she is smiling. He reaches down to touch her hair.

"How do you like that one, Agnes?" Grant asks. He has to smile when he looks down at the great hulking spread of Agnes there on the floor.

"Not much," Agnes says. She is always truthful. Grant laughs again and e has Crystal,

"Do the raven," Agnes says. It's the only one she really likes.

"No, no, don't do that one!" Crystal sits up, her heart beating fast. "Please don't do that one. Do the daffodils."

"I hate the daffodils," says Agnes.

"Well," says Grant, thumbing through the book, "How about 'I Have a Rendez-vous with Death'?"

"No, no." Crystal shakes her head until the fine blond hair swirls across her face. "That's too sad. Don't do that one."

Grant looks through the book and the girls wait. Agnes is not much for poetry, but Crystal loves it, and Agnes will do what Crystal does.

"Here we go." Always the showman, Grant smooths the book with a flourish. He pushes his glasses, which

15

have gotten too big for him now, up higher on his hawk nose, clears his throat, and begins:

> "The little toy dog is covered with dust,
> But sturdy and stanch he stands;
> And the little toy soldier is red with rust,
> And his musket moulds in his hands."

"No, no!" Crystal is almost sobbing. "Don't do that one, don't do that one, Daddy!" She pounds on his knee with her fist.

Grant grins at her, a surprisingly incongruous mischievous grin in his sick wrecked face. He raises his voice and continues over Crystal's pleas.

> " 'Now don't you go 'til I come,' he said,
> 'And don't you make any noise.' "

"Oh, oh," Crystal says, but it's hard to tell by the tone of her voice whether she's delighted or upset—intense emotion all unfocused—and her usually dreaming face is wholly alive.

Grant's voice goes soft as she hushes, and he reads the part about the toys standing faithful to Little Boy Blue through all the long ensuing years. Grant almost whispers the last lines.

> " 'And they wonder, as waiting these long years
>   through,
>   In the dust of that little chair,
> What has become of our Little Boy Blue
>   Since he kissed them and put them there.' "

Crystal bursts into huge racking sobs as she hugs her father's knees, and the tears run down her cheeks. "I can't stand it," she cries. "Oh, it's the saddest thing!"

"Don't cry, Crystal," Agnes directs from the floor, but Crystal doesn't even hear her, her face pressed tight into the old blue silk.

Grant is smoothing his daughter's hair.

"He died, didn't he?" Crystal sobs. "The one that put them there."

Agnes grows uncomfortable and begins to pick at her face.

"I think that's enough for tonight," Grant says, taking a drink from his glass and closing the book of poems.

"No, no," Crystal nearly screams. "Do the spider and the fly."

"You know you don't like that one," Agnes says. "That scares you to death every time."

"Do it, do it," Crystal begs. Crystal wipes at her eyes with her fist. She has stopped crying now, but her eyes are dark and liquid and she has bright patches of color along her cheeks. "Please do it, Daddy."

"I don't see what you want to hear it for if you know you're going to get scared," Agnes says. "I think that's dumb."

Grant smiles. He picks up the book from the floor. "Ready?" he asks.

Crystal bobs her head up and down. Agnes nods reluctantly.

Grant makes his voice deep and full of cunning malice as he begins,

> " 'Will you walk into my parlor?' said the spider
>   to the fly;
> ' 'Tis the prettiest little parlor that ever you did
>   spy.' "

When the fly answers, Grant's voice is high and innocent.

> " 'O no, no,' said the little fly, 'for I've often heard it
>   said
> They *never never wake* again, who sleep upon your
>   bed."

Unconscious of what she's doing, Crystal twists the hem of her father's robe into a hard tight ball and bites it. Grant goes on and the spider tempts the silly fly with flattery until the fly has lost all caution and the spider drags her up to his dreary den. Grant's tone is gravely serious as he reads the moral lesson at the end.

> 'And now, dear little children, who may this story
>   read,

17

To idle, silly, flattering words, I pray you ne'er give
  heed;
Unto an evil counselor close heart, and ear, and eye,
And take a lesson from this tale of the Spider and
  the Fly."

Crystal shivers and lets all her breath out in one long
shuddering sigh.

"You ought to be ashamed of yourself!" Lorene flings
the door open and stands in silhouette as the kitchen light
streams in behind her. Everybody blinks. "Scaring little
girls like that! I don't know what gets into you. Look at
Crystal Renée, now she's all wrought up, see what you've
done, she probably won't go to sleep for a week. Agnes,
it's time to go home. I just heard your mama call. Crystal,
come on. It's bedtime. You ought to be ashamed of yourself," Lorene says again to Grant, who chuckles way back
in his chair.

"I'll see you in the morning," Agnes says, but Crystal
feels dazed and only nods as Agnes leaves.

"Good night, pumpkin," Grant says.

"Good night, Daddy," Crystal tells him, leaning over
the chair to kiss the top of his head before she follows her
mother out.

"Good night, Mama," Crystal says and kisses her too
and takes the jar of lightning bugs with her up the stairs,
leaving Lorene alone in the kitchen to wrap up the Velveeta and put it back into the refrigerator, turn off the
TV, wipe off her countertops with a damp rag. That done,
Lorene goes to the door and pushes it open and sticks her
head in.

"You want anything?" she asks her husband. "I'm fixing to go to bed."

There is no answer from the room.

"Grant?" she says more sharply. "Do you want anything? I'm fixing to go up now."

"Nothing, honey, thank you," Grant says from his
chair. "Good night."

Lorene closes the door and goes up the stairs to bed.
Grant sleeps in the front room, on the sofa or sometimes
in his chair, sometimes passed out and other times sleep-
less so that he wanders the house after the rest of them
have gone to sleep. Lorene knows that Odell, Grant's bas-

tard half brother, buys the liquor for him and brings it when he comes, but she never sees it and usually she never sees Odell either, since he comes late when she is asleep or while she's gone to church or prayer meeting. When Lorene does see Odell, he holds his Caterpillar hat in his hands and mumbles down into the floor. He acts more like an animal than a man. But even if Odell isn't smart, he is a hard worker, they say, and it wasn't his fault they lost the mine. Lorene wonders where Sykes is now. She peers out the window at the highway when she pulls the blinds.

All up and down the bottom it is dark except for the lights from an occasional car or truck on the road and the arc lights at the Esso station, which will be open all night, catering to truckers and men on the graveyard shift in the mines. If you go back up the road away from the town of Black Rock toward Richlands, after five or six miles you leave the Levisa River bottom and go into the Dismal River bottom and start climbing, following 460 up and up until you reach the bend of Dismal where the coke ovens are, nearly eight hundred of them, roaring and sending up smoke and red fire into the night. The coke ovens stretch in irregular lines along the Dismal River and then up the steep slopes too, above the railroad track, and the sight of them is awesome, as vast and red and terrible as hell itself. The trees on the mountains around the coke ovens have long since died, their blackened shapes like ghosts of trees on the blackened hills. This is where the high-school students come to make out, parked along the old mine road off 460 above the bend where they have the best view.

"Last year a seventeen-year-old boy fell down in one of them right there and they never did get him out or even find anything of him left. It was his second day on the job," Sykes Spangler says, rubbing the breasts of the girl he is with, Marie Hicks.

"Lord, that's awful," Marie says, turned to him, her face red and black, shadowed and fiery, close to his own.

And Lorene pulls the window down against the cool night air, goes over to her dresser and applies some astringent. Directly below her, Grant sleeps already in his chair. His arm dangles over the side, fingers open and limp hanging down. Crystal lies flat on her back in her

19

bed, while the jar of lightning bugs blinks softly on her dresser. Crystal listens to all the creaking sounds of her house, Grant's low rattling snore from downstairs, her mother clicking bottles together, then flushing the toilet, then the bedsprings creaking, a truck now and then on the road, the frogs singing rivets up from the river, loud and full through her open window which faces the river and Black Mountain out to the back. *Come into my parlor said the spider to the fly.* Crystal shivers and pulls the sheet up tight to her chin. *It's the prettiest little parlor that ever you did spy.* The jar of lightning bugs casts a soft, weird, flickering light on the wallpaper and Crystal watches it until she falls asleep.

Lorene works in the kitchen while Sykes loads his car. She opens the refrigerator door, throws out leftovers, waters the African violets on the windowsill—but this is nothing, make-work, to take her mind off the fact which she cannot get it off of today: Sykes's leaving. When the clock radio woke her up this morning it came into her mind first thing, Sykes is leaving. Lorene wears black polyester pants, a black-and-white sleeveless overblouse which looks like silk, black sandals. Her broad toenails are painted Florida Rose. Somehow Lorene has wanted to look extra nice today, leave a memory, sensing perhaps that nothing will ever impress itself much on Sykes.

Sykes staggers up and down the stairs and out the kitchen door carrying load after load. Lorene doesn't say a word about the flies. Sykes is packing his record player, a radio, records, his weights, clothes, everything. There has never been much of him here, and now nothing at all will be left. Sykes wears a cowboy hat and khaki pants. His chest and back muscles bulge as he carries the things. Lorene, seeing him now in this new going-away light more clearly than before, looks at him hard, tries to memorize his body. The muscles astonish her. What has he been building himself up for?

Sykes has let his hair grow out of the flat top he wore for years. It comes a little below his ears, black and straight, the way Grant's used to be. He looks like a pirate or an outlaw. Girls are crazy about him. He also looks a lot like his father. Sykes has black eyes which are a little off center. They never quite focus on anything at the same time, but the doctors have said there is nothing really wrong with them. He has Grant's hawk nose and a wide mouth which wears, when he wants it to, a lopsided irresistible grin.

Finally he gets the car loaded, his blue Buick Sprint. Sykes totaled two cars before they sent him off to military school at Union Springs, where he couldn't have one at all. Lorene remembers going to meet him at the train station in Bluefield the first time he came home from there, seeing Sykes in dark glasses come tapping with a cane down the steps of the train with a German shepherd dog on a leash. Why, she almost had heart failure! A blind boy for a son! But it was only Sykes pretending, so he could bring that dog home on the train. And then she had to keep it for him when he went back to school, until it was hit by a coal truck. Out the window Lorene sees Sykes slam down the trunk of his car and start back toward the house. She feels funny, a hot flash.

"I think you ought to put on a shirt," she says.

"Oh Mama." Sykes grins at her.

"Well, you can't just go off to college like that."

"Mama, it's only summer school. I'm not even going to live in a dorm."

Lorene has misgivings about that too. "Well," she says, "it just doesn't look good to go without a shirt. You know what I mean."

Sykes goes and gets a blue shirt and puts it on to end the argument. He can always take it off later in the car.

Coming back down, he sneaks up behind Lorene and grabs her. "Gotcha!" he says.

"Oh Sykes, don't do that, for goodness' sakes, you scared me to death!" But Lorene is not angry at all. It's hard to be angry with Sykes, who does what he wants to and leaves everyone else alone, sliding through Lorene's hands like something with grease on it so that there's nothing for her to grab onto.

"Let me pack you a lunch," she says.

"Mama, come on. I've got to get on the road. You haven't packed me a lunch in ten years."

"Oh." Lorene is silent. Has it really been that long? But Sykes has grown up in the houses of his friends, in poolhalls, off hunting, at the drag strip at Cedar Bluff, everywhere but here.

"You study, now," she says brightly. "You know you'll have to study, Sykes."

"Oh sure, Mama." He grins so big that Lorene can't tell if he will or not. If he does, it'll be the first time.

"I'll see you, Mama," says Sykes. "I'll call you up Sunday night."

"You'll have to tell Crystal goodbye," says Lorene.

"Where is she?" Sykes shifts from foot to foot, annoyed.

"Over at Nancy's, I think."

"Well, you tell her for me, Mama," Sykes says. "I've got to go."

"Your father," Lorene says. "You'll have to tell your father goodbye."

"He won't even know whether I tell him or not."

"He might," Lorene says. "You never know."

"I'm in a hurry," Sykes says. "I told Bobby I'd pick him up at noon in Richlands, and it's twelve-thirty already."

"Go tell your father goodbye."

Sykes gives her a look she knows very well, the look which means that Sykes won't do anything he doesn't want to do, ever, that he is doing this only to humor her, and goes into the closed front room. In a minute he's back out.

"Well?" she asks.

"Well what? I'll call you Sunday night."

"I've got some tuna salad," Lorene says.

"Mama." Sykes gives her a big hug and then he's gone, spinning out in the loose gravel at the end of the drive.

Sykes has left Grant's door open, and when she goes to close it Lorene sees Grant sitting straight up in his chair.

"Honey?" he says, rasping out the word. "Honey?" but it isn't clear who he's calling. Maybe her but more likely Crystal; he wants Crystal all the time now. Lorene shuts the door before he has a chance to see her.

Then, since nobody else is there, Lorene sits down at the kitchen table and cries. "Honey?" Grant calls again, several times, behind the door. It's so hard, Lorene thinks. So hard. Like Jules, for instance. Neva always swears if they hadn't named him Jules he wouldn't have turned out like he has, wouldn't have been born so quiet and smart with his eyes set only on distance, always horsing to leave. But then Sykes doesn't act like a Sykes, is neither industrious nor practical. In fact Sykes acts kind of crazy, and Lorene doesn't know what will become of him, what he will do with this life she and Grant have given him which he doesn't much want anyhow, to judge from the daredevil things he does. She remembers in seventh grade when he blew himself up with gunpowder, one hand a red pulpy mess bleeding into the towel while they drove him to the Clinch Valley Clinic at Richlands, Grant taking the curves so fast. But Lorene can't remember a time when Sykes wasn't into some kind of trouble. Even when he was in the nursery-school Bible class at church, that little, he took things. Stole the snake out of the handmade Garden of Eden set that Mr. Pritchard had carved for the church. Everybody was looking for it at church and then one day at home Lorene found it, when she was cleaning under Sykes's bed. It's a gun, Sykes had said, pointing the carved wooden snake at her head. And Sykes used to wiggle so much when he was little. He wouldn't sit still for anything, wouldn't mind at all. Jules always minded and Lorene didn't know what to do with Sykes. From the time he opened the door he was gone.

Lorene remembers a time three years ago when Sykes was fifteen and the river flooded, the big flood of '55. Sykes got into somebody's boat and rode the flood from Little Prater all the way downtown where people were lined up all across the bridge and along the river to see him. Somebody had called Lorene and she went, too, nervous inside, embarrassed at the crowd on the bridge. When Sykes came around the bend, grinning and waving from the bucking boat in the middle of the brown swirling flood, she had to laugh and cheer with the rest of them. It was so outrageous to ride a flood. But Sykes was like that, and of course he wrecked that boat.

She hopes he will study, but she doubts it; it's her rivet money he's going on, of course. Like a lot of people around Black Rock who never had one, Lorene has great faith in the power of what she calls a "good education," not realizing yet that the children you work so hard to send out will probably never come back, or will come back all changed and ashamed of you, with new ideas of their own. Jules was already different before he left, so his is not a case in point. Anyway, Lorene is proud of that big degree of his even if he has been known to hang up the phone when she calls. Sykes and Crystal will have one, too: a good education. VPI was the only place Sykes could get into, but you can't ever tell. He might take to it yet. Every cloud has a silver lining, Lorene reminds herself. Faith can move mountains. But probably Neva is right and there's only so much you can do with a boy.

When Sykes got a new toy, the first thing he'd do was try to take it apart. But when Crystal got one, she held it up to the light and turned it this way and that. Lorene feels completely lost in her kitchen with Sykes gone and Crystal off playing at Nancy's; for a minute it's as if she never had children at all. I could be a registered nurse, she thinks. I could start a little dress shop downtown. But then Lorene sits straight up, thinking of Garnett's sermon last week about the little house by the side of the road. She shakes her head slowly and decisively back and forth, like a swimmer coming up from under the water. It's not noon yet. She has things to do. And anyway she's not through with Crystal; Crystal is still at home.

One Sunday Crystal goes up to spend the night with her aunt Nora Green and her aunt Grace Green Hibbitts (who are her great-aunts, actually) and her uncle Devere Spangler, up at the old Spangler home place on Dry Fork of Six-and-Twenty-Mile Branch. Crystal visits them often and Lorene doesn't mind her going. Lorene has always gotten along fine with Grant's family, much better than Grant ever did. Crystal loves to go up there, but she hates it a little bit too, and the same lump comes up in her throat every time they round that last bend, the curve where the Halloways' grocery store is. Crystal and Lorene bounce in the front seat of Lorene's white Pontiac, and Crystal's overnight bag bounces by itself in the back. The road grows narrower and narrower. Every time Lorene hits the shoulder, she raises a cloud of dust which hangs in the air until they are gone around the next curve and Crystal can't see it anymore.

"This road is getting awful," Lorene remarks, impersonal behind her sunglasses. "I hope they fix it before winter comes." Lorene always heralds the approach of any new season as if it were a person: "Spring is late this year" or "Fall is on the way." Crystal sits still and looks while the road climbs up closer and closer to the West Virginia line and they drive it, steep dusty green mountainside on their left and then a sheer drop down into Dry Fork Creek on the right. The big gray stone gates rise up ahead, anachronistic, a monument to her grandfather's colossal vanity. It's like entering a book. LITTLE EMMA MINING CO. is engraved on the smooth stone in the center of the arch. Lorene turns off the main road and drives under the arch.

Crystal tries to imagine it as it was once, in the thirties maybe, when her grandfather Iradell Spangler was living out his vision of grandeur here and running things in his crazy, flamboyant fashion, and the two tipples were operating around the clock and they were bringing coal out of the big drift mine at the Little Emma and all the other shafts that went out from it and shot through the mountain until it was like a honeycomb under there. That whole opposite hillside was full of identical green wooden houses where the miners lived with their families, and on that side too was the company store. Crystal has heard them talk about Iradell and how he wouldn't let the union in and wouldn't modernize his mine, how he himself perversely engineered the long fall of the Little Emma, which was finished finally sometime after his death. Now the company houses that are left are crumbling, and vines grow up through their floors. One tipple has caved in and the other is ready to go. Long since, Odell sold the machinery and scrapped the company store and most of the houses for lumber, so that everywhere up this holler there are half-overgrown roads leading noplace, pieces of falling-down structures, and POSTED and NO TRESPASSING signs tacked up to tree after tree. Lorene drives past the family graveyard on the left, where Little Emma herself, Crystal's grandmother, lies beneath the columned monstrosity, a little Greek temple of sorts, which Iradell had constructed there. One truck mine still operates, and a coal truck comes rumbling now from a road to their right and passes them, the dusty-faced driver waving his hand. *Tennessee Nights* is the name stenciled across the top of the bed of the truck.

"Who is that?" Crystal asks.

"One of Odell's people, Johnny Goff probably," Lorene answers absently, negotiating a pothole in the road. Crystal knows that Odell, Iradell's illegitimate son by Mae Peacock, lives alone in a little house up that road, and a bunch of redheaded Goffs live up there, too. But Crystal has never been there. They are close enough now so that Crystal can hear Devere's dogs barking, and then Lorene brakes to a stop by the tin mailbox.

"Here, honey," Lorene says, getting out to open the mailbox, "take this to your aunt Nora, it's still here from yesterday." She puts a pile of mail into Crystal's left hand and her overnight bag in the other hand and gives her a kiss on the cheek. "I can't come in!" Lorene calls before anybody has a chance to ask her, waving to Nora, who has appeared at the door. Then Lorene jumps back into the car and pulls out in a cloud of dust, already late for a meeting.

"Law, honey, I'm glad to see you," Aunt Nora calls, stepping outside the screen door and wiping her face with her apron. "Shoo!" she says, flapping her apron back down at the chickens which come pecking around at her feet. "Shoo, now, I ain't got nothing for you."

"Here's your mail," Crystal says, giving it to her, glancing down once at the little booklet on the top of the pile; it is named *So You Sew!* Grace must have ordered it. Grace is always sending off for things.

Aunt Nora smothers Crystal, pressing her into her giant bosom, then pushes her back out to arm's length and looks at her. "Getting prettier every day," she says. "You look a little peaked, though. Come on in, we're waiting dinner on you." She pushes Crystal across the porch and into the old frame house where the air is cool even in August. The Spangler house is built in the old style, with a breezeway going straight through it from the front door to the back, four high square symmetrical rooms on the first floor, four identical ones above. The furniture, once considered very grand, is heavy, dark, and clawed, made in Grand Rapids forty years ago. Every available surface is covered with lacy things or little breakable figurines or pictures in curly gold frames.

"Where's Grace?" Crystal puts her overnight bag down on the settle in the hall.

"Right here." Grace's small, shy voice comes out of the shadowed parlor. Grace is as thin and delicate as Nora is massive, smelling like lilac and old things as she hugs Crystal tight.

"Crystal, you're growing every time I look at you," Grace says gently. "I'm so glad you're here."

"I'm so glad to *be* here," Crystal says politely, but it's true, she is glad to be here, and she sits down at the big round table for Sunday dinner and looks down while Nora says the blessing. Crystal eats enough of everything to make even her aunt Nora happy. The food is good, all the vegetables right out of the garden, sweet corn on the cob, green beans cooked all day with slab bacon, chicken and dumplings, big round thick slices of tomato on a green glass plate. Everything is served in big bowls with steam coming off of them. Crystal eats and eats. She always eats things here she wouldn't touch at home.

A fly buzzes in from the kitchen. Nora slaps at it and it buzzes back out the door; no fly or anything else would dare to disobey Nora. Nora has surprisingly delicate table manners for such a big old woman, manners which are all that remain of her long-ago girlhood in Baltimore; she sits straight up and eats slowly, does not pile up her plate although she takes helping after helping of the food. Nora is in her sixties now, but she has not shrunk up the way that Crystal has seen other old people do. Instead she seems to grow larger with the years, erect and strong behind her giant bosom, wearing the men's shoes and shapeless dresses which vary in color but never in style. Nora's gray hair is so long she can sit on it, and she wears it pulled straight back into a knot at the back of her neck. Nora wears her eyeglasses on her bosom on a long gold chain, but Crystal has never seen her use them and can't imagine that she would ever have to, Nora's eyes are so bright and so black. Her strong face falls down from chin to chin and into the neck of her dress.

"How's your father holding up?" she asks Crystal, wiping her mouth.

"Not very good," Crystal says. "He doesn't get up much anymore at all."

"He never was a stout one, even as a boy. Took after Emma," Nora comments, shaking her head sadly.

Down at the end of the table, Devere eats slowly and

placidly, lost in the process of eating. He is Grant's younger brother and he looks so much like Grant that it sometimes makes Crystal cry to see him. Except that all the things in Grant's face which have gone hard and haunted and hollow are full and smooth in Devere's. There is a calm, baby look to his face. Devere dresses in a clean flannel shirt every day regardless of the season; he moves slow. There is nothing much wrong with him that Crystal can see. She knows that Devere fell off the foot log crossing Dry Fork when he was a little boy, and did something to his head. She knows that he was in a methane gas explosion in the No. 6 mine when he was not yet twenty. But he doesn't seem retarded to Crystal, not like pictures of retarded people in books in the public library with their tongues all hanging out. Devere does odd jobs for people up and down Six-and-Twenty-Mile Branch and Dry Fork, he works in the garden, and he keeps his tools in the toolshed all shiny. He raises hunting dogs that people come from everywhere to buy. He will speak right back if you speak to him, although he never has much to say. Sometimes he just stands still like he's listening to something far away. Once Crystal told her daddy she thought Devere heard a different drummer after Grant read that to her in a book. "That's about right, honey," Grant had said. Devere loved her father and used to follow him everywhere, people said. But he never sees Grant now. Devere won't go into town, hasn't been there for years and years. When they need something, Odell gets it for them or Nora and Grace go to town in the pickup, and oddly enough it is Grace who drives.

Devere folds his napkin carefully, pushes his chair back, and stands up. He's a big man.

"Not yet, not yet," Grace twitters. "I made a coconut cake for Crystal." Grace is also the one who makes the desserts.

Obediently, Devere sits back down and unfolds his napkin and puts it back into his lap.

Grace moves into the kitchen in her skittish, sideways fashion and comes back with the cake on a platter, little strings of coconut all over the white icing.

"How is it?" Grace asks anxiously after she has cut and passed it.

Crystal thinks she will die from eating. "It's the best cake I ever ate," she says with her mouth full.

"Too much vanilla," Nora says.

"Oh, Nora." Grace's pretty little wrinkled face falls beneath the wisps of her hair. She tastes the cake herself. "Why, I think it's pretty good," she says.

"Too much vanilla," says Nora. But she eats two pieces all the same and Grace is pleased. Devere rises again and leaves, looking out the window.

"I'm going to do the dishes," Nora says, "if you all will help me carry them in."

"I'll help you do them," Crystal says, although she never volunteers to help out at home.

"I will, too," Grace says.

"Not you," Nora says to Grace. "What kind of help would you be? You'd just get in the way, that's all, and besides you know how the heat does you. Go on in the parlor now, you all, and get out of my kitchen."

Crystal and Grace sit on the dark curved furniture, and out the window they can see the garden in the sun. Grace sighs automatically as she gets comfortable in her little chair and puts her feet up on her stool. "Heat does do me bad," she confesses to Crystal. "Makes me feel dizzy, and I don't know." She stops abruptly. Crystal is used to Grace and the way her mind wanders off. Crystal loves Grace, and at home she has boxes and boxes of the tiniest clothes that Grace has made for her dolls.

"Tell me about Grandmother," Crystal says.

Grace's blue eyelids flicker and she begins, telling it all again, the way Crystal wants her to. "Well, we were all brought up in Baltimore, Nora and Emma and I, by our cousin Sam. We lived in a big house on the corner with poplar trees in the yard and we went to Miss Jenny's school. Not every girl went to school in those days, but Cousin Sam said since we were orphan girls we would have to make our way in the world, so he was training us up to be schoolteachers." Grace pauses and then giggles. "*Amo, amas, amat*," she says. "*Amor vincit omnia.*" Crystal stares. Grace giggles again and goes back to the story. "After we finished up at Miss Jenny's, we all went out into the world. But I only went next door, that was all, to teach the children there their lessons. Nora taught school on the Eastern Shore of Maryland and had one whole little school to herself. But Emma! Emma was the religious one, you know, the smart one. She used to go around with a bow in her hair. Well, Emma had a vision that she wanted to be a missionary of God and knowledge, that's how she put it, and so she read in the paper about the Methodist Day School being started in this county and she sat right down and wrote them a letter and they took her right away."

Nora sings a hymn in the kitchen, clanking plates together in the sink. Grace whispers out the story in her soft, soft voice, and Crystal is getting sleepy. She grinds her hand into the starched antimacassar on the arm of the love seat where she sits, rubbing the stiff lace against a sore place on her finger to keep herself awake.

"Emma came here on horseback. That was the only way you could get here in those days, and after she had been gone a year we received word that she was engaged to be married to a Mr. Spangler. So Nora and I, we came, too."

And never left, Crystal knows that. "What was Grand-daddy like then?" she asks.

"Oh my," Grace says, a watery opaqueness dropping now over her eyes. "Why, he was *something,* your grand-father was! You never saw a handsomer man. He was a wild one, of course. But he was crazy about our Emma, I'll say that for him. He loved the ground she walked on. Nothing was too good for our Emma. If she hadn't died so soon, he would have been a better man."

"What did she die of?" Crystal doesn't know this part of the story.

"It was when Devere was born," Grace says, nearly whispering now because Nora doesn't like it for her to talk so much. "And your daddy was three years old. We were all living in this house, it was almost new then. Something went wrong when Devere was born, some complication. I don't know. It was one of those things they would know what to do about now. But she just never stopped bleeding, our Emma didn't. A hemorrhage of the womb, they called it. Oh, your grandfather almost went crazy. He carried her to Richmond in his lap, and then he brought her back. There was nothing they could do, they said. They could slow it down, but they couldn't stop it."

"Did Emma die then?" Crystal asks. "Grandmother, I mean?"

"No, honey, she lived on five months longer, and she was just the bravest thing. Even after she couldn't stand up anymore, she still had them dress her up so nice every evening—we used to have help then—and she used to call me to put up her hair. Emma still had them fix a big dinner every night, just as nice as ever, and we all fixed up to come to the table, and your grandfather and one of his men would carry her down in her chair. She never ate anything, toward the end, but she was so brave. She pretended to eat. She tried to sit up in her chair. We used to have candles . . ." Grace trails off, then adds inadvertently, "Toward the end, the smell of the blood was so bad that the rest of us could hardly stand to eat. But we never told her that, poor thing. She was such a lady, she couldn't have stood it to know."

"And then what did Grandaddy do?" asks Crystal.

"Do? I'll tell you what he did!" Nora comes sputtering in from the kitchen and sits herself down hard in the big old rocker. "He went right back to his awful ways and left us to manage those children the best we could. Do? I'll tell you what he did. He went right back to sinning, that's what he did, and went on sinning for the rest of his life." Nora pulls a handkerchief from her bosom and wipes her face.

"Do you think he went to hell, then?" asks Crystal with her father's scorn in her voice.

"Yes," Nora says.

"Now, Nora, you don't *know*, you shouldn't tell the child such things . . ." Grace twitters on like a bird in her chair.

"She's not a child," Nora says. "These are things she has a right to know."

Through the window Crystal sees Devere coming out with a big pail of food for the dogs, and the dogs start jumping against the wire fence and barking like crazy.

"I think I'll go help Devere," Crystal says.

"I think I'm getting a headache," Grace says faintly as Crystal leaves, and Nora says she is not surprised.

Anyway, Crystal knows most of the rest of the story: how they buried Emma, and Iradell imported her monument from New York City itself at enormous cost; how

Nora kept house for Iradell and hated him for twenty years. How her grandfather brought a woman named Mae Peacock and his own blood son by her, Odell Peacock, into this house and kept them there without even marrying her while she brought two more illegitimate children into the world; how Mae Peacock died, too, finally and Iradell sent her body back to her people at Caney Creek for burial, would not have her lying anywhere near his Emma; how Iradell was losing it all by then and how he brought a young girl, Goldie Coe, to live there and then took Goldie Coe to Charlottesville and bought her some new teeth after which she left him as everyone said all along she would. How Nora and Grace and Grant and Devere still lived there after Goldie left; how Odell drove her grandfather everywhere in the car after Iradell could no longer drive; how once Iradell got away from all of them and crashed his big car in the middle of downtown Black Rock, where the road takes a sharp bend in front of the barbershop, running his brand-new Lincoln into the gray cliff face beneath the Bulova Watch billboard, Iradell breaking his own neck and paralyzing a young high-school teacher from the waist down as she crossed the street with her groceries. And now Iradell too is buried in his own graveyard.

But wait. Crystal nearly forgot the surprise in the story. It is a slight surprise, nothing much to compare with the grandeur of Mae Peacock having her bastard babies in the bed Little Emma died in, or with Iradell Spangler crashing into the cliff on a payday afternoon. But here it is: sometime during those stormy years. Grace slipped off and got married. Nobody took much notice of Grace, she was so quiet and agreeable. She was always making flower arrangements and taking courses by mail. She was almost invisible in the war that raged on and on between Iradell and Nora, their hatred so intense it was mostly like love, their dependency on each other so total. But somehow, sometime, Grace managed to meet a traveling sewing-machine repairman named Mr. Hibbitts, a rheumatic mousy bald little fellow, and somehow she managed to marry him. Their marriage was kept inexplicably secret for seven years while Mr. Hibbitts made the rounds of his mountain towns, repairing sewing machines, seeing his wife presumably on the Black Rock run. In fact, the marriage might never have come to light at all if Mr. Hibbitts had not died suddenly of a heart attack, leaving his entire estate of six thousand dollars to his wife. Then how sick Grace was, how long she wore black clothes in mourning! while Nora paused in her work to shake her head and mutter, "I'll swan!" over and over in complete amazement, and Iradell roared with laughter. But Mr. Hibbitts too is in the graveyard down the hill.

Crystal shakes her head to clear it and goes out into the yard. Devere is in the dog pen and the dogs are leaping all over him. He is covered with bluetick hounds and spotted spaniels. Their frenzy seems crazy in this hot late afternoon, and Devere among them is as immovable as a wooden man. He sees Crystal and smiles. "Looky here," he says, and brushes the dogs off him like bugs and takes Crystal by the hand around to the little pen where Dollie has got some new puppies.

"Oh, *Devere!*" Crystal cries, getting down on her knees to feel them, warm and blind and squirming. They lick and lick at her hands with their little tongues no bigger than her thumbnail. She plays with them for a long time and Devere stands still, smiling and watching her, until the sun starts slanting down and it's time for him to do some chores. Crystal helps him, and then it's time to sit on the porch.

Nora goes to bed early because she gets up every morning at five o'clock. There is not any particular reason for Nora to get up so early, but she has done it all her life almost, ever since she came to live in this county with Emma and found out that she was a country woman at heart; she took to the place and the life in a way that neither of her sisters ever had. Devere goes to bed at nine-thirty every night. So Crystal and Grace are left in the parlor and Crystal makes Grace tell her everything she can remember about Baltimore, about Cousin Sam's house, and about her daddy when he was a boy. Crystal likes to hear about her daddy best of all.

Crystal goes to bed in the feather bed in the downstairs bedroom where she always stays when she's here, and waits until Grace has tiptoed in like a fairy in her long diaphanous gown to see if she's asleep. Then Crystal sits up in bed.

Crystal used to play a game when she was little and visited here. She made the game up so she wouldn't be scared if she had to go to the bathroom at night, and now that she's older and knows it's nonsense she still believes it a little bit, sometimes plays it still. This game involves wood. If you have to get up in the night, you will be all right if you touch wood all the way wherever you go. In her grandfather's house this is easy because dark wood-work runs along everywhere. If you fail to touch wood, though, the ghosts will come, and then it will all be over. This is Sunday and the yellow ghosts come on Sunday nights with yellow smoke around their heads and long hot teeth. There are different-colored ghosts for different nights of the week. The green ghosts, on Fridays, are not as bad as the others, because they are very sad. It makes them sad to hurt you, but they can't help it if you don't touch the wood. Behind all the ghosts, beyond and above them, stands Clarence B. Oliver, the Ghost King, greatest of ghosts. Clarence B. Oliver is as big as the world. He can do anything he wants to. He can kill anybody he wants to, anytime. If you touch wood and are obedient and fair with the colored ghosts, then Clarence B. Oliver will be there when you need him to help you out. But you don't mess around with Clarence B. Oliver. You don't ask him for anything unless you really want it so bad you will die if you don't get it, whatever it is.

Moonlight comes in the window and picks out the fan pattern on the old quilt at the foot of Crystal's bed. She smiles and traces a fan, green-figured feedsack calico, thinking of Clarence B. Oliver. Somewhere out there she hears an owl. Closer by, one of the dogs yelps in sleep and another wakes up to bark for a while and then hushes. It's just light enough in this room to see. Crystal gets out of bed, touches the night table, stretches over to touch the dresser and holds to its grainy old wood while she tiptoes the three steps over to it and stands squarely before it, looking into the wavy, tilted mirror. She sees herself in shadow, backlighted; the dog barks again. Who is it there in the mirror? She sees long bright hair and no face, no eyes, no nose, no mouth. Moonlight spreads over the quilt. Who? she wonders, shaping the word with the mouth she doesn't have. *Who?*

Touching the chair rail all around the room, she moves to the window and stands looking out for a long time, her fingers on the sill. Again and again she traces the initials carved deep in the wood. W.G.S. William Grant Spangler. Her father's initials, and he must have carved them there, must have stood sometime at this window where she is standing now, with a new sharp knife, young then, maybe just a boy her own age, leaving his mark. She wonders what he was thinking about when he carved those initials. W.G.S. Crystal thinks of her father as a boy passing through this house, walking up the stairs. But now her father is a grown man; that boy is dead. W.G.S. is dead whoever he was who carved these initials here, and she thinks of all the other people, of Grant and Devere as little children, of Mae Peacock, of bleeding Emma, of big rough Iradell and all the others who have passed through this house, sat on this furniture, breathed this air and slept in this bed and used this space she is using now. And in ten years she will be dead, too, the Crystal who stands here now, this Crystal up so late in the night. She'll be all different, all grown up and changed. Who will she be then? *Who?* The dogs are barking loud now. They have heard something off in the woods. The yellow ghosts have thin long fingers just like wire, but Crystal holds on to the wood.

"How long is this going to take?" Crystal asks as politely as she can. She sits on a straight-backed kitchen chair in the conversation area of Lorene's kitchen, surrounded by women. They have poked holes into an old tight-fitting aqua rubber bathing cap and put it on Crystal's head. Now Lorene and Neva are into the slow process of pulling Crystal's hair up through the holes with long silver crochet hooks, jabbing them down into each hole and then jerking, the slow pull up until a whole long strand of hair emerges. It is incredibly painful, especially around the temples and the ears. Susie Sykes, Neva and Lorene's youngest brother's wife, rocks in the rocker, giving her baby a bottle. The baby is a two-month-old boy named Denny. Her aunt Susie keeps Denny so dressed up that Crystal has never yet really seen what he looks like. *Days of Our Lives*, which Lorene watches every day, has just come on television, and every now and then the women pause in their conversation to see what's going on in Meadville and then resume, jabbing and pulling and talking, while Neva's cigarette burns itself out in the ashtray and Crystal bites her lip. Neva lights cigarettes and lets them burn out. It's hot and getting hotter in the kitchen, damp August heat that makes it hard to do anything active or even breathe.

Every morning Crystal plays a private game, trying to guess what kind of day it will be. She has plenty of time to guess, because the sun doesn't come up until ten o'clock or so. It comes up, that is, but it only hits the mountaintops and never makes it down into the bottom until ten or eleven o'clock. If Crystal has guessed *pretty day*, and it is, she buys herself a Coke at the Esso station. If she guesses wrong, she has to pay a penalty, but these penalties vary from day to day. One time it was clean up her room. Another time it was be nice to Chester Lester. It depends.

"Crystal, honey, turn your head over this way a little bit," Neva directs. Crystal turns her head. Her eyes are on a level with Neva's armpits and she sees a wide wet patch of perspiration on the blue uniform; Crystal sniffs but it doesn't smell. Lorene always says that horses sweat, men perspire, and women glow. But Neva sweats. Neva looks a lot like Lorene, but she is larger all over, a bigboned energetic woman. This year her hair is auburn red.

"I cannot go on like this!" says a beautiful woman in Meadville, clutching at a doctor in a hospital corridor. "Let me tell Gregory! We cannot live this way. Always meeting in secret—the motels, the deceitful lies. It's killing me."

"You must calm yourself, Karen," the doctor says dispassionately, looking quickly up and down the hospital corridor to see if anyone has heard. "Remember my position. Remember your own. Besides, there is something I must tell you." He smooths his white coat.

"Let me tell Gregory, please! *We could live together*, Paul! Who cares what people think?"

"Darling," the doctor says rapidly, "we will discuss this at another time. Just now there is something I have to tell you. It is not good news. I want you to brace yourself, Karen. Are you ready?"

Karen gulps and bats her eyelashes tremulously. It's clear that she is not ready at all.

"The test results from your physical have come back, darling, and I regret to say they indicate that you may have a—"

Organ chords crash and a commercial for Oxydol appears.

"Well, shoot!" Lorene says.

"I bet she's got a malignant tumor," Neva says, jabbing.

"She might," Lorene admits. "You know she hasn't been feeling so good. But I thought it was just nerves."

"Maybe she's pregnant," says Susie, tilting Denny's bottle up so he can get it all.

"I don't think I can stand this anymore," Crystal says suddenly, surprising everyone including herself. Usually she has such nice manners. "It really hurts."

"That's because we're around your face right now, honey," Neva soothes her. "We'll be all through in a minute. Go get her some aspirin, Lorene."

Lorene gets a glass of water and two aspirins and Crystal takes them. Through the screen door she sees Babe in a two-piece red bathing suit, playing in the sprinkler. Jubal Thacker rides by on his bike. Crystal would give anything to be out there. August. She can't believe that the summer has come and gone so fast and now she can't even remember what she did with it, long days out riding her bike, reading, going to the movies with Agnes every time the picture changed downtown. Just sitting, mostly, in different places: by the river, on the back steps, on Agnes's front porch. Mooning, her mother calls it. But she wasn't mooning. She was biding her time. Only now that it's August that time is nearly up, and she can't imagine why she agreed to have her hair streaked in the first place. She would rather be out in that sprinkler with Babe.

"Well," Susie says, standing up and giving her pedal pushers a hitch, "if you all don't mind, I think I'll leave Denny right here on his blanket on the floor, he's sleeping so good, while I run on down to the Piggly Wiggly and do my shopping. You don't mind, do you?" She's asking Lorene, but her eyes travel nervously back and forth between the two women.

"No, honey, you go ahead," Lorene says. Susie's out the door in no time flat.

"I knew she was going to do that," Neva says.

"Well, but you know how it is being cooped up in the house with a real little one," Lorene says, "and Edwin don't do a thing to help out."

"Those big kids could help her a lot if they weren't spoiled rotten," Neva goes on. "I told her about that. You could see it coming as plain as the nose on your face. But you can't tell Susie anything, she knows it all."

"Edwin could have done worse," Lorene remarks, and Neva says, "I guess so."

"What do you mean, you spent the night at your friend's house? You don't have any friends. That's a miserable lie," cries Mrs. Bennett in Meadville. "Sandra, answer me."

Sandra, a long-haired skinny teenager, rushes up a flight of stairs. Mrs. Bennett goes into the bathroom and takes a pill.

"If you give them an inch they take a mile," Neva says to no one in particular. "OK, honey," she says to Crystal, "now shut your eyes while I put this on." Neva pulls on her rubber gloves and mixes up some terrible-smelling purple solution and spreads it over all the hair that the women have pulled through the cap.

"Can Crystal come out now?" Agnes is at the screen door sun-blinded, trying to see in.

"No, she can't," Lorene says. "She won't be done for a long time. How long, Neva?"

"Depends on how fast she turns. Hour and a half, anyway. I've got to wash it and roll it up after this."

"I can't breathe," Crystal says.

"Run along, Agnes. You can see Crystal after a while," Lorene says just as Denny starts crying and she has to pick him up.

Agnes disappears and Lorene sits down in the rocker with Denny.

"*Anyway*," Neva goes on, back to an earlier conversation they were having before Susie came in, "don't you breathe this to a soul, but they say you can hear her screaming every time you go around that curve at night, right by the big pine, that one with the split top was the one she crashed at."

"I don't believe a word of that," Lorene says.

"What? What?" Crystal's voice is muffled by the towel around her face.

"I'm just telling you what I heard. I'm not saying if it's true or if it isn't. But you know as well as I do, if you die in an upset frame of mind your spirit don't just lie down."

"Who?" Crystal asks.

"Nothing, honey," Neva tells her, and takes Crystal over to the sink. "Turned out good," she announces in a minute, fingering the squeaky pinkish strands of hair.

"Why, that looks awful!" Lorene almost drops the baby and he starts to cry again.

"Well, it's got to have a toner on it," Neva says. "It won't look like anything till you get a toner on it."

"What does it look like now?" Crystal asks.

"What did the doctor say?" Neva has pulled off the cap and now she's washing Crystal's hair, kneading the scalp with her knuckles, holding her head under the faucet. Neva nods her head at Grant's closed door.

"Said there's five stages of emphysema and he's in the last part of number four," Lorene answers, glad that the doctor came and went and that she has a big name to put to Grant's illness now, whether it's the right one or not.

"Lord, Lord," Neva says.

"Who—Daddy?" Crystal tries to ask through the towel, but the women are watching TV because Karen is telling Gregory everything. Crystal thinks about that time in August two or three years ago, when her daddy took her over to the miniature golf course at Richlands and they played through windmills and castles and over lakes in the sun. Once Grant left his putter at the hole they had just finished playing. Crystal went to get it for him and came up behind him and said, "Here, catch," real quick, and tossed it, and it clattered down to the green artificial grass while her father, all shaken and gray with surprise, cringed and mumbled something nobody could understand. Several people were staring at them. Crystal went and picked up the club and put it back nice into his hand.

"Of course I will keep the children, Karen," Gregory says coldly.

"The children? *My* children? No, Gregory, you wouldn't." Karen is sobbing again.

"Oh, but I would!" says Gregory.

"Now what are *you* crying about?" Neva asks, as soon as Lorene has got Denny quiet.

"It's just taking so long. I didn't know you had to roll it up too." Crystal tries hard not to cry.

"Well, sure I've got to roll it up if you want it to look like anything," Neva says.

Lorene comes over and gives Crystal a Kleenex. "Honey, don't you want to look real cute for high school? School's going to start in ten days."

"I don't care," Crystal wails. "I don't care if I look cute or not, I don't care, I don't care!"

Neva bites down on a bobby pin. None of her children would act like this. But then if it was her, she wouldn't have stayed married to Grant Spangler long enough to have had any children in the first place.

But Lorene is patient with Crystal, explaining, "It'll be done pretty soon and you'll like it, you'll see, honey. Oh, honey," she says, hugging Crystal, "you're just going to be so pretty!"

High school is like a movie that Crystal has almost seen, starring herself and Kim Considine and Annette Funicello and a lot of other ex-Mouseketeers. It's like *American Bandstand,* which Crystal and Agnes watch most days after school. But it's not exactly like these things either, and it confuses Crystal to be in this movie.

Fall comes and drifts into October, frosty cold and dark in the early mornings so that there's something secretive and exhilarating about getting up and dressing, getting books together, and eating while the windows outside are still black. Crystal leaves her house every day in this excited, trembling state. She feels like she used to feel when she was swinging very hard on the big swings at her old school, the moment when she was up in the air on a level with the bars before she bailed out.

Agnes's father takes them to school each day on his

40

way to work. In the closeness of the car he smells strongly of Aqua Velva, so that Crystal has to open the window to keep from throwing up. Some mornings they have to pick up old Miss Marvell, who boards with Nancy's grandmother, whenever she is substituting for somebody at school. Incredibly ancient, Miss Marvell has dyed her hair black and has bought herself a hairpiece to match. But this hairpiece is not as big as her bald spot, which causes Crystal and Agnes to roll over and over in the back seat every time they pick up Miss Marvell, shaking with awful, silent giggles at the way it looks from the back, the pale-blue rift of skin.

Agnes's father drops them off at the old Black Rock High School where he went to school himself. The school has not changed much since then. It is large, two-storied, rectangular, with a lot of windows with small rectangular panes of glass in them. Some of the panes have been broken out and have not been replaced. Behind the school building itself is a collection of prefabricated shacks built to catch the overflow of students. No grass grows in the schoolyard. It is red dirt and has been that way for years, hard as rock in dry weather, clammy, red, sucking mud whenever it rains, the kind of mud that makes excellent mudballs. Part of the schoolyard in front is paved in concrete, a sort of terrace, lined by the wooden fence with the green paint peeling off of it. It separates the concrete from the red dirt yard and runs along the sidewalk in front of the school. Boys sit on this fence or lean against it, watching the girls go by. In the mornings they are always there when Crystal and Agnes get out of the car. Three scraggly maple trees have been planted in the schoolyard by the Junior Women's Club as a part of their town beautification project. A flagpole is planted in a concrete block. Each week a different home room must put up the flag. Across a big gravel parking lot at the side is the elementary school where Crystal and Agnes went last year, a different world. Where they had their eighth-grade graduation wearing white dresses and wrist corsages and picked "Climb Every Mountain" as their class song. But they never go back there now.

Now they rush into their home rooms, terrified of being tardy. They are never tardy. In home room Crystal checks her things carefully to be sure they're all there: the three-

ring notebook with the colored dividers, one for each subject she's taking, English, alg. 1, French, social studies,
biology. Crystal also takes chorus and phys ed on alter-
nate days. If she makes cheerleader, she'll have to drop
chorus. Her home-room teacher is Miss Dale, who teaches
home ec in her little kitchen in the basement of the school
between the cafeteria and the locker rooms. Miss Dale
makes all her own clothes. Her home room is a boring,
efficient procedure, something to be gotten through every
morning. Miss Dale calls roll and then somebody, usually
Jubal Thacker, gives a prayer, and announcements take
up most of the rest of the time. When the P.A. box
crackles ominously, they can tell that the principal, Mr.
Viers, is listening in. Agnes is not in Crystal's home room.
Pearl Deskins, who has been kept back two grades, is.
Pearl wears a little round pearl collar on her sweaters, and
straight, tight skirts; she's becoming quite friendly to
Crystal. They whisper in home room. Crystal's home
room also has rough boys in it who drop their pencils so
they can look up the girls' skirts; Pearl Deskins warns
Crystal of this. It has a couple of junior varsity football
players, and it has a lot of kids from up in the hollers who
are poorly dressed and more nervous than Crystal. She is
always nice to them. Once Crystal found one of the girls,
Suellen Clevinger, eating her lunch in the girls' bathroom
because she was ashamed of what she had brought, cornbread and milk in a pint jar.

Classes go by fast. Crystal's French teacher is Miss
Martin, who wears very short skirts and sits up on top of
her desk. While they are working, Miss Martin moves
around the room and puts her hand on the back of the
boys' necks. The football coach, Mr. Swiggert, is Crystal's
biology teacher. He's a nice man, but he doesn't know any
biology. He assigns a section each day and gives a test on
it the next day from his teacher's book. In class he tells
jokes. One day when they are studying the circulation of
the blood and poor Bobby Lukes is reading aloud, stumbling over all the words, Crystal has to get up and leave
the class because she feels like she's going to scream; she
can't stand to think about the circulation of the blood. She
can't stand to look at the little blue veins in her wrist.
Crystal also has trouble with algebra. She doesn't understand the signs. Her teacher, Mrs. Marshall, gives her

extra work whenever she misses the problems in class. But she doesn't understand the extra work either, so Agnes does it for her.

Crystal likes English class, though, where her teacher is Mrs. Muncy, a blue-haired stocky woman who won't put up with any foolishness. If you have Mrs. Muncy, you learn the parts of speech. You also have to read one outside reading book every six weeks from a list Mrs. Muncy made up. Everyone else hates Mrs. Muncy and thinks this is unreasonable, but Crystal likes her. She loves to go to the board and diagram compound-complex sentences.

At the end of each class, the bell rings and they have three minutes to get to the next one. Crystal is always late. Sometimes it's because she can't work the combination on her locker. Most times, it's because some boy is carrying her books for her. Often, too, she starts to drift when she walks down the tiled, crowded halls and sees all those faces coming up at her, so many faces, all different. You can pick out the kids from the hollers easily: they look different, somehow, from the town kids. A few are paler, or wall-eyed or crook-necked, but most seem bigger and healthier-looking. However they look, they look different. Crystal smiles and smiles at everybody; she really wants to be popular. At the end of the day, her mouth hurts from smiling so much.

Agnes and Crystal could ride the bus home if they wanted to, and sometimes they do. But the bus smells. It's so full of people, so slow. It takes forever to go the two miles from school to home, and then they can't get off in front of their own houses but have to get off at the Davidson Apartments, a bad place where a lot of people on welfare live, the men sitting out sometimes on old wooden Coke boxes right by the road, smoking, with their hair greased back and their T-shirts on, and they yell things at Agnes and Crystal. Nothing bad, usually something like "How's school, honey?" or "What'd you learn today, sugar?" but there's some tone, some insinuation in their voices. Several of these men have tattoos. And a passel of children runs off the bus each time and into the Davidson Apartments, whooping and grimy, rushing behind the thin doors where their mamas wait with another new baby, as likely as not.

Things happen in high school.

Crystal makes cheerleader, much to her surprise. She is the only ninth-grader chosen. The football team elects the cheerleaders and it is whispered that Crystal got it for her looks, that Becky Ball has a higher jump, that Susie Knight can do a cartwheel and land in a split. Crystal hears these rumors and cries. But no matter. At the first game she's right there, running out onto the field in her gold-and-black uniform, the black V-neck sweater with the big gold letters BR, the short black skirt with the gold pleats, the gold knee socks, the new black-and-white saddle oxfords. Lorene is so proud. The football games are held at night and Crystal can't see much of the crowd because of the lights. She's surprised when the crowd actually cheers along with the cheerleaders. Lean to the left, lean to the right, stand up, sit down, fight, fight, fight. Crystal is amazed that the crowd does all these things. It's cold out there on the field, but Crystal isn't cold. She feels something like a fire inside her every time she jumps, each time the crowd yells. When they make a touchdown, she thinks she'll die.

Crystal attracts attention out there on the field. Boys start calling her up, even juniors and seniors. One of the boys who calls the most is Roger Lee Combs, a football star. His father owns the Family Dry Goods Store downtown. Roger Lee is a nice boy with a nice family and a yellow Ford of his own. He is very tall, with wavy brown hair, and it's rumored that he will make all-state.

Crystal dates Roger Lee Combs and holds his hand in the movies. They switch hands when their hands get too sweaty. She goes to the Homecoming Dance with him and dances very close when they play "The Twelfth of Never," her favorite song, and Roger Lee's sports jacket leaves an indented crossweave pattern which lasts for a minute or two on her face. At lunch he buys Peppermint Patties for her and she saves the wrappers in a little silver stack in her bureau drawer at home. She has decided to be in love with Roger Lee.

But there's this boy in her biology class, Mack Stiltner, a mean country boy that she keeps looking at. She knows she shouldn't look at him, but she can't help it. Most days he isn't even there; he cuts school all the time. Mack Stiltner has long dark hair and bad teeth and a bad reputation. He wears shiny black boots and terrible-looking loud shirts. But he has ropy white muscles in his skinny arms. He has a way of putting his feet up in class and leaning back, head cocked, like he doesn't give a damn. He stares at Crystal all the time out of his strange eyes, half blue and half greenish gray, no color really. He does not smile. In the hall when Crystal is laughing and talking with her friends or flirting with Roger Lee Combs, she sees him: just staring. He knows she's too good for him. Crystal knows this, too. But she can't help herself—she begins staring back.

Now that Crystal has to go to cheerleading practice and all the away games, Agnes takes up 4-H. Immediately she becomes an officer. She wins the school 4-H contest with her demonstration of how to make potato salad. Agnes prepares the potato salad in front of the judges, describing the nutrient value of each ingredient and the history of the potato as she goes along. Now Agnes is practicing for the district 4-H contest, making potato salad and giving her speech at home, until Babe refuses to eat any more.

On Saturday mornings Crystal takes piano lessons from Miss Belle Varney, at Miss Belle Varney's house, where the walls inside are stucco and Miss Varney has cactuses growing everywhere in pots. Miss Belle Varney raps Crystal hard on the knuckles with a ballpoint pen if Crystal has failed to practice. There's a funny smell about Miss Belle Varney's house, as if she's always cooking meat loaf. Crystal memorizes "The Trisch-Trasch Polka."

Crystal can't fix upon a handwriting. She writes a different way each day. Sometimes she favors a tight, small, back-slanted hand. Other times she writes in a forward sprawl similar to the signatures on the Declaration of Independence. Sometimes she prints: rounded, uniform letters with squatty capitals. It changes every day.

There's a stir in the neighborhood; it is discovered that Chester Lester has never learned to read. A dressed-up lady comes to tell his mother, who has a bad back. Chester Lester is furious, setting fire to the inside of his mother's Chevrolet. But the Chevrolet doesn't burn well, and by the time the volunteer fire department gets there Chester is bored with all of it and helps them extinguish the blaze.

The young French teacher leaves mysteriously in November. She is replaced by a fat blond young man named Mr. Roach, who waves his hands a lot and cooks quiche Lorraine for the class. They are astonished, and several parents protest. Mr. Roach is so strange. But he remains until the end of the year, when he goes back to graduate school at Charlottesville.

Crystal reads *Madame Bovary* and *Miss Lonelyhearts* from Mrs. Muncy's list. She writes a poem comparing life to a candle flame, and Mrs. Muncy reads it aloud to the whole class while Crystal blushes furiously in her seat.

One Friday night, her aunts Grace and Nora appear at a football game, wildly out of place, to see Crystal cheer. They sit with Lorene. Mack Stiltner sits on the second row hunched over in an old red plaid shirt, smoking cigarettes and talking to some other wild boys, staring at her, and Roger Lee Combs makes a sixty-yard run. Crystal thinks she'll explode, but she doesn't. Her color deepens and she jumps higher and higher and shakes her pom-poms wildly, and everyone says she's the very best cheerleader of all.

Crystal's daddy is dying, but she doesn't allow herself to realize this. He's a lot like he has always been, only now he lies down all the time on his sofa. When Crystal comes in, he seems animated. When she's not at home, he does nothing. Lorene's brother the Reverend Garnett Sykes mounts a stiff campaign to talk to Grant, who refuses. The Reverend Sykes comes into the front room several times, but Grant turns his face to the wall. "Well, we can't pray him into heaven, honey," Garnett tells Lorene.

Once when Crystal goes to see *Thunder Road* at the drive-in with Roger Lee Combs, she gets out of Roger Lee's yellow Ford to go over to speak to Pearl Deskins, who is in another car, two cars away. It's November now and cold at the drive-in, and a lot of people have their car heaters on so they can't see the screen at all since their windows are all fogged up. Also, a lot of the drive-in speakers don't even work, but there's nothing much else to do in Black Rock on Saturday night. Roger Lee says wait a minute. He says he thinks Crystal ought to stay just where she is. "No," says Crystal, "I want to talk to Pearl a minute," and she crunches through the gravel and opens

46

the front door on the shotgun side. Pearl's date, some boy Crystal has never seen before, is sprawled out on the seat. Crystal can't see very well in the dark. "Excuse me," she says, "I was looking for Pearl Deskins." "Shit," says Pearl Deskins's date. He fiddles around and then sits up, and then Pearl sits up, too, holding her dress up in front of her chest. In the pale light from the movie, Crystal sees Pearl's white shoulders and back, and her hair all messed up. "Crystal," says Pearl in a voice with no tone to it at all. She sounds like she's only stating a fact. "Excuse me," Crystal says, and shuts the door.

She shivers in the cold air. Petting! It was all abstract before. Now she wants to know exactly what they do, how they go about it there in that foggy front seat. Crystal is in love with Roger Lee, of course, but they have never petted. Should they? Crystal can't imagine how it would be with Roger Lee, how they would ever begin. *Petting.* Even the word is animal, all tied up with kittens and barnyards and goats. Nobody will respect you; Lorene has said it so many times. You've got to save yourself for Mr. Right.

When Crystal gets back to Roger Lee's car, she won't talk to him at all. She doesn't even thank him when he brings her a vanilla Coke, but sits huddled up on her side by the window. "What's the matter?" asks Roger Lee, but Crystal isn't talking. "Look at that," he says when Robert Mitchum wrecks three state troopers in a row. Crystal won't look. Roger Lee, not used to moodiness, is charmed. In the darkness of that drive-in, he falls in love. Even though Crystal won't speak to him right now, he vows to make her happy for the rest of her life.

Agnes wins the potato salad contest at the district level and goes on to compete in the state contest held at Longwood College in Farmville, Virginia, all the way across the state. She practices and practices. But she is disqualified in the final elimination because she fails to wear a hair net. "Unsanitary procedure," rules a trio of snippy state judges, even though they eat big helpings of her potato salad. So Agnes comes back on the Greyhound bus with her mother. She is not so unhappy. After all, she did reach the top level of the 4-H hierarchy in the whole state, she did get her picture on the front page of the

Black Rock Mountaineer, and she did get a free chopping block just for being there.

One day while Agnes is out of town on the potato salad trip, Crystal walks over to town after school by herself and buys some creme rinse in the Rexall. Then she calls Lorene to come pick her up. She stands outside on the sidewalk to wait for Lorene, facing the gray stone courthouse with the clock in the tower and the black benches out in front. It's cold and the benches are empty now, and nobody much is downtown. There are empty parking places all around the square. "Think it'll snow?" asks Edwin Sykes, her uncle, hurrying by with his coat collar up.

"I wish it would," Crystal says. She looks up at the close gray clouds. There's a cold place between the top of her knee socks and the bottom of her coat, and she wishes her mother would hurry up. Trash scuttles along the sidewalk.

"Hello, Crystal," says Mack Stiltner. It's the first time he has ever spoken to her. But suddenly he's there on the sidewalk beside her, wearing somebody's old navy pea jacket. Crystal is surprised to see that he's not much taller than she is.

"Hi," she says. Then a terrible embarrassment descends and Crystal looks away from his strange light eyes that close to hers, nods to a friend of her mother's rushing by, and Mack kicks the toe of his boot on the sidewalk. The wind comes down the street and Crystal shivers in her coat.

"Cold?" asks Mack.

Crystal nods yes. There does not seem to be anything else to say.

"Listen to this," says Mack, and to Crystal's astonishment, although she knows Mack has the reputation of being liable to do anything, anytime, he whips a harmonica out of some inside pocket in the pea jacket and starts playing "Blue Eyes," playing really well, right there in front of the Rexall. His hair falls into his eyes while he plays. Somebody opens the door of the Rexall to see what's going on, then closes it to keep in the heat.

Oh, I'm thinking tonight of my Blue Eyes
Who is sailing far over the sea

Oh, I'm thinking tonight of him only
And I wonder if he ever thinks of me.

Crystal moves closer to Mack. Now she's so close that she can see how his skin is greasy and he has hair growing in the V of his plaid shirt collar. Mack finishes playing with a long sad trill and wipes off the spit on his sleeve.

"OK," he says and puts the harmonica back into his pocket. Crystal stares. She's very close to him and she feels funny, weak at the tops of her legs, the way she feels when she considers the circulation of the blood.

"It's starting to snow," she says.

Mack Stiltner grabs her shoulders with both hands and pulls her to him, roughly, and kisses her on the mouth. He never closes his eyes and neither does Crystal. He puts his tongue into her mouth, and Crystal is kissing him back. Then suddenly he lets her go, almost pushing her, back against the Rexall wall and he's gone, rushing off into the wind. Snowflakes swirl around him until he disappears, never once looking back, and snowflakes fall all over Crystal's face. She looks straight up at the sky and catches them in her mouth. They melt on her tongue immediately, sweet and cold and utterly strange. Then Lorene is honking the horn.

"Didn't you see me?" she asks, cross, when Crystal finally gets in.

"No," Crystal says. All she can think about is how Mack Stiltner's tongue felt in her mouth. That night she sits by the telephone, but Mack Stiltner doesn't call, and the next day he isn't at school.

One Sunday afternoon, Roger Lee borrows his daddy's Jeep and picks up Crystal and another couple, Sue Mustard and Russell Matney, and they go way up on the Paw Paw fork of Knox Creek for a picnic. The day is crisp and cold and sunny, the sunlight pale but strong. All the leaves have fallen off the trees. For a while they are on a hardtop road, going up Paw Paw, although it narrows until there's room for only one car at a time. They pass the three-room Paw Paw elementary school, pass several independent mines, pass all the houses and trailers crowded along the road.

"Look at that," says Roger Lee, pointing and slowing down.

He says something else, but Crystal can't hear him over the roar and clank of the Jeep. She looks where he points and sees it, a house with polished hubcaps all over the front. The sun hits the hubcaps all at once and they shine together, a single incredible jewel in the cold bright light.

"That's the tackiest thing I ever saw," Sue Mustard says, swishing her pony tail.

"I like it," says Crystal.

Roger Lee grins at her. He knew she would like it. He wears a yellow hunting cap with green fur earflaps, turned up. His brown eyes are steady, flecked with gold. They leave the hardtop and go onto a dirt road which has big ruts in it, so that Crystal has to hold on to the edge of the seat. She loves the way the jeep smells, like leather and oil and sweat, like a hunting trip. The wind on her face feels cold and new. The road is steep, and off to their right is a sheer drop down. Way below them they can see the town like a toy down there. One more curve and then they're right up on top of the mountain, which has been leveled off for strip mining and then left, a huge dirt expanse with no trees and nothing growing on it, the biggest piece of flat land Crystal has ever seen in this county, something like the surface of the moon. Roger drives figure eights all over it, and they know they're the only people around for several miles.

Roger stops the Jeep and they get out, Sue Mustard and Russell Matney holding hands in their matching His and Her sweatshirts. There's a kind of pool, like a quarry but not so deep, and they put their blankets out by that and then eat Lorene's fried chicken and potato chips and some chocolate cake that Sue Mustard made. Russell eats pistachio nuts, his trademark. You can always tell where Russell has been because he leaves a little pile of the bright-red shells behind. Then Russell and Sue go off to make out, and Roger takes Crystal's hand and leads her over to a mine entrance. Crystal wonders if he wants to pet, and she thinks of Mack Stiltner again. It makes her stomach feel weird. They go into the mine pretty far, until Roger says it's not safe. The timbers are rotting now. He takes a railroad stake from the little old railroad track that goes into the mine, as a souvenir. Suddenly Crystal remembers a time years ago, when she was about seven or eight, and her daddy took her up into the mountains to see a man he had to see about some land, and there was a small mine like this one, where they still used ponies to pull out the coal cars. The mine ponies were small and shaggy, just the right size for Crystal. The ponies blinked in the sun. The men let Crystal ride them, in and out of the mine. The men all grinned and waved to her each time she came out. Her daddy stood there with them, smiling. Suddenly Crystal is sure that this mine will cave in. She can see the timbers giving, the rocks pouring in on each side. She can practically smell the dust. Panic thuds in her chest and she grabs Roger's arm. "Let's go! Let's get out of here." Her words echo way back in the mine. Then she lets go of his arm and starts running and runs all the way back out.

"Hey!" yells Roger. "Crystal! It's all right. Wait a minute."

Crystal collapses on a rock outside, breathing hard. Of course she's being so silly. The sun feels good out here, and everything is totally calm and peaceful. Flat red dirt, the town down there, the other ridgetops across the valley, all the cliffs and big rocks showing everywhere with the leaves gone. The vertical line up the opposite ridge where the power line runs.

Roger Lee finds her and sits down, too. "What happened in there?" he says. "Something spook you?"

Crystal only nods and stares around at the strange terrain. It's just too complicated to explain. It seems particularly odd to be so high, up here above the town, where the sun would come right up in the morning. Roger Lee takes off his Black Rock High class ring and puts it into Crystal's hand.

"What are you doing?" she asks, although of course she knows. The ring is warm and heavy in her fingers.

"I want you to go steady with me," Roger Lee says. He's all choked up. "I know you're real young, and I hate to tie you down, but next year I'll be going off to college, you know." College seems crazy to Crystal right now, like any other idea of the future. She can't even think about college. In fact, she can't think about anything beyond this ridgetop, this rock, this day. She turns the ring in her hands.

"Try it on," Roger says. He puts it on her finger. The

ring is much too large and they both laugh at how funny it looks on Crystal's small hand.

"I guess I could tape it," she says.

Roger Lee turns Crystal around and kisses her, but Crystal doesn't pay too much attention. She's thinking about what her mother will say, about showing the ring off to Agnes and Babe and everybody else, about wearing it to school on a chain around her neck.

Sue Mustard kisses Crystal, too, later, on the cheek, when they all get back together at the Jeep and Roger breaks the news. "I just knew it!" says Sue. "You all make the cutest couple!"

Even Crystal knows this is true.

Lorene claps her hands when she sees Roger's ring, and hugs Crystal tight, and then she calls Neva to tell her the news. "Such a nice family," Crystal hears her say into the phone. Grant, though, is sick that afternoon, napping, and when Crystal goes in to tell him the big news his response is unsatisfactory. All he does is smile into the shadows, beyond the glow of his lamp. "That's nice, honey," is what he says, and then he turns over to sleep. So Crystal feels disconnected, funny in the middle of her stomach, and at supper she doesn't eat much even though Lorene has made three-bean salad, usually one of her favorites. She puts Roger's ring in the middle of the table and it sits there, shining at her, while they eat.

"Haven't you got some homework, honey?" Lorene asks her after supper. After all, it's Sunday night: school tomorrow. *Algebra.* Crystal doesn't think she can possibly face algebra when she's so much in love. It ought to be morning and she ought to be wearing a long lace dress, running through flowered fields. Instead it's Sunday night, dark and cold, and she's got fifteen problems which she can't possibly solve by herself. Crystal puts three Band-Aids on the inside of Roger's ring, to keep it on her finger, and then she gets her books and puts on her coat and goes next door, where Agnes and Babe and their parents are all in the front room around the television, watching *Sea Hunt.*

"Look!" Crystal drops her books on the floor. "Look what Roger gave me today!" She holds out her hand in the air.

"Well, shoot!" Hassell hollers. "You girls are growing up too fast for me."

"Ooh, let me see," Babe cries, running across the room. "Ooh, it's so *big*," she says.

"I suppose this means that you and Roger are going steady." Agnes uses her passing-judgment voice, which Crystal has heard before. Agnes sits on the love seat in her church dress, the navy-blue knit for the fuller figure which her mama made, adding a sailor collar onto the pattern to make Agnes look more her age. She doesn't get up to see Roger's ring.

"That's right," Crystal says. She sits in the chair by the window; when she looks out, she can see her own house, and she wonders if Grant's asleep.

"Now, what does 'going steady' mean, exactly?" Agnes's mama looks up from the crocheting in her lap.

"Well, I don't know." Crystal giggles. She hasn't thought about it just that way.

"I guess we'll finally get some peace and quiet out in that driveway now," Hassell teases. "It was getting so busy over there on the weekends I was getting ready to ask the town to put up a traffic light."

"Yeah, you sure are popular," Babe says without a trace of envy. "When I get in high school I'm going to be that popular, too." Babe pirouettes on the plastic runner in the middle of the floor.

Their mama smiles. "You'll have to learn how to stand still first," she says.

Agnes stares straight at the TV, where a clue has washed up on the beach and Lloyd Bridges, out walking his dog, has found it.

"Well, you all were just made for each other," Babe goes on, and Crystal is getting embarrassed. "I'm not going to go steady until I'm about twenty-seven," Babe adds. "I'm going to play the field." It's something she has read in a magazine.

"Why, Pauletta," her mama says faintly, and Hassell guffaws.

"Whoever I marry is going to give me everything I want," Babe says. "He's going to be real rich and real

53

handsome. One thing I want," she adds after she's thought awhile, "is about forty pairs of shoes."

"What're you going to do with that many shoes, Pauletta?" Hassell asks.

"Dance," Babe says. She's dancing right now.

While everybody is still laughing at this, Agnes gets up heavily and goes upstairs to take off her church clothes, not even looking once at Crystal as she goes. In her room she avoids the mirror as she undresses. It's upsetting to Agnes that she is still growing. Crystal has stopped, apparently, at five-six, but Agnes is pushing five-ten already, with no end in sight. Her arms and legs are so long and heavy, like furniture parts. Agnes was not made to be a teenager. Already she looks like a woman, and not a young woman either. Somebody thirty at least. She hangs up her dress carefully and pulls on some green knit slacks and a long loose top that her mama made, with vertical green stripes to take away pounds. Except it doesn't work. That morning Agnes sat by the window biting lipstick off her lips and watching Crystal come out of her house with Roger Lee, wearing tight blue jeans and a little red knit hat with a tail on it and carrying a basket of food. Roger Lee and Crystal ran holding hands to the Jeep, got in and roared off, spewing gravel exactly like Sykes used to do when he came and went, leaving Agnes still staring out the window at Crystal's empty yard, her house, her driveway only fifty feet away. And now Agnes sits on her bed. Crystal said going steady. *Going steady?* High school is happening so fast that Agnes has not had time to consider that. But her own little sister Babe appears to know all about going steady, as well as everything else in the world. Babe might be obnoxious, but she isn't dumb. Agnes feels dumb and clunky right now, like a big homemade machine. Going steady! It wasn't so long ago that she and Crystal cut their fingers and mixed the blood and swore to have nothing at all to do with boys. But it seems like years and years. Even this summer Crystal was too dreamy and too absentminded, playing on the river bank. Now she's too grown up.

All the way down the stairs, Agnes can hear Babe still talking about her husband, and Hassell is laughing so much he coughs.

"And also I'm going to get married in the Luray Cav-

erns," Babe is saying. "You can do it, Mama. You really
can. I saw somebody do it on television. A lot of people
do it down there. Way down there they've got this crude
but natural cross."

"Why, Pauletta!" their mama says. Hassell wipes his
eyes. Crystal is looking at Roger's ring.

"What you ought to do is use wax in it," advises Babe.

"How would *you* know?" Agnes snaps.

"Well, everybody knows *that*," Babe says. "Haven't
you got any wax in the kitchen, Mama? Haven't you got
any old candles or something? Let's go do it right now,"
Babe says.

"There's some jelly wax in that cabinet under the
breadbox," their mama says. "You've got to be real careful with it, though. Melt it in that little old blue pan and
don't turn the stove up too high."

When Crystal and Babe go off to the kitchen, Agnes sits
down on the couch. She feels tired, which is funny, since
she hasn't done a thing all day except go to church.
Hassell snores, his newspaper flat on his lap. Agnes turns
to her mama. "Don't you think Lorene is too easy on her
children?" she asks. "Don't you think she's too permis-
sive?"

Agnes's mama is never asked for any opinion at all and
she looks startled. She pauses for a minute, biting a thread,
before she answers in her sweet slow voice. "I think
Lorene has a hard row to hoe," she says finally, and that's
all she says.

After a little while, Agnes gets tired of sitting there
watching her mama sew and listening to her daddy snore,
and she can't understand *Sea Hunt* either since Crystal
came in and made them all miss the beginning of it, so
she gives in and goes out to the kitchen where all the giggling is.

Babe and Crystal have made a big mess, which figures,
but they've gotten a thick glob of wax to stick in the ring
and Crystal is tickled to death with it. The wax makes the
ring stick out so far from her finger that nobody in the
world could possibly think it was her own ring; everybody
will know she's going steady. "Look at it now," Crystal
says, holding her hand out to Agnes.

"Well," Agnes says. They look at each other across the
spilled wax on the oilcloth tabletop until Crystal flushes

and looks down, twisting the ring on her hand. She has gotten beautiful, Agnes sees. Some spots in her face have filled out, but her eyes are still hollow and huge, deep blue, when she raises them up to look steadily at Agnes.

For some reason Crystal feels like she ought to apologize, which is crazy. Apologize for what? For a minute Crystal wonders if Agnes might be jealous, might have a crush on Roger herself. Could that be it? But then Crystal understands and she says, "I was hoping you could help me do my algebra," so Agnes will know that nothing has changed. Of course they can still be friends. Even if Crystal *is* going steady, which she is!

"I don't know," Agnes says stiffly. She sits down in a chair at the kitchen table and draws her legs up like an old woman.

"Algebra!" Babe says. "Yuck!" She goes back in to the TV.

"I've got some homework myself," Agnes says. This is a big lie and they both know it, because Agnes always does all her homework right after school on Friday afternoons. She won't do anything before she gets it done.

"Thanks anyway," says Crystal, who feels like she might cry all of a sudden, but then, looking at her face, Agnes says "Oh, *OK*" and does all her algebra for her in fifteen minutes flat, and they've got the rest of the night to watch TV and make fudge together, and Crystal is having so much fun that she doesn't even mind when she gets melted chocolate down in all the little decorative tracings around the stone in Roger Lee's class ring.

Christmas has come and gone and now, five days later, Crystal's in the kitchen helping Lorene take down the tree. Crystal has felt jittery and peevish ever since school closed for the holidays. School was something regular, a schedule to hold on to. As she reaches for the ornaments she turns her hand back and forth slightly, looking at the new pearl ring which Roger Lee gave her for Christmas. Now she wears his class ring around her neck, the pearl ring on her right hand. The pearl ring has two real pearls in it, entwined by golden leaves. It's called a friendship ring. Unfortunately, Crystal doesn't like Roger Lee so much now that football season is over, but she doesn't see him so much either. Since the end of the season he has been working at the American Oil station downtown. That's how he got the money to buy her this ring. Sometimes when she's driving through town with Lorene, Crystal sees him out there all grease-stained and dirty, and she waves and waves from the car. Other times Roger calls her from the pay phone at the gas station. She loves to hear the dime drop into the slot, the traffic noise of the street behind his voice. She likes to drive by the station and wave to him or talk to him on the phone more than she likes being with him. Mack Stiltner has never called her, not once, and sometimes she thinks she imagined that time at the Rexall. Of course Mack Stiltner is so trashy anyway —he wouldn't dare to call! And Roger certainly is sweet to her. He had her over to his house for dinner on Christmas Eve and she watched all of them open their presents, which all the Combses do on Christmas Eve. Mr. Combs had bought the whole family a new twenty-one-inch TV and it was all wrapped up with a bow and they were all pretending that they didn't know what it was. Then they sat surrounded by wrappings and watched Bing Crosby. Later, in the car, Roger Lee gave Crystal the ring. "I love you," he said. "I love you too," said Crystal, and when she said it she meant it, but as soon as he had taken her home she wasn't so sure.

Crystal's hands move silently like birds, wrapping up the ornaments in tissue and putting them into the box. It's an easy job, since Lorene didn't have much of a tree. Just an artificial one from the dime store, three feet high and white, sitting on a round table in the conversation area. Lorene had put mostly blue ornaments on it and then sprayed it with blue spray. Crystal thought it looked pretty, but Jules said, "My God!" when he came in and saw it for the first time. He hurt Lorene's feelings. Jules hurt everybody's feelings, in fact. Crystal didn't like him at all. Neither did anyone else, including Babe, who came over to deliver presents and after observing Jules reading a book for a while asked in a loud stage whisper how come he was such a fruit. When Jules lowered the book and looked at her, Babe said, "Lordy!" and scatted home. Crystal didn't know why he was such a fruit, either. Jules was thin and very pale, with a high, balding head; his horn-rimmed glasses made his eyes huge when you looked at him head on. Behind the glasses, one eye had a tic in it that it had had for years. Jules's fingers were skinny and twitchy, plucking here and there. His smile was heavily sardonic.

When he opened the set of polished wood coat hangers that Lorene had ordered for him, he said, "Oh, *thank* you, Mother," sarcastically. Then he got up and went over and kissed her on the forehead, which she had wrinkled up anxiously while she watched him open his gifts, and said, "Thank you," again, in a nice voice. Then he went over to the window and leaned his forehead against it while everyone—Crystal, Lorene, and Sykes—was quiet, and outside they could hear the littlest Thackers yelling, "Bang, bang," as they raced through their yard. "Oh shit," Jules said, and went upstairs.

Grant was so sick on Christmas Day that Dr. Lewis had to come and give him a shot. He had a virus, the doctor said, with some complications. The trouble with a virus, the doctor added, is that you never know where it will settle. Fat little Dr. Lewis looked around at all of them in the front room by Grant's side when he said it. Dr. Lewis sighed; he had to get on home. Like everybody else in town, he knew all the Spanglers and the Sykeses and all about them, he had known Grant as a young man, and he remembered quite well the day that Iradell drove into the cliff. "Merry Christmas," Dr. Lewis said, and after he gathered up his things Crystal turned the overhead light off in the front room and fixed her daddy's covers. "Keep your chin up," Dr. Lewis said to Lorene as he went out the back door.

Sykes had brought expensive presents for everybody: a mohair sweater for Crystal, a watch for Lorene, a new red silk robe for Grant, a Scheaffer fountain pen and pencil set for Jules. Sykes didn't say where he got the money. He didn't say how he was doing in school either. He did say he didn't see why anybody should pay to go to school when the Army would educate you free. Sykes ate a lot while he was home and told Lorene what a good cook she was, and every time Crystal came into the room he winked at her. It was as though they shared some secret, but they didn't. It made Crystal really nervous the way Sykes winked.

One night when Roger Lee came over, Sykes stayed at home and they all watched a bowl game on TV, Roger Lee and Sykes deeply engrossed in the plays and hollering out just like they were really there, Lorene smiling in the rocker, Crystal on the floor leaning back against Roger's knees. Jules stayed two days and Sykes stayed three, and now they both are gone.

But the house seems different somehow and empty, and Lorene's bustle and talk get on Crystal's nerves. This afternoon she doesn't feel like doing much of anything, and Lorene is trying to get her to go over to Neva's. All the Sykeses will be there: they're having a potluck dinner. Lorene puts the last of the ornaments into the box and seals it with tape. She puts the tree into a plastic bag. Crystal sighs, thinking of her aunts' tree, which Nora and Devere cut down in the woods. It reaches to the ceiling, standing in front of the fireplace, and the smell of it fills the whole parlor.

"I wish you'd go," Lorene says.

Crystal opens the kitchen door and looks out. Only four-thirty, but it's already dark. The snow by the steps is gray and dirty, trampled. Black Mountain is invisible, but Crystal can feel it there.

"Shut that door," Lorene says.

Crystal shuts the door.

"Go on and get dressed, honey. Put on that new jumper, I want to show it to Neva."

"I guess I'll stay here," says Crystal. "You can tell them I'm staying with Daddy."

"Your daddy is better. He can stay by himself." Lorene is large and insistent; it seems to Crystal that she's swelling up to fill the whole kitchen.

"I just don't want to," Crystal finally says. She tries to think of a reason Lorene will accept. "Roger's going to call."

"Oh," Lorene says. "Well, all right, then. But I wish you'd go." What Crystal doesn't say is that she doesn't want to see her uncle Garnett because she knows he will take her aside and tell her it's about time she accepted Jesus Christ as her personal Lord and Savior, the way he always does. Or listen to her uncle Edwin's jokes, or say how cute Susie and Edwin's baby is, or have Neva discuss her hair, or do anything at all with her loud Sykes cousins.

Lorene goes upstairs to get dressed and Crystal goes in to see her daddy. She finds him half propped up on his couch, holding a deck of Bicycle playing cards.

"Want to play some blackjack?" he asks. His old blue robe is wrinkled around his chest.

"Sure," Crystal says. It's a long time since he has felt like playing cards.

Grant deals her two cards and they start. In a little while Lorene comes back down all dressed up in a forest-green pantsuit, and comes to stand by the sofa.

"You look good, honey," Grant says, looking up. The virus has left his eyes brighter and his face even thinner than ever.

"Thank you, sir," Lorene says, as chipper as can be, but she clutches at her purse in an unaccustomed fluster and tells them about the ham turned to Warm in the oven.

"OK," Crystal says without looking up. " 'Bye, Mama. Tell everybody hello."

"Don't you let Roger Lee come over here if I'm not home," Lorene says.

Grant deals Crystal a five of clubs and a four of diamonds.

"Hit me," Crystal says as Lorene leaves.

Grant deals her a seven of clubs and then a jack of hearts and she's busted the way she usually is; she will never hold her cards, but always goes for more. It tickles Grant the way she plays.

In a little while Crystal says she thinks he ought to rest, but Grant wants to talk. Lately he has been talking more and more, rasping on in his hoarse voice, telling Crystal all the old stories he knows. And even Crystal, who loves stories, sometimes gets tired he tells so many. Some are grotesque. Once, he said, when he was a boy, he had to go and take a letter from Iradell to a man who lived way up on Hoot Owl. He rode his black pony named Bud. And when he got to the house with the letter, he could see in the window where they were all sitting around having Sunday dinner. He could see the man inside at the head of the table facing the window, his napkin at his neck. But just then, before Grant the child rode his black pony into the clearing, along came a man on foot with a rifle, out of the tall trees on the other side of the house, and walked right up in front of the house, where he raised the rifle, took careful aim, and fired through the open window. Then he turned and left. Grant saw through the window how the man inside fell over, face down in the gravy.

And now Grant is telling her about the time they hanged John Hardin. Crystal sits on the floor by the sofa and listens. "It was cold, Crystal. Somewhere around the middle of December. I was little then. And people came from all around, Dickenson and Wise and Pike Counties, to see John Hardin hang. They slept anywhere they could find, some of them in wagons, in spite of the cold. They built up fires in the road to keep warm." Grant coughs and stops to get his breath and Crystal asks, "But what did he do?"

"He shot a man, honey," Grant says. "On the day before the hanging, John Hardin wanted to be baptized, and so the sheriff brought him out and took him to the river, where Elder Wallace Compton from the Regular Baptist Church did the baptizing. John Hardin told everybody then that he was prepared to die and didn't want to live any longer. He never did show any sign of breaking down or weakening.

"At twelve o'clock the next day, they brought him out dressed in a neat black suit that the sheriff and some others had bought for him, and he looked as cheerful as if he was starting out to a wedding and not to death. He jumped up on the wagon, sat right down on his coffin, and they drove him over to the scaffold, which was about where the Magic Mart is now. At the scaffold Hardin walked right up to the trap, joined in the singing and the prayers, and shook hands with everybody there in reach. He said he wanted all the people to know why he was there, that it was for killing a man on account of his wife, and his wife was the cause of it all. He said he hoped she was sorry now. He said he thought he was doing right when he killed Mounts, but now he saw he was wrong. But the Lord had forgiven him for it anyway, he said, and he was ready and willing to die. He told all the men to keep away from liquor and low women—" here Grant smiles—"as that was what had brought him to the gallows. He sang a song that he wrote himself.

"The sheriff told him he had nine minutes to live, and

he smiled and said, 'That is a short life.' He told the sheriff he had a piece of tobacco in his pocket which he wanted him to take out of his pocket after he was hung and give to your aunt Nora."

"Nora!" Crystal sits up straight. "What did he do that for? Did he know Nora?"

"I doubt it, honey. He just admired her, I suspect. He was a little bit crazy too, I guess. A man in his position would have to be."

"What else did he say?" asks Crystal.

"He told the sheriff not to tell him when they let him drop, and then he told Professor Mullins he was going to heaven. As he stepped onto the trap door, he took a stub of cigar from his mouth and told the sheriff he'd leave that to him. Then at one o'clock the sheriff adjusted the rope and sprung the trap, and they took him down at two and then his people took him home."

"Then what happened?" Crystal asks.

"That's it," Grant says. "That is the end of the story." Grant's eyes are closed and he seems almost to sleep, so Crystal moves to go.

"No," Grant says. "Not yet. Listen, Crystal. Listen. A long, long time back, in the late seventeen-hundreds, an Englishman named John Swift rescued another white man, named Mundy, from the Shawnees around here. While he had been living with the Indians, Mundy had heard tell of a silver mine, and so he and Swift set off to find it. They found it here, honey. Listen. Right here, somewhere up on Black Mountain. They started mining it. They traveled with pack mules, supplies, and a crew of men every fall, down from northern Virginia. They mined all winter long. It was sort of a secret operation, but it was considerable. Swift put in a furnace to melt silver and a mint to make the coins. They say that one spring he packed out two hundred mules and all of them loaded down.

"But the Indians raided the mine, again and again. Listen. There were no white men here then, and the Indians captured Swift's boy because he couldn't keep up with the rest of the miners who were running away from the Indians. Swift looked back, and when he saw that they had got the boy, he shot one time and killed him so they couldn't torture him to death. Then Swift left and he never came back. Some people say he was caught and sent back to England for some crime, other people say the Indians destroyed the trail and the silver mine both."

The wind is coming up outside. Crystal knows it's time to take their supper out of the oven, but she sits still and says, "Then what? Hasn't anybody ever found it?"

"No, nobody has ever found it. But plenty of people have looked. One man thought he found it, Joe Vandyke's grandfather I think it was, but when he went back again he never could find the place."

"Did you ever look for it?"

Grant's laugh is short. "Yes, I used to look for it," he says.

Crystal fixes their supper and brings it in and they eat in the half-light of the front room. The phone rings once, but Crystal doesn't answer. She's carrying the tray back.

"Crystal!" her daddy calls while she's cleaning up the sink. "Crystal!"

When she goes back into the front room he says, "Crystal. Listen," but he pauses too long and falls asleep. Crystal straightens up the room a little. She notices the new red robe from Sykes still inside its plastic wrapping. She takes it out and takes out the pins and lays it across the back of the sofa: tomorrow, maybe, she can get him to put it on.

Five minutes later Lorene is back, full of gossip and malice and loud good humor, and the television goes on and the phone rings. "It's for you, Crystal," Lorene says with her hand over the receiver. "It's Roger Lee," she whispers.

Crystal picks up the receiver.

"Hello," she says.

"You wouldn't believe how Susie is spoiling that baby!" Lorene says.

"Whatcha doing right now?" asks Roger Lee.

Her daddy takes a turn for the worse after that, and for the next two weeks Lorene and Crystal are so busy taking care of him that Crystal gets way behind in school and makes a D on her algebra midterm. Finally Grant seems better, still weak but the fever is gone at last, so Crystal goes up to spend the night on Dry Fork with her aunts and Devere. She hasn't been up there—or anywhere—for a long time, so she was glad to say yes when Nora called.

In fact she feels better with each turn as they climb the mountain road. It's so cold—maybe Nora has made a fire. When Crystal arrives it's already dark, dinner time, and sure enough the fire is blazing. Devere is not there yet, but they go ahead and eat without him since everything is ready, and after they're through eating Nora sends Crystal out to tell Devere to come in from the toolshed. Sometimes he loses track of the time. Crystal pulls her sweater tight around her going across the dark back yard, and the wind goes right through her corduroy pants as her shoes sink down in the mushy grass.

Crystal comes into the shed. "Hi, Devere," she says. "Nora says it's time for you to come on in the house."

Devere stands absolutely still, holding his open-end wrench carefully in one red hand. Crystal doesn't feel so good all of a sudden. She feels like she's going to faint.

"Devere," she says.

Devere stares at the wrench like he doesn't know where it goes, but he has a place for everything in his toolshed. Devere stares at the wrench.

"Watcha doing, Devere?" Crystal says. He's always still and slow but not this still. Usually he will answer back. In the harsh white light from the single hanging bulb, Crystal sees Devere's face moving. Some expression on it is struggling to get born. Crystal doesn't say what she was going to: she stares. It's so funny. She has never seen any expression at all on Devere's smooth face, the face so much like her father's, but different and softened out. *"Devere?"* she asks again but he won't answer, circling her, until he gets between her and the door. He holds the wrench easily and lightly now, as if it's a part of his arm; it shines in the light from the hanging bulb. Without even thinking about it, Crystal is backing up, backing up, until her back is against Devere's work table, as far as she can go. She strokes the wood and whispers the words for the ghosts, who do not come. Devere comes and pushes her down on the cold dirt floor, and the wrench drops at last from his hand. Later Crystal can never remember this or anything about it, but by the time Odell comes in looking for Devere to fix a truck, Devere has left the toolshed and is already out at the pen with the dogs and Crystal is sitting on the damp dirt floor.

"Devere around?" Odell asks. He holds some machine part in one gloved hand. Odell wears a black leather cap with the earflaps down, and coal dust rings his eyes like makeup. He looks like a raccoon, Crystal thinks. But something hurts her so bad. Odell's raccoon eyes squint down at her, move away, travel the shed, come back.

"You all right?" he asks. Odell doesn't talk much to women, and his voice is rough and short. "What you doing down there?" he asks.

Crystal sits hugging her knees. "I must have fainted," she said. "I came out to look for Devere." She feels really weird, lightheaded and cold all at once. Her legs hurt and she's got cramps. "I guess I've got a virus," she says.

"Well, you'd better get up from there." Odell's black eyes dart back and forth. "Nora's been calling you. It's time to come on in the house."

Odell helps her up and then they leave the toolshed, Odell going toward the dog pen and Crystal back across that grass to the house. The dogs are all barking and in the light from the house she can see Devere's big outline in the pen, the dark jumping shapes of the dogs. Feeding them late, most likely. She has to concentrate to make her legs work right to go through the back yard.

"Crystal! You Crystal!" Nora's on the back steps, looking out.

Crystal breathes in the cold dark air, walking. Walking gets easier. Smells like more rain in the air, with a slight sulphur scent from the slag heap up at the fork. Odell comes out of the dark. He chews tobacco and smells like it, holding her elbow, looking at her. "How do you feel now?" he asks shortly.

"Not very good," Crystal says. *"Awful."* But then she has reached the house and Nora is giving her aspirin, making hot tea with mint in it, putting her on the horse-hair sofa in front of the fire with an afghan around her. That night she sleeps hard in the bed in the room with her father's initials on the windowsill, W.G.S., the room where she always stays, and she does not dream.

The next day Crystal eats a big breakfast with her aunts and Devere, pancakes Nora made and fat hot sausage cakes and apple butter. She feels much better although she still aches. *"Must* have been a virus," Nora says. "You know how you ache with a virus." Grace wears a fancy white crocheted shawl at the breakfast table and sneezes delicately into pink Kleenex. Cold does her bad, too. Devere eats methodically.

Odell comes knocking, holding his hat in his hands and turning it, bringing in the morning. First he takes Devere up and leaves him off at his mine to look at a radiator; then he comes back and gets Crystal and drives her down into town. It's still early morning, and all their words make smoke puffs in the air. Crystal tells him she's feeling much better and thank you. Odell stays in the truck while Crystal gets out in front of her house, goes around the house and in the open back door. She hears the roar of Odell's truck as he goes away.

"Mama?" Crystal calls, but Lorene is not in the kitchen. She must be over at the McClanahans', because her car's still there in the drive.

"Daddy?" Crystal puts down her overnight bag and goes into the front room. "Daddy?" she says again. She's still wearing her coat.

Grant lies back on his pillows, one hand on his chest with the fingers curled like he's trying to hold on to something, the other arm hanging off the sofa with the fingers open and limp. His neck is at a funny angle, hanging slack over to one side against the pillow. When Crystal goes over to straighten his covers, he does not move. He doesn't open his eyes. Crystal takes his hand, presses the fingers together, rubs them. He doesn't move his fingers; he won't hold her hand like he used to. Crystal lets go of his hand and touches his cheek, softly, her fingers fluttering over the skin. His skin is still warm to the touch, but he's dead and she knows it now. Of course he's dead; he's not even breathing. It's funny how that's the last thing she looks for. No breath: under the blue silk robe, his chest is still, so still it's almost sunken. Crystal sits down on the floor where she always sits, and leans back against the sofa. Back and forth, back and forth she rubs the end of the tie of the blue silk robe between her fingers, back and forth, and the whole world falls away from her by degrees until nothing at all is left.

* * *

Lorene comes home thirty minutes later, yodeling in at the door, "Crys-*tal?* Crys-*tal?* You back, honey?" Lorene takes her coat off, puts it over the back of a kitchen chair, and claps her hands together briskly to get the cold out of them. She glances around her kitchen. It's all clean, all straight, everything from breakfast dried and put away; she did that before she went over to the McClanahans' to look at the new book of spring patterns from Simplicity that Agnes's mama sent off for. Little specks of dust dance in the shaft of light that comes in the kitchen window. The whole house is still and quiet. Out of the corner of her eye, Lorene notices something: Crystal's overnight bag on the floor by the wall. "Crys-*tal?*" she yells. Dust twirls softly in the path of light and nobody answers her call.

Without hesitation or haste, Lorene crosses her spotless kitchen to Grant's door and pushes it open and goes in. It takes a minute for her eyes to adjust to the dark. When they do, she gulps in her breath sharply and one hand flies straight up to her mouth. She has always known she would come in here one day and see this, find Grant dead. He's had death in him for years, as plain as the nose on your face. Lord, Lord, she prays, I hope you have got some kind of a place for Grant. Since he never found a place on this earth, she adds. *Amen.* Lorene leans against the wall for a minute, remembering all things the first house they lived in, one of Iradell's company houses up on Dry Fork, her mother's old brass bed with the log cabin quilt, and the wide pine planks on the floor. Young then, Grant fascinated her. She never knew anybody like him, she who was such a worker and lived by the clock. She never knew anybody so full of dreams. Well. Lorene straightens up and smooths her skirt. What's done is done. But you can't throw the baby out with the bath water, and all the things she has to do now come crowding into her head. First, Crystal Renée.

Lorene goes over to the sofa. Crystal sits on the floor, looking down, holding one end of the belt of Grant's robe. Crystal's hair divides evenly down the back of her head and falls down in front of her shoulders. When Lorene leans over, she can see the white line of scalp in the part at the nape of Crystal's neck. This makes her want to cry in a way that nothing else does. But she doesn't cry. She puts her hand gently on Crystal's head.

"Come on, honey," she says. "Let's go."

Crystal neither moves nor answers, though her fingers work at the silk.

"Crystal," Lorene says in a firmer voice, "your daddy has passed away, honey. You come on and lie down. We have to call the doctor, we have to do a lot. Or you could go over to Agnes's for a little while right now."

Crystal doesn't move.

"Come on, now," Lorene says quite firmly. "Get up from there."

Crystal doesn't move.

Lorene shakes her daughter's shoulder hard. "You come on, now," she says.

Crystal's long hair swings back and forth in the half-light. She won't look up at Lorene.

"Well." Lorene snaps on a light. The room grows suddenly smaller and dirtier, becomes any old neglected room. Lorene sees the dust on everything and wonders what people will think. If she can just get Neva over here. If she can just get Crystal to get up from that floor. Grant looks terrible in the light, worse than she had thought he would. At least those eyes are closed.

"Crystal!" she says.

"Yes, ma'am," Crystal says in a perfectly normal voice. "You go ahead. I'll just stay here with Daddy, I think."

Lord God. Lorene almost runs back into the kitchen, and her fingers shake as she dials the Clip-N-Curl. She knows it's their busy day. "I need to talk to Neva," she says when somebody finally answers. "I don't care if she's doing a permanent or what she's doing," she snaps. "Get her on here."

But when Neva gets on the line, Lorene can barely speak. "Neva," she says finally, after Neva has said hello three times in a row, "you've got to come over here. Grant has passed away. This morning, I guess. I don't know. I don't know exactly. Crystal did. I don't know. No, I haven't had a chance to call him yet. I will. I will. OK. I will. But, Neva, you've got to come on over, I can't get Crystal out of there. I don't know. She was up at Nora and Grace's spending the night. I don't know. 'Bye."

Lorene hangs up the receiver, wipes her hands on her

skirt, calls Garnett and Edwin, looks in the phone book and starts dialing again. She has one moment of pure anger after she calls up Bill Hart at the Black Rock Funeral Home. She might have known Grant would go like this! He always loved to get Crystal all wrought up.

Pretty soon Neva is there, as fast as she can make it from the Clip-N-Curl, along with two of her operators and about half of the people from the beauty shop, all in different stages of getting their hair done. They park in front of the house and come right in and take over.

Before she knows it, Lorene is seated in her rocker with three women hovering over her and one of Neva's operators, Loretta Hurley, has got two pots of water already boiling on the stove.

"It'd be better if you can cry," Mrs. Ruby Wright tells Lorene anxiously. Mrs. Ruby Wright's little eyes are glistening and darting around. "The best thing is to get it all out." Mrs. Ruby Wright, a member of Lorene's prayer circle, has three brush rollers on the top of her head and none anywhere else at all. She still wears a Clip-N-Curl towel at her neck.

Loretta, skinny and competent in her blue uniform, steps back from the stove. "Anybody want Sanka?" she says.

"You go on and just cry your eyes out if you've got a mind to," Mrs. Ruby Wright tells Lorene.

"Sometimes it's a blessing in disguise," remarks Ludie Compton. "Do you reckon he passed in his sleep?"

"Well, poor thing. He'd been sick so long," adds Neva's other operator, Jean Potts, handing some sugar around. She has never seen Grant in her life, but she knows all about him because she has heard it from Neva for years.

Lorene leans back and lets their voices rise up all around her. "You all are so sweet," she says.

Neva, big and able, appears at the door to the front room. "I can't do a thing with her," she tells Lorene, her voice high-pitched in exasperation. "She's just sitting in there. She won't get up for nothing. She won't even answer me back."

"Who?" asks Loretta quickly.

"Crystal," Neva snaps. "Her girl."

Loretta goes in to see and the others follow, a high tide of voices and then a hush as they enter the front room, and they're whispering at first when they come back out. "Now, isn't that the saddest thing?" says Mrs. Ruby Wright.

"Shock," pronounces Hester Suggs, who used to be a practical nurse with the County Health. "She ought to go right to bed. We need to get her out of there, it's not healthy."

Neva takes a deep breath and squares her shoulders. "You just stay right there," she tells Lorene.

Loretta and Neva and Hester Suggs go in to get Crystal, and then Jean Potts has to go in there, too. Crystal won't come; she's fighting them all the way. Finally Neva just picks her up around the waist and hollers at Hester to get her arms and somebody else to get her feet. Loretta, who is as tough as she is skinny, makes a grab for the legs, but Crystal kicks and kicks. She kicks Loretta right in the nose and blood comes out of one nostril. "That's enough of that," Loretta says, pulling off Crystal's saddle oxfords and getting a good hold at last on her legs. Crystal is not very heavy, but she fights like a wildcat all the way as they carry her through the kitchen and finally get her up the stairs and hold her down in her bed. By then Lorene is there, too, leaning over, trying to stroke the face that keeps thrashing so wildly back and forth on the ruffled pillows.

"It's just shock," Hester Suggs says again. "I've seen it a lot before."

"Well, it's better to get it all out," Mrs. Ruby Wright repeats, but even she looks doubtful as she tries to help them hold Crystal down.

Crystal is embarrassing them all—she won't stop screaming for Grant. Finally Neva sits on Crystal's legs and stays there.

"Everything is going to be all right!" Neva shouts at her. "You shut up that hollering, now. That's not the way to act, Crystal Renée. I'm surprised at you. Look at your poor mother. She doesn't know what to do, you're acting so wild."

"Daddy," Crystal screams, a weird muffled scream into the pillow, and she keeps on doing it until Dr. Lewis comes. He gives her a shot immediately and she calms down, goes glassy-eyed and then to sleep. Neva sits on her feet until they are sure she's asleep.

"Now how about this nose, Doc?" Loretta says. "She like to broke it, I think."

While the doctor is still upstairs looking at Loretta's nose, Neva helps Lorene back down and now the whole house is full of people: Agnes's mama from next door, in her apron; Neva's silent husband, Charlie, his truck parked out on the road in front of the Thackers'; Edwin Sykes, in a suit, asking everybody if arrangements have been made; his wife, Susie, wet-eyed and shaky beside him; Jubal Thacker's daddy stiff as a post beside the door; smiling Bill Hart from the funeral home; others. The Reverend Garnett Sykes makes a spectacular entrance, coming in the kitchen door and taking off his hat with a flourish, lifting wide his arms. "May God have mercy on this house!" he says in a deep voice, and everybody there says amen. "Lorene," Garnett says, still holding his arms out but lowering them a little, and she goes into them, held and comforted against the big wool coat. "Honey, it's a blessing," Garnett says.

Lorene says something about the fit Crystal is taking, and Garnett says time heals all. Upstairs, watched over by Agnes's mama, Crystal grinds her teeth in sleep.

"We need to clean up that front room some," Neva says, and several of the women go to help her.

More people come, neighbors from up and down the bottom, men from downtown. A fidgety group of neighborhood children has gathered in the yard at the front of the house. People keep going in to see Grant. Lorene asks them not to at first, but after they get the room cleaned up she lets them all go in. Of course they're curious. Most of them haven't set eyes on Grant Spangler for years. Dr. Lewis clears the room for a while and examines Grant.

"Heart failure," he tells Lorene when he opens the door. "Pure and simple. That virus on top of the emphysema and the cirrhosis." He adds, "I'm sorry."

"Well, it's not your fault," Neva says.

"No," adds Lorene.

"No," Dr. Lewis says, almost absentmindedly, looking around, and a small silence falls. The question of fault almost surfaces but does not; it's not anybody's fault, anyway, they know, all of them—nobody's except Grant's himself or maybe Iradell's, but not theirs either, not really: you just never know how things will turn out.

The question of the arrangements is debated; where will he be laid out?

"He never left this room, poor thing," Susie ventures timidly, but Neva says, "Well, he's left it *now*," and that decides it for Lorene. She will lay him out at the funeral home.

"That's the best," Hester Suggs assured everybody. "You still have to live here, you know. I know I wouldn't feel right about sitting in here after I had sat in here with *that*."

Odell pulls up in the drive in his pickup, still black-faced from the mine, with Nora and Grace in the seat. Nora comes in, nods shortly to everyone, and straightens up the sink. Grace is tearful and trembling. "I had a dream," she says. "You might even call it a vision." She looks so frail and weird and old-fashioned in Lorene's bright kitchen, so different from the women there.

"Don't you think we should bring him home?" she implores Neva, and then Edwin and Lorene. She means lay him out up at Dry Fork, they see; and it takes the Reverend Garnett Sykes himself to hush her up and explain the arrangements.

Agnes's mama comes down to say Crystal is awake and will somebody please bring her a Coke or something to drink.

Neva turns up the heat because it's getting so cold in the house, the way the doors are being opened and shut all the time. Some people leave and others come; they're bringing food now, too, and Mrs. Thacker lists each dish and who brought it as they come in. Like the others, Mrs. Thacker knows exactly what to do.

Bill Hart is back with the hearse and his two assistants, but Odell won't let anybody help him carry the body out. Odell acts like he might even hit Garnett Sykes, so everybody stands back while Odell picks up Grant, wrapped in a blanket now, and carries him out to the hearse. Odell's black eyes are fierce and he mutters wildly under his breath and they all stand back out of his way. It's hard to watch Odell staggering down the front steps with the body over his shoulder, Grant's long legs swinging out from under the blanket behind, bony feet bare in the cold. Bill Hart turns away. He could have taken care of it all so tastefully.

Upstairs, there's another commotion. Crystal has gotten up to go to the bathroom. She has seen the hearse. "Don't let them take him out of here," she begs Agnes's mother. "Please don't let them take him away." They call Lorene and she hugs Crystal to her as the black car pulls out, Odell in the front seat with Bill Hart.

But Crystal pushes her mother away. She turns on her a face that isn't like any face Crystal has ever worn, twisted and ugly and hateful, her eyes several shades darker and full of fire. Why are they taking her daddy? Where in the world is he going—Grant, who hasn't left this house for years, off into the winter day with somebody he doesn't even know? No one, no one may touch her. Because they may take him like that or think they take him, but in fact her daddy is all around her still, his presence filling the air. "Don't touch me," she spits at Lorene. "Get away from me. Get out of here. Don't you *think* about touching me!" she says.

"See if Dr. Lewis is still down there," Neva tells somebody, and they go to get him, but Crystal snarls at him too like some kind of an animal. After she gets a shot she goes back to sleep, and this time she sleeps for a long, long time.

That night while the others go down to the funeral home, she stays turning in sleep in her bed, and Grace stays with her, and Roger Lee Combs comes and stays downstairs. They don't want him to see Crystal right now, and he doesn't really want to, either. He would just as soon wait until she's got it all out of her system. But he has volunteered to stay downstairs while Lorene has to be at the funeral home. His mother and daddy will go by there, he knows, like everybody else in town. His mother was dressing to go when he left. Roger Lee himself is wearing a plaid sports jacket over his shirt; he thought he should. Roger Lee watches *Gunsmoke*. When that's over, he gets up and fixes himself a plate of food. Lorene said to. The whole kitchen is running over with things to eat that people have brought. The refrigerator is crammed full, and foil-covered dishes line the counters everywhere. Roger Lee takes some fried chicken, some corn pudding, rolls, slaw, two kinds of Jell-O salad, a piece of German chocolate cake and some buttermilk pie.

While Roger is eating, more people come in: Mrs. Ratchett with her famous corn lightbread, Miss Ida Rankin with a pot of green beans. "These come right out of my garden," she declares, winking at Roger Lee. She is an old, old woman from way up on Dry Fork, a little bit touched in the head. "Put them up myself. He used to like them," she adds, nodding wisely. "He used to eat them over at my house of a Sunday." Wrapping her old coat around her, Ida Rankin moves back out into the February cold. It has started to drizzle. Roger Lee shivers in his sports jacket as he closes the door behind her, wondering who she meant. Crystal's father? Crazy to bring beans to a dead man. Roger Lee eats everything on his plate and goes back to watch TV. He's still surprised that Crystal's father died. Roger Lee has seen Grant so seldom that he never really gave him credit for existing at all, and this dying seems out of place.

Roger Lee is not surprised that Crystal is taking on so. His mother has always said that Crystal is "too emotional," but Roger Lee doesn't think so. He thinks everything about Crystal is perfect. Sykes calls up long distance just then, collect, to say that he's driving home and will get there about midnight, to tell Lorene not to wait up. Sykes's voice is a lot more serious than anything Roger Lee can imagine coming from Sykes. Perhaps it's a bad connection. Roger Lee goes back to watching TV and every now and then he hears Crystal's aunt Grace say something upstairs, but he can't hear the words and doesn't want to. Her aunt Grace gives Roger the creeps.

Down at the funeral home, Lorene is holding up pretty well, holding up being naturally what she is best at. She stands by the door dressed in a navy-blue suit and kisses everybody and shakes their hands as they come into the room where Grant lies. Beside her is her brother Garnett, baldheaded and massively holy, speaking straight into everyone's heart. Garnett is a toucher—he holds on to hands a long time when he shakes them, he kisses women and children, he puts his arm around shoulders and squeezes. Garnett likes to touch people. He's always conscious of himself as a living witness of God in the world. Susie and Edwin, all dressed up, are shaking hands, too. Nora sits in a big green leather armchair, and people go over there to speak to her. Odell is an embarrassment to everyone: he sits slumped in a straight-backed chair at the head of the coffin, looking madder than hell. He never went home to clean up, and he won't say a word to anybody. Neva and her husband, Charlie, and her children are there; Edwin and Susie's oldest kids are there; some old Spanglers everybody has almost forgotten about have come, including Blind Bob from up on Dicey, with his boneheaded handmade cane. When a lot of Peacocks come in the door, Nora won't speak to any of them.

"Don't he look peaceful?" people whisper over Grant. "Looks like he just fell asleep."

Neva, who put a little bit of foundation makeup on Grant, is satisfied. Lord knows he doesn't look *good*, but he looks better than he did before she got there this afternoon. Bill Hart does a good job, but he hasn't got any eye for the fine points.

They have dressed Grant up in an old blue suit they found in the closet upstairs, with a white shirt and a solid blue tie. With him lying there, it's impossible to tell that they've got the clothes so bunched up underneath him, the pants all folded over since he had gotten so thin. He's visible only from the waist up.

"He just looks so natural," somebody says.

But he doesn't, Lorene thinks once, overhearing. He looks better than he has looked for years: eyes closed, face smooth with the foundation makeup, mouth closed, big features still hawklike but rested, out of torment. Candles burn on each side of him in long wrought-iron holders. The lights in the room are dim, with flowers everywhere. "Sixty-three arrangements," Neva whispered to her earlier, but now they've lost count. And the people keep coming and coming. Everybody from up on Dry Fork, everybody from the First Methodist Church where Garnett preaches and which Lorene attends, innumerable Sykeses and everybody who knows them, men from different places along Grant's boyhood and his past.

The crowded church is overheated for the funeral, which is mercifully short. As Neva said to Charlie earlier, there isn't much you could read out of the Bible that would apply to Grant Spangler. Garnett keeps the question of Grant's soul out of it altogether, sticking to Ecclesiastes and Psalms, and Miss Belle Varney outdoes herself on the organ selections. Agnes and Roger Lee sit on either side of Crystal, who looks at everything very carefully and steadily and doesn't cry and doesn't say a word.

Crystal feels as empty as light, somewhere outside herself, seeing herself walk up the aisle, then sit, then walk back out at the end. The coffin is closed at the funeral and she has never seen her father's body since Bill Hart and Neva fixed him up, but she hasn't mentioned it to anyone, and nobody has mentioned it to her.

Sykes holds Lorene's elbow carefully, guiding her out. To everyone's surprise, he has been a big help ever since he got here. As the family leaves the church, everybody says how sweet it is, and sad, Roger Lee and Crystal sitting together like that, and *look at Sykes!* and they all stare at Jules, who won't look back at any of them, and at the weird friend he has brought home.

Jules's friend is a man of about his own age, with a beard and a neat three-piece suit. He looks sissy, like Jules. The friend's name is Carter E. Black. Jules and Carter E. Black are very solicitous of each other and stick pretty much to themselves. Before the funeral, Lorene asked Jules—since he *is* a professor of English, after all—to write up his father's obituary for the *Black Rock Mountaineer,* but Jules refused.

Odell didn't go to the funeral, but he's waiting when the cars pull up at the graveyard on Dry Fork, sitting bent in the wind in a folding chair. Bill Hart has put a little canvas canopy over the grave, and two rows of folding chairs for the family. It has stopped raining today, but it's bitter, biting cold, with a piercing wind.

Jules, whose field is the nineteenth century, thinks suddenly of how the Brontës kept catching cold at each other's funeral and dying. But there is no way he can share his amusement with Carter right now. All Jules can do is silently turn up his coat collar and silently take his seat in the second row of folding chairs, after he has helped to carry the coffin. Pallbearer. Pall, the philosopher's cloak. Hardly. Worn by Christians instead of the Roman toga.

All palls. And is this all? Jules thinks furiously. Is this all there is to know, birth and breeding, the conqueror worm? Perhaps it is, but Jules will never know these things, not firsthand. He must make analogies, must draw them out from books. Jules momentarily envies Lorene her easiness, her openness, the way she holds on to Sykes now when she needs someone to hold on to, the way she holds on to his uncle Garnett. Jules can't reach out and hold on to anybody; and if his mother reached out for him, he knows he would stiffen and move away. Jules glares at the cool slick coffin not twenty feet away, but there's nothing to see except the coffin itself and behind it some flowers and the other graves and the fence and the hill. Suddenly Lorene disgusts him with her red-nailed grasping hands—he sees them on Garnett's sleeve in front of him, her brassy blond curly hair. *They have really fucked me up.* Jules smiles and almost laughs out loud, for this is the final irony even in his world where irony is everything: to know that this is not true, either, finally, for he knows and has always known too much, has seen both sides of every coin. Jules sits perfectly still in the funeral-home chair, folds his leather-gloved hands in his lap. What had he hoped to learn here?

Garnett sprinkles three handfuls of dirt on the coffin, in the name of the Father, the Son, and the Holy Ghost. They lower it, and everyone rises to leave. Only Grace is sobbing, ladylike but unrestrained. "Hush," Nora tells her firmly, but Grace keeps it up. She can't help but remember Grant as a child right here on this place, herself not much more than a child, either, Emma's little sister all dressed up. It's as much for Emma's little sister as for Grant that she cries now; it's as much for Mr. Hibbitts, poor thing, with the winter leaves wet on his grave. "You go on to the house now," Nora tells her, and Grace goes; she knows she needs a cup of tea. Nora follows after, heavily up the hill, and Devere is fixing a lamp in the parlor as they come in. Devere looks up and smiles. It's no loss for him; for him, Grant Spangler died years ago when he left them and moved to town.

Back at the graveyard, everyone else is leaving. But it's hard to get Crystal to go. She wants to sit right there in her chair. Roger Lee tries to pull her up, but she doesn't come. She smiles up at him brightly—after all, they're going steady—but she can't understand what he wants her to do. His voice echoes at her like he's talking way down in a well. Roger Lee looks around for help, but Lorene's back is turned.

She's saying goodbye now to Jules, who will leave right from here in his rented car and drive back to Ohio with Carter E. Black. Jules and Sykes shake hands and Lorene cries a little. *Men*, she thinks. They both are men, or nearly. Jules leaves and now everybody is leaving except Bill Hart and his men and Odell. Neva and Charlie are taking Lorene. The Reverend Garnett Sykes goes over to help Roger Lee with Crystal.

Crystal is listening to how the canvas tent flaps in the wind. It's almost like a little song. It's like the wings of birds. Her daddy has died and now she knows it. This is all she knows right now, and her mind runs around and around this knowledge—it's like a big rock in a field and she is roaming the field, playing. Every now and then she touches the rock and then skitters away. People are trying to distract her, but she's not going to let them. She's *not*. Roger Lee is talking into her ear on one side and Agnes on the other. She'd like to pull all of Agnes's red hair out by the roots; she'd like to scratch Roger's face with her fingernails. But that would not be good, that wouldn't be nice, Agnes is her best friend and she's going steady with Roger. They're trying to help her, and Agnes made all that potato salad for Lorene: smile now at nice Agnes and Roger. Crystal smiles brilliantly up at Roger and Agnes.

"Mama," Agnes calls, and Roger Lee says, "Reverend Sykes?"

They pull at her arms, but she won't come, listening to the flap-flap-flap of the tent in the wind, the murmur of voices around her. The ground is too cold today for her daddy; but *the highwayman came riding, riding, riding, the highwayman came riding up to the old inn door*. They pull her up from the chair and she screams out. There's no ground at all, nothing but empty space beneath her feet.

Garnett Sykes shoos Roger and Agnes off like chickens. He puts his arm around Crystal and presses her to him.

"Come on, now, Crystal," he says. "The Lord in His in-
finite wisdom takes care of us all." Garnett Sykes believes this absolutely. He smells like Old Spice. Because of
his voice and his huge warmth and mainly because there's
nothing else left to do, Crystal believes him. Contours,
outlines, objects return to the world. She puts her feet
down on the wet freezing ground and walks on back to
the car.

The next Sunday, Crystal goes to church with Lorene.
Lorene didn't make her. Crystal got up and got dressed
and suggested it herself. She goes the Sunday after that,
too. There's something about the program that she likes.
It's new and fresh every Sunday, smelling faintly of mimeographed fluid. A cross with lilies is mimeographed at the
top. Crystal likes the way things happen in order, the
way the program says they will, from the prelude right
down to the benediction.

She still has not accepted Jesus Christ as her personal
Lord and Savior. She has not been born again. She sits
quietly in church during Garnett's long loud prayers and
looks down at her hands. Garnett is famous for his frank,
conversational prayers: talking man-to-man to God, he
calls it. Crystal feels nothing at all during these prayers,
except sometimes her mind wanders out the stained-glass
windows and up into the mountains and she thinks of the
Swift silver mine, or John Hardin, or any long story or
song that she can. Grant's absence is still there like the big
rock and she's still skirting it warily, getting used to it bit
by bit.

Crystal goes to school, dates Roger, giggles again with
Agnes and Babe and Sue Mustard (after they have all
finally gotten over being so solicitous of Crystal like she's
a piece of cut glass), joins the Methodist Youth Fellowship, helps Lorene pick out all the new furniture for the
front room and choose a paint color for the walls from
the bright little squares on the chart. Lorene is doing it all
up in "earth tones": pale-yellow walls, rust-colored shag
carpet, little orange and green pillows here and there.

One day in early March, she breaks up with Roger

Lee. She gives him his class ring back, right in the cafeteria in front of about a million kids. She puts it down on the table beside his cardboard milk container. Then, before he can say a word, she takes off the pearl ring he gave her for Christmas and puts it down on the table, too. Roger Lee stares glumly down at his plate of half-eaten cafeteria food—soup beans, cornbread, Jell-O salad, and a square of yellow cake—and at the two rings there beside his plate, catching light.

"Are you mad about something?" he asks.

Crystal wears a lime-green V-neck sweater that day. "I'm not mad at all," she says. In Roger's eyes, she has never looked prettier. "I just don't want to go steady anymore." Big old boy that he is, Roger is near to tears. The whole cafeteria swims in his eyes.

"Why don't you want to go steady?" he asks.

"I don't know," Crystal says. This is true. "I just don't. I mean, we can still be friends and all. We can still go out."

"I'm not going to date you if you won't go steady," Roger Lee says. "You can't just up and treat somebody like that, for no reason. Just because you happen to feel like it. What did I do? Just tell me, what did I do?"

All the kids at the table have stopped talking so they can hear.

"You didn't do anything," Crystal says. "Please don't be mad."

"I'll talk to you about this later," Roger Lee says in a strangled voice. He picks up his class ring and puts it into his jeans pocket. "You keep the other one," he says. "That's a Christmas present." Without looking back, he stalks out of the cafeteria and out to the gravel parking lot and gets into his car and leaves for the rest of the day. It's the first time Roger Lee Combs has ever cut school in his life.

Crystal leaves the pearl ring on the cafeteria table and walks off to English class. As soon as she's out of sight, Judy Bond grabs the ring and puts it into her change purse. Judy Bond has had a crush on Roger for years. She will give him the ring and her sympathy and whatever else he wants besides.

Crystal moves through the rest of the day pretending not to notice all the gossip around her. Roger's best friend,

Russell Matney, pointedly refuses to say hi to her in the hall. Russell calls Roger at home from the pay phone outside the guidance office between classes and tells Roger Lee not to feel bad, that they're all bitches anyway. Sue Mustard, overhearing, flings Russell's own class ring down on the floor in front of the phone booth and stalks off. Sue Mustard goes to find Crystal and console her, join her, be friends. But Crystal just smiles sweetly at Sue. "I can't see what all this fuss is about," she says.

When she gets home from school, Lorene has already heard it.

"I just can't understand why you want to go and do something like that for," she says, meeting Crystal at the front door and following her back to the kitchen. "Hurt Roger Lee's feelings like that, after he was so nice to us when your daddy died. It's beyond me. It really is. I don't understand how you can just up and do something like that!" Lorene also can't figure out how she can ever face Roger's mother again if she happens to run into her in the Piggly Wiggly or on the street.

Crystal sits at the kitchen table eating a piece of pecan pie. She looks up and tries to explain. "I didn't mean to hurt his feelings," she says slowly. "I would *never* want to hurt his feelings, Mama. I just don't want to go steady anymore."

"Why not?" Lorene lowers her voice, remembering now that she's got a man painting woodwork in the front room. She sits down at the kitchen table.

"I don't know," Crystal says. "I just don't. I'm tired of it. This is good pie. What came in the mail today?" she asks, and Lorene stares at her. Something in Lorene says *uh-oh*. Crystal seems completely self-possessed, the way Sykes used to act. Lord, if it's not one it's the other! Lorene thinks. Now Sykes has quit school and joined the Army. He did it right after the funeral, and Lorene knows instinctively that she'll have no more trouble from him. She got a postcard from him just yesterday, from Fort Bragg in Fayetteville, North Carolina. And now it's Crystal acting up. But she's *not* acting up, not exactly, Lorene reminds herself. She remembers when her children were little, if they woke up in a bad mood she used to say they got up on the wrong side of the bed. This is more like that. Crystal has been *too* quiet, *too* normal ever since the fit she took at Grant's passing. Now she has snapped out of it, she has awakened, and there's something different about her. But Lorene can't put her finger on what it is.

Whatever it is, Crystal is not aware of it yet. She hasn't done anything except break up with Roger, and she can't see why everybody is acting like it's such a federal offense. People break up all the time. Big deal. "Well," she says, finishing up her pie, "you always said you wanted me to be popular. Looks like you would want me to date other people too."

This is true, and all the plans Lorene had for Crystal come flooding back.

"He *is* a little bit old for you," Lorene allows after a while.

"See?" says Crystal.

Later she has to deal with Agnes, who comes over full of righteous anger and pity for poor Roger Lee.

"I just don't want to go steady anymore," Crystal finally tells Agnes. She's sure she's said it forty times that day. "Roger Lee is going off to college next fall, so he doesn't need to go steady, either. Listen, Agnes," she says suddenly, earnestly. "There's not anything in the world to do with somebody like Roger Lee except marry them."

Agnes sniffs and peers at Crystal close, but Crystal clams up and refuses to say anything else about it.

When Roger Lee calls, Agnes has to answer, and Crystal refuses to come to the phone. High spots of color appear in Agnes's cheeks: it's an exciting afternoon. Agnes is the one who has to talk to Roger Lee and he sounds all torn up.

"What if he goes out and gets drunk?" Agnes said after she hangs up. She follows Crystal around the house. "What if he wrecks his car?"

"Let's listen to records," Crystal says.

"What if he *kills* himself?" Agnes throws herself down on Crystal's bed.

Crystal giggles. "He won't," she says.

They listen to records in Crystal's room and Crystal plays her favorite several times in a row: "Love Hurts." But it doesn't, she thinks.

Later, after Agnes has left and while Lorene is watching Huntley-Brinkley and fixing supper, Crystal goes to the new upstairs phone in the hall. She looks in the phone book and then dials and then speaks, keeping her voice down.

"Can I please speak to Mack?" she says.

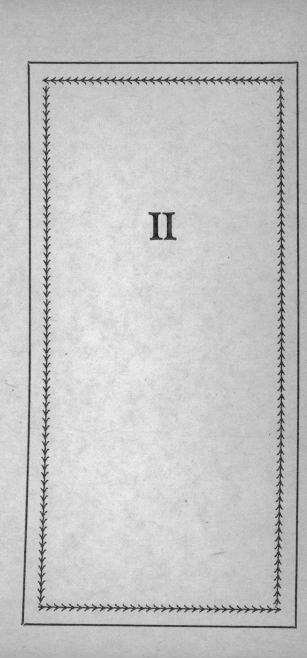

II

CRYSTAL AT SIXTEEN is everything Lorene hoped she would be, everything Grant was afraid she would be, too, only that's beside the point since nobody talks about Grant much these days, and nobody seems to remember him much either, except for Crystal. Crystal is beautiful. Her skin is still fair and clear, and the color still comes and goes in her cheeks. Her hair is very long now and very light and silky, baby fine. She is perfectly proportioned, thin but not too thin, and she moves all the time like a dancer even though of course she has never had lessons; there's no ballet in Black Rock. Crystal laughs and giggles and cuts up a lot. Find any party and she will be smack in the middle of it, dancing. She learns every new dance that comes along. At the end of last year, she was picked as Miss Best All-Around for the tenth grade. Now she's a junior and they have elected her Miss Best Personality, and her picture has been taken for the yearbook. Everyone agrees that she has a good personality. She is so popular. But her face sometimes, in repose, looks sad— it's the kind of eyes she has. "Bedroom eyes," Sue Mustard calls them, giggling, but that's not it. Crystal's eyes are too large and too blue and too deep. When she's not talking to anybody, when she's staring out a window or not listening to a teacher lecture in class, her eyes seem like lakes, as if there are secrets in them, as if a mystery is there.

For there is a mystery about Crystal: is she a good girl or not? She is a staunch member of the Methodist Youth Fellowship and the Tri-Hi-Y Club, she goes to church every Sunday, and she's always real sweet and real nice. In spite of her popularity, she doesn't seem stuck up. On

the other hand, she will date just about *anybody*. Take
Mack Stiltner. He's dropped out of school now, drives a
truck for the Piggly Wiggly and talks about moving to
Nashville. Only he can't leave town because he can't
seem to get over Crystal. She won't go steady with him,
though. She hasn't gone steady with anybody since Roger
Lee.

This should be some comfort to Roger Lee, now in his
second year at the University of Virginia in Charlottesville, only it's not. Roger Lee has pledged Phi Delt. He
has made the starting lineup in football already. His
grades are good. He dates rich girls with charm bracelets
and A-line skirts, girls from Sweet Briar and Randolph-
Macon, and they're all crazy about him, but he can't help
it. Just when he thinks he's really getting interested in
somebody, he somehow sees Crystal's face. It's dumb, but
he can't get over her. His closest friends admire this te-
nacity a lot: Roger's tragic flaw, they call it. It gives him
an even greater stature among the Phi Delts in their columned house on Rugby Lane. They identify with the Old
South and with getting drunk and with tragic flaws, tragic
flaws are big this year and Roger can't help it: sooner or
later, he sees her face. When he's home on vacation he
calls and calls, and sometimes they actually have a date.
On these dates Crystal is the same old Crystal, moody
and laughing by turns, but nothing ever happens. All they
do is talk, and Roger tries to impress her, but somehow he
never does. He impresses other girls plenty—what is he
doing wrong? Spider Marks, a Northern fraternity brother
of Roger's, has developed a theory about the whole thing.
"What you've got to do is screw her eyes out," he has told
Roger Lee several times. "You haven't ever fucked her.
That's why you're so hung up." At first Roger Lee was
appalled by Spider's gross Northern advice, but then he
saw the sense in it. Only he can't get anywhere with Crystal. For instance, he can't bring himself to touch her
breasts.

Crystal even had a few dates with Horn Matney before
he moved out of town. Horn is one-quarter Cherokee and
his father is in the pen. Lorene tried to put her foot down,
but she didn't get anywhere. Crystal is polite and nice to
her mother, but she does what she wants to and everybody knows it. Lorene deals with this problem by refusing

to acknowledge that there is a problem, so there isn't, and Crystal dates anybody she wants to and makes straight A's in English and Social Studies. The boys and Agnes do all her math. Crystal reads the *Alexandria Quartet, A Catcher in the Rye, The Robe, The Idiot, Raintree County,* whatever she can get her hands on. She's such a big reader, she's so nice, that there couldn't be anything wrong. Not with that sweet angel face.

And meanwhile, what has happened in the neighborhood? Nancy's grandmother had a stroke and they put her into the rest home in Galax, so Nancy doesn't come to visit in the summers anymore. Jubal Thacker has become a teenage evangelist. He draws droves to the Holy Pentecostal Church of God, where his frailty and youth and his burning eyes often move people to speak in tongues. Agnes has finally stopped growing. At five-eleven she is a big strapping girl but not used to it yet, not to her size or to the way she is, so different from how she would like to be. Babe has started dating now and she's a real trial for Agnes, and so is Agnes's uncle Jud who got black lung and moved in upstairs. Chester Lester is in reform school now, and his mother's back is a whole lot better. Both the Varney boys have joined the Special Forces and gone to Vietnam. Their mother has a big map of where they are, tacked up in the living room, with little pins to mark the places they name in their infrequent letters home, names like Saigon and Mekong Delta, but these names don't have much meaning here in Black Rock yet, and the map looks weird on the wall with its winding brown rivers like snakes. Sykes is over there, too. He has been promoted from corporal to buck sergeant, and Lorene is so proud.

Crystal reads *Dear and Glorious Physician* and cries. She goes to see *A Summer Place* at the movies, starring Troy Donahue, and cries. Then she goes back to see it four more times. She reads and reads. Sometimes she goes back to her old favorites, even now: *Charlotte's Web, The Secret Garden,* everything ever written by Laura Ingalls Wilder. She spends a lot of time up on Dry Fork, as much as Lorene will let her. She helps Devere add onto his pen. Grace crochets a lilac shawl for Crystal, and Crystal thanks her profusely but never puts it on; it's all queer and out of style.

One spring night she wears it, just for kicks. She has a date with Mack. It always interests Crystal to see if Mack can tell what's tacky and what's not. Usually he can't, but how could you expect him to, coming from the background he does? Crystal preens in the shawl before the bedroom mirror, waiting for Mack. She pushes her lips together in a Sandra Dee pout. Then she whirls around so that the fringe ends of the shawl flutter softly, and pretends she's somebody's Spanish mistress, then a flamenco dancer like she saw on *The Lawrence Welk Show* Sunday night; and she kicks, staccato, at the bedroom floor.

"What's going on up there?" Lorene calls, and Crystal answers, "Nothing."

Crystal hears the doorbell when it rings, but she isn't ready to go down even though she knows that Mack is uncomfortable with Lorene, who won't even give him the time of day. But he can stand it, Crystal figures.

Still looking in the mirror, she ties the shawl around her waist so that it hangs softly down all around, a peasant skirt, and she hunches her shoulders and gazes sorrowfully at herself in the mirror. The Little Match Girl. She looks so pitiful she almost cries. Then she piles the whole shawl up loosely on top of her head, steadying it with one hand, and draws herself up proud and stares arrogantly into the mirror, an untouched native with necklaces of bone and teeth, carrying some exotic burden: don't touch me, swine.

"Crystal?" Lorene calls. "Mack is here."

"Coming." Crystal takes the shawl off her head and puts it back around her shoulders. It sure is tacky. She studies herself in the mirror, applies lipstick again and blots it. She practices looking down and then raising her eyelids slowly like Audrey Hepburn. She brushes her hair.

"Crystal!" Lorene sounds mad now, so Crystal puts her brush on the dresser and runs downstairs, where Mack still stands by the door, shifting back and forth from one foot to the other.

Lorene purses her lips when she sees the shawl, but says nothing except "I expect you home by twelve."

"Yes, ma'am," Mack says and then they leave, running down the steps and across the sweet-smelling side yard, freshly mowed—Odell came and did it for Lorene that morning—to Mack's pickup truck. That grass smell always makes Crystal feel drunk.

"Hey, wait a minute," Mack says, trying to catch at the flying fringe of her shawl, but Crystal won't wait. She runs across the grass and climbs up into the cab and then locks both doors and collapses, giggling, on the seat.

"Come on, now," Mack says. "Open the door, Crystal. I left the keys in there."

Crystal grabs them out of the ignition and jingles them at him behind the glass.

"Damn it, Crystal, open the door!"

Behind Mack's black hair, Crystal sees the Venetian blind slit open in the McClanahans' living room, and somebody's eyes, Agnes's or Babe's or their mama's, come peering out. She opens the door and hands Mack the key.

"Shit, Crystal," Mack says, gunning the truck back out of the drive.

Crystal grins. Beyond the hanging dice on the rearview mirror she sees the Presbyterian church and the Esso station, and then they pass them, and she sees Bob's Drive-In Restaurant on the left around the bend, and the railroad track across the river, and the pale-green mountain on beyond that. Crystal rolls her window down and the wind comes in warm and sweet, springtime. One of the songs that Mack's band sings is "When It's Springtime in Alaska, It's Forty Below." Crystal starts giggling again. They're driving upriver on 460, out of town.

"What's got into you?" Mack asks, taking his eyes off the road to look at Crystal. He takes a sip from the beer he has in his crotch on the seat of the truck.

"I don't know," she says. "I just feel good, I guess."

"You want one of these?" Mack holds up his beer.

"I don't think so," Crystal says politely. She always refuses the beer politely, as if she might have one later but not right now, and this amuses Mack. He has never known her to drink a beer. Probably because her old man died of it, he thinks. But Crystal never talks about her old man either, so he has no way of knowing for sure. There's a lot of things it's hard to know for sure about Crystal. Mack has been dating her off and on now for about a year, over a year now, and he still can't figure her out. The first time, *she* called *him,* and he still can't get over that one. He never would have called her up. He couldn't

91

believe it when Buddy said the phone was for him. He couldn't believe who it was. Then when he went to pick her up, he couldn't believe how she acted either: she was all over him immediately, like somebody from up in the hollers. Mack had borrowed one of Buddy's good shirts for that date: he had thought they would go to the movies. They never got there, though. Mack still couldn't believe it how Crystal had been. She really wanted it, or seemed to, and he gave it to her right there in the truck parked on the high road above the coke ovens, telling her to slow down all the time, trying to watch out for the troopers he knew patrolled that road. He had some rubbers in the glove compartment, but he couldn't get one on. He didn't have time because Crystal wanted it too bad. Or did she? That was one he would never figure out. Because then she cried all the way home and wouldn't even let him touch her, much less kiss her good night, got out and slammed the door and ran straight into her house. Mack was so torn up that he went back up to Buddy's and lined up two six packs of Coke bottles under the porch light and shot every one of them with Buddy's rifle, not caring who heard or who came, until Buddy came out and got the gun away from him and told him to get on into the house. But Crystal had called him again, and then finally he had called her; it wasn't what you would call regular, but it went on. "If I was you, I'd just relax and go to it," Buddy had told him once. "You don't know what's in a woman's mind."

Mack looks over at her now, all wrapped up in that purple thing on the seat. "What you doing away off over there?" he says.

"Just thinking. How do you like this?" She spreads out her arms in the shawl.

"Come over here a little bit where I can see."

Crystal scoots over closer and he fingers the shawl, all the tiny careful stitching. "That's real pretty," Mack says. "Somebody make that for you?"

"Yes." Crystal is caught up in some secret delight. "You really like it?"

"I think it's beautiful," Mack says.

"It is beautiful," Crystal says quickly. "It is *very* beautiful." Then she grows quiet on the seat. He can feel her drawing back into herself like she does sometimes, and her good mood is going away.

"C'mere," Mack says. He pulls her over closer and puts his arm around her and she's all up against him now. Crystal puts her head back and closes her eyes, smelling him, some old tacky hair oil he uses and cigarettes, and Mack kisses her hair and her forehead and nearly runs off the road. Crystal sighs and stretches and feels better. She curls her feet up under her on the seat. They have passed Royal City, they have passed Vansant, they have passed the big Island Creek tipple all lit up. They're on their way up to Buddy's, but Buddy won't be there. He's working the three-to-eleven shift at the Harmon mine.

Mack flicks on the radio, which he listens to all the time. He picks up Cincinnati and they get Merle Haggard, and Mack whistles along right next to Crystal's ear. She never knew anybody could whistle like Mack can. It's like his mouth is some kind of a musical instrument or maybe some kind of a bird. It's beautiful the way Mack can whistle, and his breath is lifting her hair. Outside it's full dark now. They can see lights way up in the mountains every now and then, little houses where people live. Crystal wonders who lives up there and what they're doing right now: *what do people do?* She sighs and gets closer to Mack.

He pulls off 460 and turns up the holler where he and Buddy live, a holler without even a name to it, and then bounces along the dirt road and parks in front of Buddy's little shotgun house. Crystal stumbles over a beer can, going up the steps. Once she dreamed that Mack lived in a giant beer can, she remembers. Well, he might as well. But even if she has dreams like that, she doesn't care—she would rather be here than anywhere else, and she would rather be with Mack than anyone else. With Mack she feels like she can be herself, whatever *that* means! she thinks, grinning, stumbling again on the steps. It means she can wear a purple shawl if she wants to, for one thing. It means she can fuck him if she wants to, which she does. Oh yes. Mack holds the screen door open for Crystal to go into the house.

Buddy's house is nothing: peeling linoleum all over the floor, streaked paint inside, old broken furniture piled up any old place. Buddy had a woman, but she left him, so he doesn't keep house very much anymore. Mack says that Buddy still thinks his woman will come back, but Mack doesn't think she will. Mack says she's been gone too long. The only decent thing in the whole tiny house is a big color TV in the corner; but outside, behind the house, is Buddy's boat, a shiny metallic green fiberglass MonArk with an 85-horsepower motor, the boat inexplicably named the *Bud-E*, stenciled in white on its flank. Buddy keeps the *Bud-E* shined up to gee all the time, even though there's no water for miles around. He has to haul it all the way to South Holston Lake to get it into the water.

"It ain't the water anyway," Mack told her once. "Buddy don't give a damn about water. He just likes to work on the boat."

Now Mack disappears back into the kitchen to get another beer and Crystal goes into the bedroom and sits down on the mattress without turning on the light. The bed takes up the whole room. Mack sleeps in the front room, she knows, on the couch. Three rooms and a bathroom is all there is to Buddy's house, and Buddy sleeps here. Crystal sits on the edge of the mattress and feels dirt under her fingers; she lets her shawl drop down on the floor.

"Get out of here!" The kitchen door slams and she knows Mack is putting the dog out. The dog has mange and he doesn't have a name either. Nothing has a name up here. Crystal doesn't even know what Buddy's woman was named: all that's left of her is one bottle of Evening in Paris perfume, which still sits on the back of the toilet. Only Buddy and Mack have names, but Mack doesn't have his father's last name or even know it. His mother, Buddy's sister, gave him her last name—Stiltner—and that's all she gave him before she went up to Detroit to find a new life that didn't include any baby. Mack lived with his grandmother until she died, then with some cousins he didn't get along with, now with Buddy. Crystal brushes off Buddy's bed. Buddy killed a man one time, she knows. A long time ago. Crystal met Buddy once and he was smaller, slighter than she had thought he would be; Buddy has only three fingers on his left hand.

Mack stands in the doorway, blocking the light. His shirt is unbuttoned now and hangs loose around his jeans.

He's taking off the jeans as he moves forward; he pushes her back on the bed. Crystal closes her eyes and he gets off her clothes and gets on her. She comes before he does. She can come sometimes at home just thinking about him. Then they lie on the mattress all tangled up, not talking, and the fresh air from outside blows in across them as softly as breath.

Mack still can't believe it. There is nothing as nice as a nice girl. Every one he has ever had before Crystal wanted to put her clothes back on right away, or they wanted you to say you loved them, or they tried to make you feel bad about it, or they were too crazy to care. Mack used to worry about Crystal getting pregnant. Now he doesn't care. He wishes she would. Then they'd have to get married.

"What's the matter?" she asks now, because Mack gets up and goes over to stand by the window.

Mack doesn't answer. He feels around on the floor for his shirt and gets a cigarette and lights it, and in the moment when the match flares Crystal can see his face, all dark and surly, his light-colored eyes looking mean in the glare.

"What's the matter with you?" she says. "Come on back in the bed."

"I don't know," Mack says. Crystal has to strain to hear him because he's facing the window away from her. "What I told you before, Crystal. It's just gone bad. I don't know, it's no good anymore, honey. I've got to get out of here." Because except for Crystal it's all gone now and this house and the mountains are pinning him in and he knows he has to get out of here and away. He's been here too long already.

"But what about your band?" Crystal says.

Mack laughs. "Some band," he says. "It's not any good anyway, you know that. What do you expect—a butcher and somebody that works in a furniture store and then poor old Jimmy. He doesn't do nothing, I reckon."

"I think you all are real good," Crystal says. And it's true, they can get jobs whenever they can get together to take them, at Hazel's Blue Light up at the state line or at the fire department benefit or anyplace.

"No. The band is not any good. The band is shit," Mack says. After a while he says, "I'm good, though."

Crystal leans down and gets her shawl and puts it over her. "Play me something," she says, knowing he will anyway, he always does, and Mack puts on his jeans and gets his guitar, the only good thing he owns besides the dobro that belonged to his grandmother, and lays it on the bed in its case and takes it out. Mack is real careful about his guitar. He does "Honeycomb." He does "I'm So Lonesome I Could Cry," real slow, as good as Hank Williams. Mack's singing voice has got something in it that Crystal can't identify although she's thought and thought about it, something like a searchlight. Only she would never tell him that. He's not used to girls saying things like that: he'd think she's crazy. He thinks she's crazy now. Crystal lies back under the lilac shawl and lets the air come over her and over Mack playing, and some light from the front room comes in and across the bed.

"Here's one I wrote about you," Mack says, hitting an A-minor chord, and he sings,

"Angel face, angel hair,
Spread out on the pillow so fine,
Soft and fair, angel hair,
I know she won't ever be mine.
Angel hair, she don't care, my darling angel hair.
I hang the house with angel hair,
Christmastime, turkey roast,
But angel hair is sharp as glass
You never can get even close."

Crystal is sitting up in bed with the shawl around her, staring at him. He misreads her look, breaks the song for a minute while he keeps strumming. "I need me some jingle bells right in there, see? Right back there at the Christmastime part." He goes back and starts again on the chorus.

"Stop it," Crystal says.

"What?" Mack looks up.

"Stop it. Stop singing that song."

"Come on, now, Crystal," Mack says.

Crystal starts putting her clothes back on.

"What's the matter, honey?" But Mack puts his guitar back into its case and closes it carefully before he touches her. He's surprised that she's shaking all over. "You cold?" he asks.

"No." Crystal pulls her sweater on over her head; she feels all lost inside, like the bed is swaying. She remembers that the front of Buddy's house is propped up on nothing but cinderblocks and she sees it all smashing up in the road. There was a slag slide up on Dicey once, her daddy told her there was, one Sunday morning. Killed fourteen people, he said, and would have killed more if they hadn't all been at church. Only the bad people died.

"Crystal." Mack pulls her back on the bed, stroking her hair, but she fights to sit up and he lets her go.

"I don't like that song," she says. "It's about me, you said it was. It makes me sound awful. I don't like it. Why did you have to go and write that?"

"It's a good song," Mack says.

"It's not a good song." Crystal wishes for a minute that he was Roger, who could never write a song in the first place, but if he did would never write a song like that. All Roger ever did was give her rings.

Crystal bursts into tears.

"I tell you," Mack says, getting up. "You can't have it every way you want it, honey. You've got to pick, sometime."

"What do you mean?" Crystal sniffs from under her shawl. Mack sounds so serious; finally she looks at him.

"I'm getting out of here," Mack says. He speaks in his soft voice, with all the country in it, and all the pent-up ways he feels come through. "I'm going to Nashville. I don't know how good I am—I was just kidding you a while back when I said I was good. Buddy says I am, I don't know whether I am or not. But I've got to find out, see? I figure I can get a job, I can hang around some, see what's happening."

"Please don't go," Crystal says.

"Why not?" Mack sounds so serious that she can't believe it.

"Oh, just don't, please don't." He's giving her a headache being so serious this way. Crystal pauses for a minute and then does her lip in the Sandra Dee pout. "We've got a date next week for the beauty contest, remember that?"

Mack smiles a slow curling smile which she has never

seen before, full of scorn and almost hate. "The beauty contest," he says without inflection.

"You said you'd take me," Crystal says.

"I don't know," Mack says. "I don't know where I'll be by then."

"Please."

"You ought to come with me," Mack says after a while.

"Where?" Crystal moves around on the mattress, but she still can't see his face because he's back up at the window again.

"Nashville."

"What would I do in Nashville, for goodness' sake? I'm in high school, remember?"

"Fuck school. You could get a job, we could get married."

"Married?"

"Yeah. Whether you know it or whether you don't, we're two of a kind, baby, we're just alike, you and me." Mack's voice is flat and nasal, country.

Crystal draws back from it. "We are not," she says.

"You can't have it all." Mack hit the cheap wood headboard of Buddy's bed viciously with his fist. "You've got to decide sometime what you want. You've got to settle down and decide on things. You ought to think about your mother sometime, too," he adds.

Crystal doesn't know what to say.

"My mother?" she repeats.

"Sure. Old Lorene. Old dumb Lorene. What're you going to tell her we did tonight, tell her we went to *The Sound of Music?* What're you going to say?"

Crystal flares up. "You're a fine one to talk about my mother! What do you want, anyway? You know perfectly well I can't possibly get married. I don't see what you're acting this way for. I don't see what you want."

"I guess I want it all," Mack says. "Like you do. Only I know I can't have it all and you don't, baby, that's the difference. That's the only difference between us."

"I don't know what you're talking about," Crystal says. Mack is really giving her a headache now. "I want to go home." She gets all her things together and goes into the bathroom to brush her hair and fix her face in the wavy mirror. The toilet smells; there are lots of yellow stains inside the bowl. Crystal feels a lot like throwing up, but she doesn't. She puts some of Buddy's woman's Evening in Paris behind her ears instead.

"How do you like it?" she asks Mack when she comes out.

"What?" He's moody, removed.

"Smell me."

"You smell like shit," Mack says.

On the way back to Crystal's house in the truck, he doesn't say much even though Crystal tries to kid him out of it; she calls him Mr. Blue. She touches his cock one time and says, "How's your hammer hanging, Mr. Blue?" But Mack doesn't answer. He shifts into overdrive doing sixty down the road.

"You better slow down," Crystal says, and he does, and a coal train goes by on the railroad track and its whistle splits the whole spring night. "I'll see you next Saturday," Crystal calls back as she goes into her house. Under the porch light she's beautiful, like a princess in her shawl.

Mack picks up some more beer and goes back up to Buddy's and he's still up drinking it, out on the front steps, when Buddy comes in from the mine.

"What's the matter with you?" Buddy says. He hits Mack playfully on the shoulder.

"Cut it out," Mack says.

"Well, what's the matter?" Buddy says.

"Christ, I don't know," Mack says finally, because Buddy keeps standing there and looking at him. "Women," he says. Mack looks out over the whole valley and up and down the bottom, dark and lonesome, and there's not anywhere, no middle ground, for him and Crystal.

"Hell, if it's not one thing it's another," Buddy says. "I been telling you that."

It's May 4, the night of the Black Rock High School Beauty Contest, and everything is ready. The Junior Women's Club has had the auditorium closed off to students for two whole days while they worked feverishly to decorate the stage. This is the first time Black Rock High School has ever held a beauty contest, and the president of the Junior Women's Club, Mrs. Luke Wooldridge, is taking it all very seriously. She feels that the club has to do a real bang-up job on this one because they will be setting a precedent, as she told the club, just like the Supreme Court or something. Everything has to be right. Everything has to be in good taste. The club chose "A Springtime Bower" as its theme, and they have totally transformed the stage. They have made several thousand colored Kleenex carnations and hooked them up on fanciful chicken-wire frames to suggest a fairy-tale hedge all across the back and sides of the stage. They have painted a blue sky backdrop with cotton clouds on it, featuring a small migration of gilt birds in flight. They have constructed a little pink wishing well with a canopy over it at front stage right, for the emcee to stand in. They have made two large trees toward the back of the stage, fabricated from wooden bases painted like bark and real branches cut just a few hours ago for freshness. Burl's Florist and the Black Rock Funeral Home have donated generously of both time and money to place standing arrangements everywhere, and the Junior Women have borrowed the funeral home's red carpet for the finalists to walk out on. The Junior Women were not through with the stage until right before show time, but now it's just like a picture.

Mack Stiltner leans on the green wooden fence in front of the high school and smokes, watching the cars go by. He's pissed because he had to get here so early; Crystal had to be here one whole hour before the contest starts. He's also pissed because he couldn't even get close to her in the truck. Her hoop was in the way and the white net ruffles on her skirt kept jamming the gears. She looked pretty all right, but she was so excited that all she did was talk about nothing all the way. Mack is pissed, too, because he's sure she'll win, and how will he feel about that? If she was his girl, he'd be proud of it, but she is not his girl. He had to get off work early to get here on time, and Mr. Story told him if he had so many social obligations maybe he ought to think whether he wanted to work for the Piggly Wiggly or not. "I'd hate to interfere with your night life," Mr. Story said. Well, fuck him. Mack goes back out to his truck and gets a beer and drinks it, watching the cars roll in and the people get out of them.

The safety-patrol kids direct traffic with their bright-orange gloves. These are town kids, dipshits all of them, and Mack wouldn't care if any one of them got run over. He takes a long cold swallow of beer and watches with some interest to see if this might happen, but like everything else around here, it doesn't.

Down in the cafeteria, the girls prepare for the contest. The whole room is chaos and color, movement, as the girls check their faces in the mirrors in the top of their train cases or their makeup cases, and work on their makeup some more. Sisters and mothers tease their hair and then brush it back down, trying to get it right, to attain just the degree of bouffant. A lot of giggling goes on. Lorene and Neva did Crystal's makeup at home, except for the lipstick. Crystal puts it on now, Revlon's Summertime, and practices different kinds of smiles in the mirror. When Crystal turns her head, her neck and shoulders feel too bare. Neva has done up her hair in a beehive French twist, all shining and elegant, with two spit curls hanging down in front of her ears. Crystal is perplexed by her made-up face in the mirror. It doesn't seem to go with her hair. Or the hair doesn't fit the face. Anyway, she doesn't look like herself in the mirror. She twists her head around, feeling like her hair is some hat that might fall right off, but the beehive is perfectly stable.

Crystal wears a strapless white ballerina-length gown covered all over in seed pearls, with rows of net ruffles going all the way down its skirt, bright-red patent-leather high-heeled shoes with straps, a red velvet ribbon around her waist and another around her neck. Crystal takes a careful look around the cafeteria to see that no one else is wearing a velvet ribbon, and she is assailed by doubt. This neck ribbon was Lorene's big idea: she saw it in a magazine. After thinking about how mad Lorene will be if she takes the ribbon off, Crystal leaves it on.

Agnes is to be in the beauty contest, too. She never wanted to be in it, not from the beginning she didn't, but Lorene convinced her mama that being in the contest is good for your poise. The contest also supports the United Fund, as Lorene pointed out. So here Agnes is, too, in a long green velvet A-line dress that looks like a long sundress, made by her mama and guaranteed to be slenderizing. Agnes knows she'll go off in the first round and she doesn't care. She never wanted to do this, anyway.

Now Mrs. Luke Wooldridge lines the girls up, using a bullhorn. There are sixty-two girls in the contest. The girls go upstairs in a line, tripping over their skirts, and crowd the hall outside the auditorium's backstage door. There are too many girls to fit backstage all at once. They grasp each other's hands nervously, for support, as they hear the crowd. Why, there must be a million people out there! The crowd claps madly for the stage decorations, which have just been revealed, then for Arvis Ember in his wishing well, who starts things off with a few jokes. Then the music begins—the music they have practiced with until they hear it ringing in their ears as they go to sleep—and two at a time the girls emerge from backstage right and left, stepping out smartly to "That's Amore," sung by Dean Martin and amplified for the crowd.

Two by two they come, walking together to the front of the stage, turning slowly all the way around, then going to stand at each side, making a V of two double lines of girls. The applause is continuous and deafening, and the yellow tile walls of the auditorium seem to shake with the noise. Arvis Ember can barely be heard. Agnes has to walk out with Sue Mustard, whom she hates. Crystal comes out with Lynette Lukes, Bobby's sister. The Junior Women's Club, attempting tact, has matched the girls up for this first round according to both height and popularity, trying to put a popular girl with a shy one each time, afraid there might be some who would draw no applause. But the crowd is in a clapping mood, and there is deafening applause for all. The auditorium is filled to capacity and overflowing. Folding seats have been placed in the aisles, and the space between the edge of the stage and the first row of seats is filled with kids sitting right down on the floor.

Crystal turns right; Lynette Lukes turns left. Crystal can tell that she's smiling, because she feels a strain on her face. She hears the whistles and the clapping, so she must be doing all right. Out of the corner of her eye as she turns, she sees a small official group there in the wings: Mrs. Luke Wooldridge, wearing a corsage; Burl of Burl's Florist; a Junior Woman with a first-aid kit; and Bill Hart with that same wide smile. Crystal stops, just for a second, in mid-turn. Then she recovers herself and continues, finishing up and taking her place in the line.

Now Crystal can see the audience a little better. She can pick out some real people to smile at, Lorene and Neva and Agnes's mother, Jubal Thacker, Mrs. Muncy. But where is Mack?

When the curtain comes down at last, the girls go back to the cafeteria to talk about how scared they were, to fix their makeup, get a Coke from the Coke machine, and await the results of the first elimination. While the judges —a trio of Junior Women from the sister club in Richlands—are deliberating, Martha Grover provides entertainment by singing "I Enjoy Being a Girl." Before anyone can believe it, the judges have reached their decision and Mrs. Luke Wooldridge reads the list of eliminated numbers through her bullhorn: 32, 8, 14, 24 . . . it's a long, long list. Thirty girls go down in the very first round. Two of them burst into tears, but most shrug their shoulders and go out to sit with their boy friends and cheer for their friends. Agnes leaves, relieved. So does Crystal's partner, poor little Lynette Lukes, but Crystal is still in the running.

This time out, the thirty girls do an intricate crossing maneuver, and the crowd begins to shout out individual numbers and names. "Crystal!" Crystal hears, and "Sixteen!" That's her number. She finally spots Mack, sitting over to the side all slouched down in his chair, with no vacant seat beside him. Now where will she go, if they take her out after this round? Mack was supposed to save her a seat. Damn him. Crystal arches her neck and smiles brilliantly.

But they don't ever take her out. Round after round she goes, until only six girls are left and Neva and Lorene have come down to the cafeteria to work on her between rounds. "I just knew it!" Lorene says over and over. "I just knew it!" Neva bites bobby pins and concentrates on Crystal's beehive.

"Oh, Mama, I haven't won yet!" Crystal says, but she knows she will. She'd better, since Mack didn't save her a seat.

All excited and bubbling, Crystal takes the cafeteria steps two at a time as she goes back up for the final round. She feels like she's going to explode. The other finalists are more serious and nervous. Suetta Wheeler, a senior, was Miss Claytor Lake last summer; she'll be really embarrassed if she doesn't get this one too. If she could just wear her bathing suit, Suetta knows she could win. Her legs are her best feature, she thinks. But the Junior Women vetoed bathing suits twenty-six to two; bathing suits simply are not in good taste. Suetta grinds her teeth at Crystal. Crystal smiles.

At the very end of the contest, Crystal feels like she has no legs left at all. She is borne up by the noise, the applause. Then Arvis Ember emerges from his wishing well with the sealed envelopes, and a hush falls, and Crystal is sure she will fall, too—*swoon,* like people in books.

"And the third-place winner is—Sue Mustard!"

Crystal claps soundlessly in her long white gloves as Sue goes forward to get her roses. The rest of them stand in a straight line across the middle of the stage: Crystal, Suetta Wheeler, two other seniors, and a pretty little ninth-grader rumored to be related to one of the judges.

"The second-place winner tonight for our first annual beauty pageant is—" here Arvis Ember pretends to drop the envelope and a chorus of boos rises up from the crowd —"is—Miss Suetta Wheeler, forty-five! Let's give the lovely lady a big hand!" And they do, and Suetta gets roses and a banner besides. Now the suspense is killing, but Arvis Ember, having a big time, prolongs it until Crystal thinks she'll die, until at last he calls her name.

Crystal comes forward down the red carpet, takes the roses, helps Mrs. Wooldridge put the banner on her, helps them place the tiara on top of her beehive. She can't even feel it up there. She smiles and smiles, and then she bursts into tears. The applause nearly doubles at this. They love it for her to cry. It's all right to be that pretty if you cry about it. Then everybody is running out onto the stage and kissing her and hugging her, all the kids from her home room, which get a new bulletin board now that Crystal has won, everybody from the neighborhood, all her relatives, everybody. Crystal is pushed and pulled and kissed and mauled, and somebody knocks the wishing well over on its side in an effort to get to her. Only once does Crystal stop smiling and crying, when Mack Stiltner appears just for a minute at her side not smiling, like a dark ghost, and whispers in her ear. Then he's gone and she smiles even more while Lorene watches from the wings with her heart so full and her head so full of plans for the future. Oh, Lorene can see it all: the Miss Buchanan County Contest, the Miss Claytor Lake Contest, the UMW's Miss Bituminous Coal Contest—everything seems within reach. Maybe, even—who knows?—Miss Virginia!

One hour later, Agnes sits in her kitchen drinking a Dr. Pepper. She still wears her formal. Her mama and daddy are in the living room watching Paladin. Babe is out on a date. Agnes thinks Babe is too young to date, but she gets to do it anyway, if she comes back home by eleven. It's quiet in Agnes's kitchen. Occasionally she hears a burst of gunfire from the living room, occasionally Uncle Jud has a coughing fit upstairs, but that's about it. The wall clock ticks. Ten-thirty. Agnes stretches and sighs. She knows that Susie Belcher is having a party, but she has not been invited. Agnes tells herself she doesn't care. Susie Belcher is trashy anyway and so are all her trashy friends. Besides, Agnes has to get up early for Sunday school tomorrow because she's in charge of the program.

The phone rings and Agnes gets it, but there's just a funny buzzing noise on the other end of the line.

"Hello," Agnes says. She waits a minute. *"Hello,"* she says again, but nobody answers. Then Agnes hears some clanking coins, and waits.

"Will you come over here and get me?" It's Crystal, sounding far away and like she's been crying.

"What's the matter?" Agnes says immediately, a little bit put out. Crystal is the last person she expected to hear on the other end of this line tonight. The last time Agnes saw Crystal, Crystal was in that big crowd of people up on stage, and when Agnes hugged her it was just like hugging a metal robot.

"Where are you?" Agnes asks. "What's the matter?"

"I'm still at school," Crystal says. "You don't have to come get me if you don't want to."

"I'll be there in ten minutes," Agnes says.

So Agnes puts on a sweater and gets the car keys and tells her parents where she's going. Agnes's mama is full of questions: Why is Crystal still at school? Why is she calling Agnes instead of Lorene? But Agnes doesn't have any answers.

"I don't *know,* Mama," she says again from the door. "But I wouldn't mention it to Lorene if I was you."

"Well . . ." says Agnes's mama, which means yes, and Agnes leaves. Agnes got an A in drivers' ed; they know she's careful.

The school looks weird when Agnes gets there. Just one hour ago it was so full of people and light. Now it's dark, with only three or four cars in the parking lot. Agnes shakes her head as she parks the car: you never know what Crystal is going to do next.

The big front doors are still open, though, and they echo like Chinese gongs when they close. Agnes goes straight ahead, hearing her own feet walk down the long empty hall. Litter is everywhere, she notices, wrinkling her nose. When she gets to the auditorium it's really a mess, paper cups and stuff all over the place as she walks down the aisle. Some men are cleaning it up. One of them tips his hat, mistaking Agnes for a Junior Woman. The auditorium lights are on, but the curtain has been drawn. Agnes walks all the way down the aisle and goes around backstage, coming into the wings exactly where she made her earlier entrance with trashy Sue Mustard.

She finds Crystal sitting on the overturned wishing well in the center of the stage, all by herself, surrounded by the seven-piece set of white Samsonite luggage that she won for being Miss Black Rock High. Crystal looks moony and daydreamy. Her face is streaked and her beehive is askew, but the glitter on her banner shines in the full stage lights.

"Well, well!" Agnes says.

Crystal looks up. "Oh, hello, Agnes," she says.

Something about the way she says it, sounding so sorry for herself when after all she *is* Miss Black Rock High, gets to Agnes.

"I thought you were going to the party," Agnes says.

Crystal blinks. "Oh," she says. There is a short silence during which Agnes volunteers nothing, offers no help, and after a while Crystal goes on. "Mack wouldn't take me," she says, still in that nearly inaudible, oddly formal pitiful voice.

"Why wouldn't he take you?" Agnes asks.

"He said I'd be too popular now. He said I'd be stuck up. I'm not stuck up, am I?" Crystal raises her large wide eyes to look at Agnes, who stands jingling her car keys at the edge of all the luggage.

"Well, whether you are or whether you're not is not any of my business," Agnes says judiciously. "But I wouldn't go out with that Mack Stiltner anymore if I was you, anyway."

Crystal continues to stare inquiringly at Agnes. She says something that Agnes can't hear.

"What?" Agnes asks.

Crystal looks down at her feet in the red patent shoes. "He plays the guitar," she says. "He wrote a song about me last week, now he won't even take me home."

Agnes has nothing to say to that, it's so dumb. Mack Stiltner is terrible and everybody knows it. She can't see why Crystal goes out with him in the first place. Not with all the nice boys she has her pick of. You wouldn't catch Agnes dead with somebody like that! Agnes thinks Crystal should have stuck to Roger Lee all along. But the boys that Crystal really likes are always weird, and look how mean she was to Roger Lee. Agnes never would have done Roger Lee that way and neither would anybody else that had a grain of common sense, but Crystal has got a weird streak in her someplace, too. Maybe she got it from her father. Agnes knows it's wrong to think bad of the dead, but she can't help it and she doesn't really care: how she used to hate all those dumb, dumb poems.

"Well, come on," Agnes says. Then they have to make three trips back and forth to the car, loading all that Samsonite luggage, and Agnes has to carry most of it because Crystal has her roses and her trophy and her makeup case and her tiara to take care of, too. Finally they get it all in, and by the time Agnes drives back through town, carefully at the posted speed limit of twenty-five m.p.h., there's no traffic at all and even the sidewalks are empty. On the way home, Agnes looks over at Crystal every now and then, but Crystal sits wrapped on the seat in that purple shawl her aunt made her, facing away, and her hoop sticks up over the dashboard.

"Don't you tell Mama I didn't go to that party," Crystal says when they pull into Agnes's drive. Then she gets out of the car and runs across the side yard as fast as she can go, leaving all that luggage in the car, and Agnes watches her go until the white of her dress is gone.

"Thank you," Crystal calls back.

Thank you, my foot! Agnes thinks, but she knows when to keep her mouth shut, and she never tells Lorene a thing.

"Summer's on the way," Lorene announces one night, looking up from her ironing board and out the open kitchen window, and Crystal looks up from a book and says, "Well, what time do you expect him?" Then she could bite her tongue off—it's not her mother's fault that Mack is gone.

Lorene blinks and wipes her face. She can't decide if Crystal is being smart-alecky or just trying to make a joke. Crystal has been so moody lately, ever since she got to be Miss Black Rock High. Maybe it's gone to her head.

"Ha ha," Lorene decides to say, but by then Crystal has gone back to her book and so Lorene's little effort goes noplace. Lorene concentrates on her ironing, doing up Crystal's new pink formal for the Miss Buchanan County beauty pageant. This one has spaghetti straps and a big ruffle around the bottom; they bought it at King's in Bristol. Lorene applies spray starch to the ruffle and it comes out perfect, and Lorene wishes that Crystal herself was this easy to straighten out. Lorene suspects that Crystal's mood has got something to do with Mack Stiltner leaving town, but of course she doesn't mention this idea to Crystal, and Crystal never says a word about Mack. So nobody mentions him, but he's gone, as definitely as if he never was here at all, as if he has disappeared into outer space instead of going to Nashville, which he really did.

Somebody knocks on the door, three short taps.

"Come on in!" Lorene hollers, expecting it to be Susie with that new little baby girl for her to watch awhile—a glutton for punishment, that's what Neva calls Susie, who still won't get her tubes tied but has these headaches in the afternoons—but instead it's Jubal Thacker, child of God.

"Hello there, Mrs. Spangler, Crystal," Jubal says formally. He looks funny standing by the door in his tennis shoes and his dirty white socks, his cut-off jeans, his old familiar angular face and crazy tousled hair, now overlaid, all of him, with a glistening spirituality as noticeable as spray paint.

Crystal looks up at Jubal and blinks. Something clicks inside her, something shifts and settles. She hasn't looked at Jubal for about two years, she realizes. Here he has been two houses away and in her home room and she hasn't even *seen* him for years! And he looks so different now. Crystal squints at him. "Well, hello, Jubal," she says. "I haven't seen you in a long time."

"I guess I've been busy," Jubal says, looking down modestly, because he knows they know he's preaching now.

Crystal keeps staring at him, old skinny freckled-faced Jubal Thacker, and Lorene unplugs her iron and sits down and fans her face. Crystal wonders if Jubal ever hears voices, if Jubal has seen God's face.

"I wanted to congratulate you on winning the beauty contest," Jubal says formally, still standing right by the door. "She sure did look pretty, Mrs. Spangler," he says to Lorene.

"Why, thank you," Lorene says, and Crystal says nothing.

Silence hangs in the kitchen until Jubal clears his throat finally and says it's such a pretty night he just thought he'd go up to the Esso station to get a Coke and he just wondered if Crystal and Agnes wanted to come along.

Crystal gets up like a girl in a trance and follows him out the door before Lorene can say a word, and Lorene watches them go across the side yard to the McClanahans' house, still fanning herself, worried about something even though she couldn't say what exactly, that look on Crystal's face. Lorene is a good Methodist. She doesn't hold with all that Pentecostal carrying on, snakes, God knows what all they do. She sure hopes Crystal isn't going to take it into her head to date Jubal Thacker. Lorene realizes she would hate that worse than Crystal dating Mack Stiltner. It sounds crazy, but it's true. Anyway

Jubal Thacker has probably never had a date in his life. Lorene has never heard of him having one. Maybe he's just lonely tonight. Lorene is lonely herself: Sykes off in Vietnam, Jules on a trip to Greece with his friend Carter E. Black ("Greece!" Neva had snorted when she heard it. "I don't see how he's got time to go to Greece when he hasn't even got time to come home!"). Lorene shakes her head. At least she still has Crystal.

There's another knock on the door and it's not Susie this time either. It's Odell, asking if her upstairs toilet is still working good; he fixed it for her last week.

"It's fine, Odell," Lorene says. "I sure do appreciate you fixing it," and then, surprising herself, she says, "I was just fixing to have a cup of coffee. Why don't you come on in?"

Odell shifts from foot to foot outside her back door. "Well," he says finally, "I guess I wouldn't mind," and he comes in and sits down in the rocker gingerly, as if the whole bulk of him might break it down.

"It's real nice in here," he says after a while. Odell turns his hat around and around in his hands. He's used to doing for other people, not having them do for him.

Lorene fixes the coffee, still surprised at herself. When she looks over at Odell, he seems to fill her whole conversation area. She gets the coffee and sits down across from him, offers him Carnation and sugar, but he says he takes it black.

"Well, Lorene," Odell says, leaning back so the chair creaks and looking at her, "I been meaning to talk some business with you anyway."

"Is that a fact?" Lorene says easily, but her whole face sharpens up. Odell is nobody's fool.

"It's about all that land up at Dry Fork," Odell goes on, his words coming out slow since he's not used to sitting in kitchens and talking to blondheaded women, especially not his half brother's wife. "You know I've got some of it, you've got Grant's part of it now, Nora and Grace and Devere has got some of it, and all together it adds up to where you would be surprised at how much it is."

"Well?" Lorene snaps. She can't stand anybody beating around the bush.

"Well, I've been having people ask me about it lately,

just inquiring, you might say. Talking about leasing it, or some of it."

"Lord, I thought that was all over with," Lorene says.

"Maybe it is and maybe it's not." Odell finishes up his coffee. "There's some now saying that the price of coal is going up again, you can't tell how high. They say it's because of the energy crunch and the A-rabs. I don't know about that. But what I want to tell you, Lorene, is this —if anybody comes around asking you about that land, hold off. Act like you don't know nothing about it. And I'd appreciate it if you'd let me know, if you wouldn't mind. If things go like I hear they're going to, if we can hold on to that and keep it all together, we might stand to get something out of it after all."

"Is that a fact?" Lorene is all excited; she always did like business.

"Well, I appreciate the coffee," Odell says, standing, and Lorene stands up, too. Odell grins at her, his gold tooth flashing once. Flustered, Lorene opens the door and Odell leaves. She hears his truck start up. *My, my.* Lorene leans her face against the doorframe. Her heart is just beating away. What if she was to make a fortune, after all these years? It's never too late, as they say. Lorene goes back over and sits down, flipping the TV on automatically. She has always thought of Odell, if she thought of him at all, as some kind of a big trained bear, Grant's pet. Now she leans forward and examines the rocker cushions carefully, but she can't find a speck of dirt, not one. Odell wouldn't be a bad looking man, either, if he knew how to dress. Lorene is lost in thought when Susie arrives; she doesn't even know what's on TV. Menopause, she tells Susie. Lorene says she can feel it coming on. She's having a hot flash, she says. Susie says she wishes she'd get the menopause herself. That ought to fix Edwin's little red wagon good, she says.

Crystal and Jubal and Agnes sit out on Agnes's porch next door, watching the cars go by. Crystal remembers sitting out here last summer and all the summers before that, and the trumpet vine smells so sweet she thinks she's going to die. The trumpet vine makes her think about Mack, about sitting out here with him in the dark. Crystal can't see Jubal very well right now, but he intrigues her. There's something brand new about him, that shiny cast overlaid on him like he's been dipped in gold. They talk a little bit about school, about Chester Lester, now out on parole.

"I tell you, I just cross the street if I see him coming," Agnes says. "It'd be all right by me if they kept him in there for the rest of his life."

"Me too," Crystal says, although she doesn't really mean it. Chester Lester excites her, knowing how bad he is, his flat white monkey face.

"I mean it, they ought to lock him back up," Agnes goes on. "You all know how bad he is! You remember when he tied Crystal up and put those frogs all over her? Why, she was tied up for an hour." And I untied her, Agnes thinks. Lord knows if I hadn't come along!

Crystal shivers and says nothing. Jubal is silent, too, and they hear some hollering out in the night by the Esso station, then quiet, the swishing sounds of the passing cars. Crystal wonders where Mack is and what he's doing right now. It almost makes her cry to think what good care he took of his guitar.

"Well, what do *you* think about it?" Agnes presses Jubal in her strident voice. "Why do you reckon they let him out so soon?"

Jubal waits a minute. Then rather self-consciously he clears his throat. He says, "Chester Lester has got a soul, the way I see it, the same as you and me."

"Soul, my foot!" Agnes snaps. "He hasn't any more got a soul than this table here." Agnes kicks the table.

"Everybody got a soul, Agnes," Jubal says softly. "And anybody that's got a soul, they can be saved, they can be changed. I've seen it. I know. It's not ever too late for salvation."

"Hah!" Agnes snorts, but the hair along Crystal's arms rises at the sound of Jubal's voice. It's something about the way he says things, so gently and so soft, not at all loud or too much in earnest like her uncle Garnett. Crystal feels funny in the pit of her stomach, and the trumpet vine smells sweet.

"That brings me to what I wanted to tell you girls about," Jubal continues easily, still soft, a disembodied voice coming out of the dark. "We're having a revival next week. I just wanted to tell you all about it, and tell you you're welcome to come. It's going to be outside on

the football field, nondenominational. Everybody is welcome to come."

"I don't believe I'll be able to make it," Agnes says.
"I've been saved ever since I was ten years old, thank you
just the same."

"Well, think about it," Jubal says. "We've got Fred Lee
Sampson, evangelist, he's coming here all the way from
Arkansas, and the Singing Triplets are coming, too."

"The what?" asks Crystal.

"The Singing Triplets," Jubal says. "They're real good.
They've made two records already." Crystal has a wild
urge to laugh out loud, but she doesn't.

"Now, listen, Jubal," Agnes says. "I'm real glad you're
going to be a preacher and all. I think it's real nice. But
I've got my own church to go to, and Crystal does, too,
and it looks to me like we ought to just stick to our own."
Having delivered this opinion loudly, Agnes begins to rock
with a vengeance, so that the creak each time she goes
forward is the only sound for a while on the porch.

"Crystal?" Jubal says.

"What time does it start?" Crystal asks.

Crystal drives to the opening meeting alone, not men-
tioning to her mother beforehand where she is going.
Lorene is at her Garden Club meeting anyway. Crystal
drives slowly through town, stopping for the single traffic
light, remembering all the rules from the driving booklet.
It's only the third or fourth time she's driven alone, but
Lorene has said she can take the car whenever she wants.
Will Lorene be mad? Maybe, when she finds out where
Crystal is going. But she did say that, after all. The light
turns green, and Crystal steps on the gas. Everybody says
that her grandfather Iradell's wreck was what made them
get a traffic light in the first place. Crystal doesn't know if
that's true or not. She parks in the lot by the football field,
puts the keys into her pocketbook, takes her wallet out,
and examines the new driver's license behind its clear
plastic cover. "Wt 118, eyes Bl." The picture doesn't look
a thing like her. You could never tell she was Miss Black
Rock High from that. The picture doesn't even look like
anybody she's ever seen before. Crystal leans back on the

white Naugahyde seat of Lorene's Buick and lets the picture and the billfold slide back into her purse. A car pulls into the parking lot beside her and she breathes some dust, sneezes. She feels funny at the edges of her stomach. She's got no business being here. She can guess exactly what Lorene will say when she finds out about it. She can imagine how her daddy would have laughed. "I put Jesus in the same category as penicillin," Grant told her once with that old slow curling grin, "and there's some that's allergic to both." Crystal takes the car keys back out and looks at them. She could always turn around and go home. Except she has the feeling in her stomach, and she has promised Jubal. She feels the way she's felt before sometimes, like something is going to happen, like she doesn't know exactly what she's going to do but she's pretty sure it will be *something*. After she does it, she'll know what it is. Crystal gets out of the car.

The enormous tent is set up smack in the middle of the football field, looking peculiar, like a huge, aberrant growth. This is where the football games are, and where she becomes a cheerleader every fall. She used to play hopscotch out here at recess in elementary school. Dust swirls around the edges of the tent, and its flaps flap in the hot, dry breeze. People park in the lot and hurry in, stream in, more people than Crystal could have ever imagined. Stepping over a tangle of electrical wiring, she ducks in, too, joins a whole group of people moving up a narrow dusty aisle and finally finds a folding chair. She looks around. This tent is so big it's like a world in here. There are three main poles and lots of smaller poles holding it up. Away up there where the poles hit the canvas top, Crystal can see little circles of light-blue sky. Cone-shaped speakers are attached to the poles. Wires run everywhere. The tent will hold about five hundred people and it's almost full now, but people keep coming in. Here and there Crystal sees people she knows, mostly country people; only a few of Lorene's friends are here. In the front center of the tent is a stage. The stage holds a portable organ, a bass fiddle, a set of sequined drums. It holds a pulpit exactly like the one her uncle Garnett preaches from at the Methodist Church, solid oak. In the very center of the stage is a giant plyboard cross, painted gold. It's at least twenty-five feet high. Somebody has drilled holes all over it, and a colored light bulb has been placed in each hole. These lights are not shining now.

Night is falling fast outside. A redheaded woman starts playing the organ on stage. She plays beautifully, long rippling runs on a jazzed-up version of "Nearer My God to Thee," and the whole big crowd goes quiet. Crystal looks to her right and her left: a high-school couple on one side holding hands, having a date for the revival; a big, straggle-haired woman on the other side, holding a tiny little sleeping baby in a dirty pink knitted cap. Crystal cranes forward with the rest of them as people come out on the stage and occupy the chairs that have already been placed there, as the lights in the tent go dim and spotlights are trained on the stage.

Melville Reed, the preacher of the Holy Pentecostal Church of God, Jubal's church, comes forward first. He is a slight balding man with bulging eyes and a goiter, but he speaks straight and forcefully into the microphone and his voice echoes through the whole tent.

"Praise the Lord!" he shouts, and Crystal jumps. "When I look out there tonight, and I see every seat filled in this great tent, a great cry rises up inside me. Praise the Lord!" he shouts again, and several people in the folding chairs shout, too. "When we were planning this revival, we were figuring the size of the tent, and some of us was holding out for a big tent and some of us was holding out for a little one. And when we called up Brother Fred Lee Sampson on the telephone and asked him what we ought to do about it, he said, 'Rent me the biggest tent you can find, and trust in the Lord to fill it up!' and He has done it, brothers and sisters, He has filled it up!" A lot of people shout, "Amen!" and "Yes!" at this. Crystal begins to feel uncomfortable. But she knows she can't leave now.

"Oh, I look out there, and I see every seat full, and I can feel the spirit moving already, brothers and sisters, I can feel it in this great crowd here tonight, I can feel it in this tent. I look out there and I see so many dear beloved faces, and I see new faces too, hundreds of them, and I say unto all of you, get ready! Get ready to open up your hearts tonight, brothers and sisters, and let Jesus Christ come in. He's waiting. He's waiting right outside this tent tonight. Think about it, beloved. It's up to you. It's up to you! And now, to start the old ball rolling, let's hear from the Holiness Youth Choir of our own Holy Pentecostal Church of God."

The youth choir comes forward on the stage to sing two numbers, accompanied by Miss Louise Yates on the Hammond organ, but Crystal doesn't really pay too much attention. What if she had a wreck? What if she *did* die in a wreck on the way home tonight? Fear shoots straight through the middle of her like a sweet sharp knife.

After the youth choir, Jubal Thacker leads them all in prayer, so white-faced and high-voiced that several women are moved to tears. Then Brother Reed is back to announce the Singing Triplets and out they come, and at first everybody is disappointed. Just from the sound of their name, you would think they would be young and cute, teenagers at the most. But these singing triplets are about forty years old. They bound out onto the stage, big hefty men with greased-back black hair and white long-sleeved open-neck shirts and eyeglasses on, one of them with an electric guitar slung around his neck, and everybody is disappointed. But then they start to sing, and one of them gets on the bass and another on the drums, and they go into "When the Saints Go Marching In" so loud it fills the whole tent. One of the triplets has a real low voice. He throws in "Oh Lordy" every now and then, way down low. They do "If Jesus Came to Your House." Then they lay down their instruments and sing "Amazing Grace" without any music, just their loud strong voices harmonizing, and several people are crying by the time they bounce off the stage.

"How about that?" says Brother Reed. "Beloved, that was the Singing Triplets, don't worry, they'll be back. The Singing Triplets gave themselves to God when they were twelve years old, they've been God's ministers of music ever since. And right now we've got a special treat for you, a young boy here all the way from Cheraw, South Carolina, let me present *Ronnie Mills!*" Ronnie Mills, not much bigger than Jubal, comes out onto the stage carrying two cinder blocks and blinking in the light. "He might not look like it, beloved, but this boy right here is one of the junior karate champions of the whole U.S. of A., and he's got a special message for each and every one of you here tonight."

116

Ronnie Mills places one of the cinder blocks upended on the stage. Then he places the other cinder block upended too, about three feet away from the first one. Everybody leans forward to see what he's up to. Then one of the Singing Triplets comes rushing out on the stage with a two-by-four. He hands it to Ronnie, who puts it across the tops of the cinder blocks. Then Ronnie, who has not said a word yet, unhooks the microphone from the pulpit and walks back over to where the cinder blocks and the two-by-four are, swinging the wire around him and stepping over it easily, and stands behind the blocks.

"Now I am God," he drawls smoothly in his South Carolina accent, "and I live all alone up here in the sky. I'm up in heaven now, can't get down to earth. Oh, I want to get down there and get into your heart but your heart is all closed up, and I'm so sad up here, I can't get in."

Then Ronnie lies down on the stage under the two-by-four and everybody has to lean up to see him. "Now I'm a man," he says into the microphone, flat on his back, "a poor sinner man, my sins are so heavy they've got me down and I want to get up to God. But I can't get there. There's not any way I can get up there at all."

Ronnie scrambles up and pauses a minute to roll up his right shirtsleeve.

"Now, what we've got here," he goes on softly, "is your basic situation between man and God. We've got a poor sinner man flat on his back, we've got a God in heaven who wants to help. Well, nothing is going to happen until that poor sinner man quits pushing and fretting and just says, 'Jesus, come into my heart.' That's all he's got to do, he's got to invite him in. And then you know what God will do?"

There's not a sound in the tent as Ronnie puts down the microphone and raises his right arm. "HI-YA!" he screams, and chops the board in two with his bare hand. The two pieces of it go clattering over the stage and one of the cinder blocks falls down. Applause bursts out as Ronnie bows and runs off the stage and Brother Reed comes back out, shouting, "Praise the Lord!"

"Oh, thank you, thank you, Ronnie, for that fine illustration of what the power of God can do in each and every one of our lives!" says Brother Reed. "That was Ronnie Mills, beloved, he'll be with us for one more night before he has to get back to resume his summer youth ministry in Cheraw, South Carolina. And now here's the man you've all been waiting to meet, the man who has brought thousands of souls to Christ, Brother *Fred Lee Sampson!*"

Fred Lee Sampson walks out, a small man with a crew cut, in a neat gray suit and a tie. Fred Lee Sampson looks a lot like George Gobel. He goes to the pulpit and gets behind it, looks around, and begins. Fred Lee Sampson has a quiet, quiet voice, so soft you have to strain to hear the words. Fred Lee Sampson speaks in a near monotone with no accent at all. His voice is like a newsman's on TV, like Huntley or Brinkley or somebody like that. He does not use the old revival style. His style is an oddity, an anomaly here in this tent. Fred Lee Sampson starts off slow, telling a story about a man he knew with seven children, a man who refused to take out an insurance policy. His wife begged him to do it. The insurance man came to see him and begged him to do it. But the man didn't want to pay that premium, small as it was. He didn't want to commit himself. I'm a healthy man, he said. Forty-six years old and never been sick a day in my life. What do I want with some insurance policy? I'll get an insurance policy when I'm an old man. The insurance man came to see him again and offered him a special cut-rate deal, but again the man refused to take it. That night, going home from work, this apparently healthy man suffered a fatal coronary and was dead on arrival at the hospital. The old ticker was weak, Fred Lee Sampson said, and the man never knew it at all. Fred Lee Sampson delivers this story to the crowd in the same way that Walter Cronkite might report what the Senate did that morning. Just the facts.

He pauses a minute to let the facts sink in. "Now, I tell you," he says in a minute, "that man was a fool. A *fool*, I tell you. He knew the facts. He heard the offer. But he refused to pay the price, the price which was *so small* compared to the results. He even refused to take the bargain rate. He was a fool, my friends.

"And looking out here tonight, over this sea of faces, I wonder how many of you have come here tonight in this man's shoes. How many of you know the facts but don't do anything about it? How many of you think you've got time to do it later, always later?"

Fred Lee Sampson takes off his gray jacket and folds it across the back of a chair. He loosens his blue tie. His voice too is changing now, taking on the twang of wherever he came from, going into the old rhythmic cadence.

A rustle runs through the tent and Crystal looks around. It seems to her that all the people in the audience are sitting up suddenly, leaning slightly forward in their seats. Something is going to happen here, and they're ready for it. They want it. It's hot and dry in this tent and Crystal licks her lips. Her stomach feels funny. She leans slightly forward with the rest as Fred Sampson goes on.

"So you want to know, you're asking me tonight, I can feel it, you're sending me a message loud and clear. 'Fred Lee,' you're saying, 'I'm no fool. I don't want to go to hell, but how can I be saved? You talk about salvation, but how do I get it? How can I be saved?'

"Well, the answer to that is easy, my friends. It's so simple you won't believe it. But let's look first at how you can fail, for that's easy, too. It's oh so easy to fail. You cannot enter the kingdom of heaven by good works. I don't care what kind of a good person you are, I don't care how many good works you've done. Don't make the mistake of mixing blood and works.

"There's one way into heaven and only one way, my friends, and it's easy. The Lord loves us so much that he has made it easy for us. He has given us a bargain rate, and that bargain rate is Jesus Christ His son. Jesus Himself said, 'I am the way and the truth and the light—no man cometh to the Father but by Me.' Now, Jesus is not saying that He's *part* of the way, that you have to pile up good works on the side. Oh no! He's telling it like it is, friends. Jesus is the only way to salvation, the perfect gift for us all. The shed blood of Jesus is the only thing that will remove the curse of sin—the only thing! There is no other way!"

Fred Lee's voice has been loud and rhythmic, but now he drops it again, a monotone whisper into the microphone. "God's messsage to us is clear, my friends. We cannot afford to tarry. There are no rest stops along the road to salvation. God's message is urgent. For I tell you, and I tell you right now, tomorrow might be *too late!* It is not given to us to know the day or the hour of death. It *is* given to us to decide of our own free will whether we

119

accept the beautiful gift of salvation through the blood of Jesus Christ, or not. We have to decide right now, friends, where we want to spend eternity. This is the word, this is the message I bring to you tonight."

Fred Lee's words crackle through the speaker directly above Crystal's head. She feels as if electricity is shooting straight into her head and all down her body, crackling in every nerve. From her biology book she remembers the outline of the human body, sexless, a black outline on the white page, with the thin red lines of the nerves. A current arcs through her body, making her feel like she felt when she was with Mack—alive, fully alive and fully real, more than real.

"Now," whispers Fred Lee Sampson, *"now*. I ask you to bow your heads and let the sweet message of Jesus enter your hearts tonight." The organ begins to play softly while Fred Lee Sampson goes on. "With every head bowed and every eye closed, let us join together, my friends, in singing 'Just as I Am,' you know that one, it is the sweet voice of Jesus from the cross speaking to you now, my friends, calling down through the centuries for you."

The crowd sings, "Just as I am, without one plea, but that Thy blood was shed for me, O Lamb of God, I come, I come."

The organ continues softly and Fred Lee Sampson continues softly, too, after each verse, over the strains of the organ. "He's here. Jesus is here with us in this tent tonight, waiting for you to open up your heart to Him. Maybe you've never known Jesus before. Maybe you were saved once but now you're a sinner fallen by the way. *It don't matter*. Jesus wants you. Behind this tent is a small tent, my friends, where Jesus is waiting. You can be baptized right here, right now. You don't have to be a sinner anymore. Oh, lay that burden down, friends, give up those sins to Jesus Christ who died that you—*you!*—might have eternal and everlasting life. Give those sins to Jesus. Give them to Him now."

They sing another verse, and all over the tent now the people get up and come forward. There's a lot of incoherent calling out and crying as Fred Lee Sampson praises the Lord for each soul. Crystal sits still and electrified, the sense of sin in every pore. She tastes death in her mouth all sugary and metallic, like sucking a scab. But she doesn't want to die.

"One more chorus, friends," whispers Fred Lee Sampson. "One last chance for you to find perfect happiness with Jesus. Oh, He wants you tonight. He's calling you tonight. Won't you listen? Won't you let Him into your heart? Won't you come?"

Crystal rises. As she stands, she notices with some minuscule part of her mind that the two seats on her right are vacant; the couple has taken advantage of the closed eyes to duck out. On her right, the woman is nursing the baby and Crystal sees a swell of fat veined breast and the baby's mouth on it and its moving cheeks. Crystal's stomach feels awful. She's sure she'll throw up, but then she doesn't and she's moving steadily, blindly down the dirt aisle, tripping over wires, straight to Fred Lee Sampson where he stands holding out his arms. "O Lamb of God, I come, I come," they sing. Crystal reaches Fred Lee Sampson and falls on her knees at his feet. Every part of her mind and body is on fire, flaming, a keen high white flame like a giant Bunsen burner in the chemistry lab, all through her. Crystal is nothing but flame.

Fred Lee Sampson praises God and closes the revival. Thirty-four souls have come into Christ. They line the stage, sobbing. They cling to all their relatives and friends. Jubal Thacker holds Crystal around the waist and his heart is full of thanksgiving; it was surely the voice of God which sent him that night to her house.

Four at a time now they go to the smaller tent behind the big tent, where a large plastic swimming pool stands filled and ready. When it's Crystal's turn, some women and Jubal take her in and she's dazzled by the bright light and the figure of Fred Lee Sampson standing waist deep in the water still wearing his gray trousers and his white shirt and tie. Fred Lee Sampson's legs look little and wavy down in the water. Crystal plunges in and it's not even cold. He takes her head and says the words and pushes her down and Crystal comes up sputtering, saved. On the way back to her car, she is surprised to see two of the Singing Triplets sitting in the back of a pickup smoking cigarettes. It doesn't seem right. Yet nothing can spoil the moment of being saved, of being gone and lost in all those flames, of giving herself to Jesus Christ and being nothing at all.

By the time Crystal gets home, dripping wet and holy, Lorene is waiting grimly by the door. Crystal hands her the car keys and goes upstairs to pray without a word, leaving wet marks all over the floor.

Yet Lorene adjusts pretty fast. The next day, several people telephone her to say how pleased they are that Crystal has been saved, how sweet Crystal looked walking up. Lorene certainly can't say that she's *not* pleased, for hasn't she been worrying all along about Crystal's eternal soul? At first she's afraid that Garnett's feelings might be hurt, since Crystal has gotten herself baptized in a tent and not sprinkled in Garnett's own Methodist Church. But Garnett proves magnanimous. He comes over to the house and questions Crystal the next day, and he is convinced that this is the real thing. In fact, he is somewhat jealous, secretly, that Crystal's conversion was so intense. Garnett himself has always yearned for the burning bush, the voice from out of the clouds. Yet these things have not been vouchsafed to him. So be it, he concludes, and when he comes back into the kitchen from the hall where he has been talking to Crystal, he nods significantly to his sister.

"It's all right, honey," he tells Lorene. "I wouldn't worry about it if I was you."

Lorene grinds her cigarette out slow. "That's all right for you to say," she allows. "But here I am, I've got the total care of that child all by myself, and you know how high-strung she is, Garnett. You remember how she carried on when Grant died. And now she's acting so strange again today, like she's in another world or something. I don't know what to make of her."

Garnett smiles. "She *is* in another world," he says, speaking forcefully as always out of his greater experience with the workings of God. "But she'll calm down."

If I could just get her to eat some Jell-O, Lorene thinks. She wanders aimlessly over to look out the window. "I don't know," she says. "I really don't think much of all that Pentecostal carrying on. She gets too worked up."

Lorene pauses and then adds, "Now she wants me to go to the revival with her tonight." She looks hard at Garnett to see how he will take this.

Garnett smiles. "Well, go on, then," he says. "It won't hurt you."

"Well," Lorene says, and sighs.

"There are many roads to Christ," Garnett says, and leaves her with this thought.

And that night at the revival, even Lorene is impressed by the high-school karate champion. Word about him has gotten around, and the crowd is enormous. Lorene is also impressed by the general appearance of Fred Lee Sampson, who is not at all like she expected. She does not think much of the Singing Triplets, nor does she approve of that part in the service when all those who have been saved by Fred Lee Sampson so far go up and screw in their own personal colored light bulb in the giant plyboard cross while the Triplets sing "Let Your Little Light Shine." Crystal has a yellow bulb. She screws it in like somebody in a trance, and her mouth forms a silent O when it lights up. When the meeting is over, eighteen more people have been saved, and they are given light bulbs, too. By the end of the revival, Fred Lee Sampson hopes to have every bulb on that cross lit up.

Crystal is quiet on the way home, turning only once to Lorene to remark that she hopes Lorene will consider re-dedicating her life to the Lord. Lorene opens her mouth indignantly to say she thinks that won't be necessary, then closes it without saying anything when she sees the look on Crystal's face.

Besides, there are some advantages for Lorene in Crystal's salvation. Crystal is a different person during the two weeks of the revival. She sings hymns around the house. She's always asking if there's anything she can do to help her mother. She pulls weeds and washes dishes. She spends a lot of time with Jubal, studying the Bible, and in those old stories she finds blood, death, destruction, redemption and grace, battles, and, most of all, miracles, until she thinks she can't stand it anymore. It worries Jubal considerably that Crystal prefers the Old Testament to the New. The New Testament is more important, he tells her. Christ is what's happening. Crystal and Jubal pore over their Bibles with serious, exalted faces, even though Lorene tactfully mentions that Crystal really ought to start laying out in the sun to get some tan; the Miss Buchanan County Contest is only two weeks away. Crystal attends the revival every night. She loses five pounds during the two weeks while the revival lasts, and at the end of it every bulb on that cross is lit up.

Fred Lee Sampson leaves then, going off to hold another revival in Durham, North Carolina, and Crystal is a part of the big crowd that gathers in the early morning one day to see him drive away forever in his camper. The camper has a picture of Jesus on the back of it. That's the last thing Crystal sees as the camper leaves the school ground and goes down the road and turns left at the bend of Slate Creek.

But about four days later, Crystal suddenly decides that she doesn't want to read the Bible with Jubal after all. It's too hot—ninety-four degrees. So instead of going over to Jubal's, she calls Agnes up and asks her if she wants to drive out to Pikeville, Kentucky, and go swimming. Agnes agrees. They invite Jubal to come along with them, but he's busy, he says. Even over the telephone Crystal can tell he's disappointed in her although he doesn't say anything about it, just by the sound of his voice. In fact, he sounds pretty put out, which makes her feel awful. So Crystal looks out the car window and doesn't say much on the way. Suddenly everything along this road looks new to her, fresh and green. The mountain woods on either side of them look almost violently green, in fact, and the sky is blue as a shout, and as exciting. She's been inside, Crystal realizes, for days.

Agnes drives them carefully over the mountains, and when they arrive the pool is already crowded. They pay at the gate, change, and spread their towels out on the cement. Crystal loves the way the hot cement burns right up through the towel into her body, the grainy scratchy way it feels when she shifts around on the towel. The air is full of pool smells: chlorine, suntan lotion, popcorn. The sun is blinding; she should have brought her sunglasses. She should have brought some cotton pads for her eyes, too. Crystal hasn't been out in the sun for so long, she's forgotten how to act. She jumps in and swims up and down, bumping into people everywhere and splashing, but Agnes can't swim and so she stays in the shallow end. Agnes doesn't want to get her hair wet, either. She has to go to a 4-H picnic that night.

When they emerge from the water, they are surrounded almost immediately by a gang of rough Pikeville boys, pushing each other around at the perimeter of their towels and showing off for Crystal. Crystal wears a black two-piece bathing suit and lies on her stomach. Every now and then she looks up, pushes her hair back, and grins at the boys. It seems like it's been a really long time since she's seen any boys.

After the boys finally go back into the water, Agnes sits up. She's in a bad mood. Of course she's glad that Crystal has been born again, but she doesn't think much of the way in which Crystal went about it, and Crystal has been so busy with Jubal ever since that Agnes hasn't seen her for days. And now all she wants to do is pay attention to these dumb boys.

"I saw you flirting just then," Agnes says.

"Flirting with who?" Crystal's voice is muffled by the towel. Oh, here we go again! she thinks. Agnes can be so hard to get along with sometimes.

"That boy in the red bathing suit."

Crystal shifts position slightly and doesn't reply.

"Well, if you're so religious I don't see why you were flirting with that boy," Agnes goes on.

"The Lord wants us to love one another," Crystal explains in her new sweet voice, the voice Agnes already hates. "I love *you,* for instance," she adds.

"Oh, for goodness' sakes!" Agnes for once is at a loss for words. Also, strangely, she's blushing.

"Why don't you just lie back down on your towel?" Crystal suggests equably. "You're getting in my sun." Most summers, she's been real tan by now, she remembers. She stretches her legs out as far as they'll go: they're *white.* "You're getting in my sun," she says again.

Agnes ignores this remark. "Another thing I don't understand," she goes on, determined to have it out, "is, if you're so religious, how come you're still going to be in that beauty contest? You have to wear a bathing suit in this one, don't you?"

"Yes," Crystal says. "That's why I wish you'd get out of my sun."

"Well?" Agnes pursues. She sees the boys pulling up at the far end of the pool and then looking this way; she knows they will soon be back.

"Oh, come on, Agnes," Crystal says. "Jubal thinks it's fine and so does Mama and so does Uncle Garnett. And so do *I*," she adds grimly, remembering how Mack had told her she couldn't have it all. She'll show him. She can't think of any good reason not to be in that beauty contest, anyway. The body is a temple of holiness, Jubal said—or something like that. Besides, you have to do *something*, don't you? You can't just sit around for the rest of your life.

"Well, what are you going to do for your talent?" Agnes asks. "Don't you have to have a talent in this one, too?"

Crystal rolls over on her back, shading her eyes with one hand. She's been thinking about that. "I think what I'm going to do," she says slowly, "is a dramatic reading from Ecclesiastes. You know that part about for everything there is a season?"

Agnes's mouth drops wide open, but Crystal has taken her hand down and she's staring straight up at the cloudless sky and her eyes are that same color blue. Then soon the boys are back, splashing water on them, and then they have to leave before Agnes gets too much sunburn.

Crystal wins the Miss Buchanan County Contest on June 19, placing first in the talent and evening-dress competitions and second (she's still a little thin since her salvation) in the bathing-suit division.

On August 2, Crystal and Lorene and Neva make the long drive across the state to Richmond, where they will stay in the John Marshall Hotel for four days while Crystal competes in the Miss Virginia Contest. Crystal hates the trip: Lorene and Neva insist on driving with the air-conditioner on and the windows all rolled up so the wind won't blow their hair, but they smoke so much that Crystal, in the back seat, feels slightly sick the whole way and spends most of her time lying down pretending to be

asleep. Another advantage of riding this way is that
Lorene and Neva will gossip without restraint when they
think she's sleeping, so Crystal hears it all. She learns that
Mrs. Belle Drury had her tubes tied in the Richlands Hospital without telling her husband right after she recently
had her third baby, a boy, and that this made Mrs.
Drury's husband, Roy Drury, so mad—because he is a
Catholic from Ohio, Neva adds—that he took a
sledgehammer to her brand-new Singer sewing machine
and busted it all to pieces. Which upset Belle Drury so
much that now she has moved back in with her parents,
bringing both kids and the new baby too. This story
amazes Crystal, who knows Mrs. Belle Drury only from
seeing her at the public library: a small, pale young
woman with runny-nose children who hang on her skirts,
checking out two Gothic novels a week at the desk. In her
mind Crystal has a clear picture of the girls on the covers
of these novels (in despair, wearing long pastel satin
dresses, fleeing across some dark landscape from the
gloomy castle in the background) but no clear image at
all of Mrs. Belle Drury who is living through such a hard
time. Neva goes on to say that Charlie, her own husband,
has been suffering from a hiatal hernia lately and it has
not improved his disposition one bit. "Charlie never was a
figure of fun, anyway," Neva says, and Lorene remarks
that he has his good points all the same. Neva says she
guesses so, and mentions that Grant did, too, she supposes, and Lorene agrees. "But I don't see how you did
it," Neva says, and Lorene changes the subject to Louise
Altemose whose thyroid gland turned out to be malignant
when they took it out last week. Then they talk about
floor coverings, Armstrong versus the cheaper Sears, and
about whether Neva ought to put indoor-outdoor carpet-
ing in the Clip-N-Curl or not. This conversation leads to
the condition of Loretta Hurley, one of Neva's girls, who
is ruining all her chances of getting married by living with
her mother and dating the same boy for five years when
he is not, Neva swears, the marrying kind in the first
place. He eats supper every single night with Loretta and
her mother, apparently. And he never *will* pop the question, Neva says, if Loretta won't stop giving him a free
lunch all the way around, if Lorene knows what she
means. Crystal knows what she means.

The two women talk on about marriages and divorces, death and birth and illness: it's soothing, and has nearly put Crystal to sleep when Lorene says, "Neva? Do you remember that party we had for Saint Patrick's Day that time?" "What party?" Neva asks. "You and me. It was when I was fourteen and you were sixteen and we had it in the old Moose Lodge before it burned. Don't you remember? We put green crepe paper all over the place." "We sure did! We had those little sandwiches," Neva says.

This whole party is news to Crystal, who cannot imagine such a thing. Not green crepe paper, or Lorene at fourteen, or Neva ever young at all, for that matter. Lorene was probably a lot like Babe. Crystal wonders where she'll be and what she'll be doing when she's Neva and Lorene's age. They might even be dead then, for one thing, whether they had a party or not. Crystal shivers. She can't imagine herself old. But she can see herself some years from now, and a whole series of tableaux goes through her mind. She's a movie star, world famous, and at her side always is her short swarthy husband with the cigar in his mouth, who masterminds her career. Gossip columnists analyze this marriage all the time, but nobody can figure it out. They have a magnetic attraction for each other, that's what, a psychic pull which extends beyond the grave. *What grave? Lord.* Crystal shivers. Or she is in Nashville with Mack who has become a legendary star himself, and they are both wearing cowboy suits emblazoned with red sequins, posing for photographers. Then Mack runs all the photographers out with a masterful sweep of his hand and locks the door. He pulls her toward him and rips off the top of her cowboy suit, scattering sequins all over the white shag carpet. They make love on the carpet, in the red sequins, and it is wonderful and Crystal is the envy of millions of his fans. Mack leaves his cowboy hat on while they make love. Or she is some kind of a church worker in a high mountainous visionary country like Tibet, where she sees herself pushing open a massive carved door and being immediately surrounded by thirty or forty sweet little starving children who have brought her hundreds of flowers. A man in this country loves her, a poet with burning eyes who sits cross-legged on a flowered rug and smokes opium in a pipe all day long, and although she responds to the spiritual passion of this doomed poet, she can never be his; she has dedicated herself to God, to these children in this remote and austere mission, even though she has contracted amoebic dysentery and TB. "I am here but to serve," she tells the poet sorrowfully.

"What, honey?" Lorene asks.

"Nothing, Mama." Crystal sits up. "Where are we, anyway?"

"We're right outside Lynchburg," Lorene says. "I've got a pimiento cheese sandwich right here whenever you're hungry." Neva and Lorene pack everything when they travel; there's no sense throwing money away. They have even brought a coffemaker to plug in, in their room at the John Marshall Hotel. They won't stop, either, although Crystal would like to see Natural Bridge.

"Tourist trap," Neva snorts.

And of course they are not tourists. They are here on serious business, which Lorene makes clear right away to the man at the desk when they check in that night at their hotel. He's polite but not impressed: this whole hotel is full of contestants like Crystal, and all their mothers and sisters and aunts. Crystal sits in a chair in the lobby of the John Marshall Hotel, watching the people come and go, their luggage carried by grinning red-suited Negroes. Negroes fascinate her; there are no Negroes in Black Rock and there's no reason for them to move there, either, Lorene has always said. Nothing to do except work in the mines, and there's not enough of that to go around in the first place. Crystal watches one boy about her own age, carrying somebody's bag. He wears earplugs, and wires run down inside his red suit to some invisible radio, tuned to jazz. He bops and shuffles, all caught up in the beat. Crystal would like to hear it, too. She would like to be him. Or she would like to be that frail elegant woman in the hot-pink linen suit, smoking cigarettes, looking distraught. Maybe her lover is late. Crystal would like to smoke cigarettes. She used to have a lover but he's gone. And anyway that was a sin, she reminds herself, but she has never been able to really feel that connection between her life and her salvation—which after all applies to the *after*life primarily—so she abandons that idea as being beside the point. It *is* beside the point.

After Lorene has signed them in, they go straight up

to their room on the eighth floor, accompanied by a porter
with their bags. Lorene tips him, then shuts the door.
Lorene and Neva are worn out, they say. And Crystal
needs her beauty sleep. The definition of beauty sleep, according to Lorene, is any sleep you get before one A.M.
After that, according to her, doesn't count. Neva locks
both locks and pulls an armchair up against the door.
"You can't ever tell," she says. Neva retires to the bathroom and comes back out in a billowing green lace negli-
gee which makes her look enormous and weird, like an
overgrown fairy from Shakespeare. Lorene sits down in
front of the mirror to count her money and cream her
face.

Crystal sits by the window and begins to read her Bible
dutifully, but she can't keep her mind on the words. She
stands up and raises the window to let the hot city air of
Richmond come into the room, and she gulps it as if it
could tell her something; it smells like gasoline, fried food,
garbage, indefinable city things. Down below her on
Broad Street, traffic is all snarled up, and in the night she
hears sirens scream. Somewhere down there, people are
stabbing each other, people are killing other people, rob-
bing stores, fucking each other, people are yelling and
screaming, houses are burning down to the ground. All of
life is going on down there without her. Even Revelations
is boring compared to Richmond. "Shut that window,"
Lorene says.

The next day they go shopping before the official round
of activities starts with a Coke party in Capitol Park at
two. Before they leave the room, Lorene puts her money
into her bra so that it won't be stolen by Negroes. Crystal
looks up and down the streets of Richmond carefully.
There's so much going on here; it's a new world, hot and
busy and rushed. They go into Miller and Rhoads, where
Crystal fingers dress after dress on the long racks. Sales-
girls hover around her; Lorene has told them why she's
here. "That's just your style!" they say when she tries a
sleeveless blue-and-white stripe. "It was made for you!"
they say when she tries on a flowery pink shift. But Crystal doesn't believe them. She can't decide. She is thor-
oughly bemused by herself in the three-way mirrors of
Richmond. Finally Lorene steps in and picks a black cotton

sundress with a square-cut neck and a geometric border around the bottom.

Crystal wears it later to the Coke party, where all the girls pose on children's play equipment while the children, dispossessed, fight in the sand or look on. "Isn't this fun?" all the girls say brightly to one another, except for one tall girl from Manassas who whispers, "This is a lot of shit, isn't it?" to Crystal, even while they both smile brilliantly and a photographer clicks away. Crystal stares at this girl and doesn't answer. Is it a lot of shit?

Several times during the next few days she manages to get away from Neva and Lorene, and go out alone. She walks for a block or so, shielding her purse. She passes a Greek restaurant, an Italian restaurant, a dancing school, a shop that sells handmade leather goods. There's an antique shop with a grandfather clock in the window and a whole family of antique china dolls. Grace would love them. The faces of the people she meets are so various, their clothes so different, that Crystal is breathless by the time she arrives back at the John Marshall Hotel. Pigeons perch on the edge of its roof. Neva says they are nasty and carry diseases, but Crystal loves them. They are impudent city pigeons which add some sort of a finishing touch to the fluted roof. Well-dressed men sit in dark leather chairs in the lobby, reading newspapers. After the second day, the doorman nods to her. The man at the desk smiles. At the elevator, people kiss each other on the cheek in greeting. She can't get enough of Richmond.

Richmond is so wonderful, in fact, that the contest itself becomes secondary in her mind and is something of a letdown anyway. Her dramatic recitation from Ecclesiastes is not a hit. She places fourth, though; the first three spots are won by older girls. Lorene is put out. The first runner-up is bowlegged, she declares. Actually she feels that Crystal would have won the whole thing if she had a better talent and if she hadn't been a junior in high school. The first prize was a college scholarship; after all, as she points out later to Neva, they couldn't very well give it to a junior; and Neva agrees. "We jumped the gun," she says. *Next year,* Lorene thinks.

Crystal doesn't care. She's famous. By the time they get back home (after stopping at Natural Bridge to please her, where a loud symphonic recording of "How Great

Thou Art" comes from some mysterious wooden source while they view the bridge; where Lorene buys four placemats with a picture of the bridge on them and Neva buys a pink glass vase) her picture has been on the front page of the *Black Rock Mountaineer*, and Arvis Ember interviews her on his radio program. "It's a memory I will always cherish," she tells him, with that girl from Manassas in the back of her mind. "Everyone there was so sweet."

Lorene puts all of Crystal's trophies and ribbons up on the mantel in the front room, and boys from the surrounding towns—Pikeville, Richlands, Haysi, Welch—begin to call her up. Crystal has a different date practically every night. She likes all these boys. They all have cars and they have change in their pockets. They adore her and Crystal likes them all, even the dumb ones, even the sarcastic ones, even the ones with deep, fake laughs. She likes their pressed pink shirts and their yellow shirts and their Madras pants. It's a funny thing, but she doesn't feel real when she's by herself, or perhaps it's only that she doesn't feel again the way she felt with Mack or the way she felt the night when she was saved. Crystal continues to read her Bible and to discuss with Jubal the workings of the Lord, but the glory is fading fast. It's only when she's talking to Jubal or to her uncle Garnett and sees in their eyes herself—*Crystal saved*—that she is conscious of her salvation.

Youth group is a bore. One night their leader, Mrs. Robert Haskell, tells the girls of the MYF never to pet, because boys can become so excited during the act of petting that they can literally *die* if they don't have a chance to relieve themselves. Girls have more control, of course, so girls are responsible for seeing that petting does not occur. The girls of the MYF nod seriously. Life-and-death decisions are safe with them. Crystal looks out the window. There's a silver mine out there someplace, and a hollow tree a man lived in.

The next afternoon she has a date with a boy named Woodrow Morris, a tall lanky boy, a doctor's son, from Richlands. He has driven all the way over here to date her after meeting her at the MYF district meeting a month before. Crystal introduces him to Lorene, who is impressed, and then gets into his baby-blue convertible and they drive across Fletcher's Ridge to the Breaks, a picnic area maybe forty minutes away from Black Rock. It's early fall, September, and red and gold leaves fall on her hair and all over her new plaid A-line skirt; they rustle in the back seat of Woodrow's convertible. Woodrow asks Crystal if she has any hobbies. He parks on an overlook. Woodrow's adam's apple sticks out; he wears loafers. "I hope to become a surgeon like my father," he says. "Let's go sit over there," she suggests, pointing, and they get out of the convertible and sit in the fallen leaves at the edge of the cliff for their picnic.

After they eat their sandwiches and drink their Cokes, Woodrow kisses her, tentatively. Crystal kisses him back, harder. "Oh Crystal," Woodrow says. She guides his hand to her breast, unbuttoning the monogrammed shirt she bought last summer at Miller and Rhoads in Richmond. "Oh baby, Crystal, you don't," he says. *"Oh Crystal."* He tries to say a lot more, but Crystal kisses him and puts her hand between his legs and finally she says, "Listen, Woodrow, would you please please please just shut up?" He does. After they're through, they lie on their backs in the dusty leaves and Woodrow plans out their whole future. He's going back to Hampden-Sydney in a week; Crystal will come for a weekend. Crystal will come for Winter Weekend. Crystal doesn't even bother to listen. Woodrow thinks this is a big deal, but it's not. Because she knows something that Woodrow does not know even if he is so smart: this doesn't matter. This doesn't make any difference. Woodrow kisses her neck and her hair. "Oh Crystal," he says. *"Oh Crystal."*

Other times she lets other boys touch her and she doesn't care. Sometimes she lets them go all the way too and she doesn't care about that either. She doesn't care what Mrs. Robert Haskell thinks about it either—or what Mrs. Robert Haskell would think about it, if she knew. Because it's only when she's with boys that she feels pretty, or popular, or fun. In the way they talk to her and act around her, Crystal can see what they think of her, and then that's the way she is.

During her senior year, Crystal wins two more beauty contests before she gets tired of them altogether. She dates more boys. She reads two books by William Faulkner which she stumbles upon quite by accident in the public library. The grammar in these books is complicated. She loves them. She reads some foreign books, such as *Les Misérables* and *Fathers and Sons*. Jean Valjean of *Les Misérables* is just her style: a lot of anguish and intensity, as she tells Agnes, who is not very interested in either one. Crystal writes a sonnet comparing life to a rose: first the bud, the bloom, then the falling petals in a high, cruel wind. She writes a term paper on "Nature in Mark Twain," with twenty-six footnotes, but Miss Hart gives her a B on it because she typed the bibliography wrong.

Agnes is accepted at VPI, where she plans to major in home economics, but VPI is not good enough for Crystal. Oh no. Because Lorene is in charge of that. Lorene has plenty of rivet money laid by, plus insurance money from Grant, and she has her sights set high. Even East Tennessee State University is not good enough. Lorene envisions herself as a visiting mother-in-law, with Crystal married to a brain surgeon. It's time for some culture, Lorene feels, some society. Crystal should meet a better class of people. Jules writes a letter of advice on the subject, in which he tells Lorene above all to get Crystal out of the South. Lorene sniffs and throws this letter away. She pores over college bulletins, checking the clothes and the prices, ignoring the course offerings, settling at last on a fancy school in Maryland. Crystal doesn't care about college. She won't even look at the booklets. She dates boys and daydreams and reads books, and then it's spring again, then graduation and summer and she and Agnes go off to Girls' State.

Girls' State, an annual occurrence, is held each summer at Radford College, while Boys' State is held simultaneously on the campus at VPI, up the road in Blacksburg. A fine sum of state money goes to support both these projects. The purpose of Girls' and Boys' State is to teach future leaders about representative government. So Girls' State is just like the government in Richmond. There are elections; lobbies and factions; bills to be considered, rejected, or passed; caucuses to attend.

Crystal is only a Congressman from the Ninth District, but Agnes has been maneuvering for the first three days and on Thursday she gets herself elected Secretary of the General Assembly. Today, Friday, she will take the minutes and call the roll at the General Assembly meeting, and she has bought a special notebook for this event, plus three new ballpoint pens in different colors.

The girls sleep thirty to a bunch in a cluster of giant, barrackslike dormitory halls at Radford. Agnes and Crystal have been placed in the same building, but they are not in the same dormitory hall. Each morning they are awakened by a bugler playing reveille, and they must get right up and wash their faces and dress and show up fifteen minutes later, ready to say the Pledge of Allegiance and salute the flag. In many ways, Girls' State is like a big camp. Most of the girls are really too old for this sort of thing, and there are not many budding politicos among them. A lot of them are just waiting for Saturday night, when they will have a dance with the boys from Boys' State.

That Friday morning, Crystal awakens an hour before anyone else. This in itself is strange, because although she often has trouble falling asleep, she always sleeps dreamlessly and interminably until someone or something wakes her up. She never wakes up by herself. She never wakes up for no reason. But this particular morning, she's suddenly wide awake and tingling from head to toe. Lying flat in her bed in her top bunk, Crystal runs her fingers over her breasts and down over her pelvic bones sticking up, down over the length of her body. She knows it's not time for her period. Maybe she's sick. But she doesn't feel sick. She's simply wide awake, and she knows that something's going to happen.

Crystal raises herself up on one elbow and pushes the hair out of her eyes and looks around to see what it might be. The vast gray room is shadowed and furred in the funny light of the early dawn. The twenty-nine other girls are all sleeping, heads on their pillows or their pillows pushed to one side, some arms hanging limp off the beds. The air is palpable, light gray. It stirs and sways with their breathing in sleep. Sometimes, somebody murmurs something that Crystal can't hear distinctly, something absorbed immediately into the thick sleeping air of the room. Crystal leans down to look at the girl on the bottom bunk; Diane Phillips from Danville, Virginia. Diane sleeps with her black hair in green foam rollers. Her sheet has twisted down to expose her to the waist, flat-chested under a cheap pink nightgown. Diane's head is skewed to one side and her eyes appear partly open, the pale lids fluttering, but she too is sound asleep, breathing with her mouth open. Crystal watches Diane for a long time and sees one saliva bubble form, then burst, then reform on her lower lip. Maybe Diane has sinus.

The window is level with the top bunk, so Crystal turns to stare out, but she can't see much—the corner of another building, brick too, a part of a courtyard, a tree, a fountain, a wall. Her view is partly obscured by the mist that clings to everything here in the mornings, persistent mist which rises only when the girls have pledged allegiance and the sun is fully up. While Crystal stares out the window, the air around her seems to move, the sounds of breathing intensify, and there is a swell, a rising movement of the air. At first she feels disconnected, then oddly terrifyingly buoyant, borne up on the gray moving air and floating. It's being in this top bunk, she thinks. That's all. I've never slept in a top bunk before. She wishes it would stop, expects it to stop—maybe it's something she ate. Only the rising current never stops, and even though Crystal lies, or falls, back on the bed, she's in it now and it has taken her up and up and up. She struggles to sit up, but she can't. Her body doesn't respond or move although she can raise her head, can thrash it from side to side on the pillow to stare out wildly into the softening, lightening room where no one stirs, no one moves, no one is yet awake. She can't believe they're still sleeping when all the air has turned to wind now, loud and roaring, tossing her and sweeping her along. How can they be asleep? Crystal twists her neck again and looks out the window. Something moves in the mist by the single tree. She tosses her head to get the hair out of her eyes and looks again. It moves.

Suddenly, with no warning, the wind stops. There's no sound at all. Crystal hears her own heart beating, and the blood runs like a creek in her veins. She expects to plummet down some awful immediate spiral into the lack of wind and sound. But she doesn't. She's suspended, and it grows lighter and lighter in the hall as surfaces everywhere grow distinct once more. Edges appear.

"Crystal!" It's a man's voice, very deep, mournful, and somehow familiar, coming from far away. Coming across unbelievable distance, echoing in empty places, but close too. Close to her.

"What?" Now Crystal can speak, and she does, and she can sit up too. Pulling her knees up to her chest and pulling her sheet up tight around her, she hugs her knees and looks everywhere carefully, bunk by bunk. He could be anywhere in this big room, hiding behind any bed.

"What?" she says again. She waits.

"Crystal," he calls again, drawing her name out long, making it last forever, and it becomes clear that he's not here inside this room.

"Wait!" she calls out. "Wait!" She pulls her bathrobe off the rail at the head of her bunk and puts it on, not stopping to button it, and climbs down the iron ladder.

"Please wait!" Crystal calls again.

She runs up the rows of bunks the length of the hall, not looking back once to see Diane Williams sit bolt upright in bed, not noticing the girls all around her waking up now, getting up. She runs straight out the front door onto the cement sidewalk, then around the side of the building and along its length, past shrubs and windows, to where the fountain is, and the tree. The mist is not so thick now. The sun is up, and only wisps of gray are left. Her feet are wet from the grass.

"Where are you?" Crystal stops and holds on to the fountain. "Where are you? Here I am."

The bugle sounds reveille very close, so loud and brassy it nearly scares her to death. Crystal runs around the fountain and the tree, along the facing wall. No one is there. A coke bottle is wedged in a crook of the tree. "Where are you?" she screams although she knows that nobody could hear anything over that bugle.

When the bugle stops, she hears all the girls, far away and babbling, getting dressed. Crystal sits down in the grass where she is. It's still wet, feels good. She gets a blade and looks at it, licks it, chews it. She doesn't think the man will call again. He called, and she couldn't find him, and now it's full morning and he won't call again. She has missed him. Crystal puzzles over who it might have been: it wasn't exactly her father's voice; it wasn't anybody here; it wasn't anybody she knows. Not anybody she *really* knows, that is, even though in a way she knows it as well as she knows her own. When Crystal was little and Grant told her about China being on the other side of the earth, she used to dig and dig for it at the edge of Lorene's tomato patch. Then when that didn't work, she took to imagining another girl or maybe a little boy, a Chinese mirror self in China, sleeping when she was awake and playing when she was asleep. Everything she dreamed was what the other did, and everything she did was dreamed by the Chinese mirror child. Maybe that was who was calling her, grown now. Maybe it was Clarence B. Oliver. More likely it was God. Whoever it was, she has failed to find him. *Shit.* She sits exhausted in the grass at the side of the dormitory with no will to go in and dress to go to the General Assembly, which seems totally meaningless anyway. More shit.

The bugle blows again and the girls come out at the front of the building. When they say the Pledge of Allegiance it's like a litany, just far enough away so Crystal can make out the words, close enough for her to catch the rhythm. Crystal looks up at the bare flagpole across the roof of the dormitory and here comes the flag. It droops and furls and then is caught by a breeze.

Crystal sighs and gets up. Maybe she can find Agnes. She can always count on Agnes to tell her what to do. Holding her nightgown up, Crystal runs around to the front of the dormitory, where the straight lines of girls are breaking up, forming groups, and starting off to breakfast. Everybody stares at her, but Crystal doesn't care.

"Agnes!" she yells. "Hey, Agnes! Wait a minute!"

Agnes, way up the walk with two other girls from her own hall, stops, pauses, and looks back. Then she says something to the two girls, who look back, too, before they walk on. Agnes moves quickly and officiously back to where Crystal waits in the grass near the flagpole, with one hand shading her eyes.

"What's the matter?" Agnes asks immediately. "Are you sick?"

Crystal looks so pale and funny, and she has grass stains all over her bathrobe. She feels funny, too. She grabs Agnes's arm, hard. "Listen," she hisses, but then, looking at Agnes all dressed up in this bright morning light, she doesn't know what to say. Suddenly, she's just plain tired. The girls of Girls' State stream by them on either side, staring curiously at Crystal.

"What?" asks Agnes. *"What?"* she asks with less patience, as Crystal continues to hold her arm and say nothing. Agnes begins to realize that Crystal isn't sick at all, and she suspects that this is another one of Crystal's stunts. But this morning Agnes has no time to waste. Girls' State runs on a tight schedule, and since she's Secretary of the General Assembly she has to be on time. Agnes grips her new notebook and her ballpoint pens firmly.

"Calm down, I'll talk to you later," she says. "Right now I've got to go."

"Listen," Crystal says.

Agnes looks at her good. Color is flooding her face and she seems to be much too excited.

"I had this vision," Crystal says.

"What kind of a vision?" Agnes is looking around. Nearly all the girls have left for breakfast now.

"Well," Crystal says, speaking slowly so she can get it right, "I woke up real early this morning and I was just lying there, with everybody else still asleep, and all of a sudden I heard somebody call my name." Crystal decides not to mention the wind.

"So what?" Agnes says.

"It was a *man's* voice." Crystal pushes her fingernails into Agnes's arm.

"Well?" asks Agnes, fidgeting.

"Well, *there aren't any men in Girls' State.*" Crystal pauses to let this sink in. "Then I heard it again. I heard it two times in all."

"Who do you think it was?" Agnes is partly scornful, partly impressed.

"Probably God," Crystal says solemnly. "It had to be." Her heart beats just like thunder in her chest and this is how she wants to feel forever and ever, this much alive.

"I bet you've got the flu or something. You better calm down and I'll see you at lunch," Agnes says. She pulls away from Crystal's fingers and runs up the sidewalk after the others. She looks back once at Crystal standing stock still there by the flagpole, staring off at nothing with that excited look all over her. Even the way she's standing, you can tell that something is up.

Crystal feels a lot better after she brushes her teeth. While she's dressing, she remembers something she read once in Lorene's *National Observer* about visitors from outer space who come down in UFOs and try to contact earthlings. There are thousands of mysterious disappearances in the United States alone. The dining room is closed when Crystal arrives, but she persuades the kitchen help to let her have two doughnuts, and then she puts her name tag on and walks over to the General Assembly, where later that day she will vote against water pollution.

III

FIVE YEARS LATER, Agnes is in the kitchen making a Lady Baltimore cake for her poor old daddy's birthday, and while she mixes and measures she looks over every now and then at the postcard lying on top of the stove. She butters and flours the pans. She pours in the batter, licks the spatula, and throws it into the sink. She puts the pans in the oven: 350 degrees. She wipes her hands down her sides on the apron and looks at the card again. One side has a picture of some big pink birds sticking their heads into the water. The other side says: "Hi! We're in Key West. Will come through Black Rock on our way back North. See you probably on Thursday. Best, Crystal."

Agnes tightens her mouth and puts the postcard into the trash. Today is Thursday, February 16. You could have knocked her over with a feather when she got this postcard in the mail. Good thing she was the one who looked in the mailbox, so Mama and Daddy don't know a thing about it. And won't, if she can help it! Not that Daddy knows much of anything these days anyway, they keep him so doped up. "Best, Crystal." Well, Crystal's best is not good enough for Agnes anymore. Imagine writing somebody a card that you haven't seen for three years, expecting them to say oh goody! Agnes fixes herself some instant coffee and sits down heavily in a kitchen chair. She has been up since 6 A.M. Crystal takes too much for granted, always has.

Maybe if Crystal hadn't been born looking like that, Agnes thinks, maybe that was the trouble all along. Crystal's famous beauty. Maybe if Grant hadn't been so crazy. But things happen the way they do, and if you look back you think, "Oh, if I hadn't closed the door just *then* when the carpet salesman from Bristol was here that time," or "What if I had gone over to Knoxville for the summer that year Aunt Donna asked me, what *then?*," but you didn't do it, you didn't go, and so you never know, and looking back it's hard to say when the important things happened or even what they were because all the days went along so fast back then, like water under the bridge.

Well, they're gone now. You've got to salvage what you can and keep ahold of what you've got, and not be looking off in the clouds someplace. If Agnes's daddy hadn't gotten so bad off, she never would have taken over the hardware store, for instance. She didn't know a two-by-four from a hole in the wall that day she started. She didn't know she was starting it either; she thought she was just going in to see how everybody was getting along with her daddy so sick.

And if Lorene hadn't sent Crystal off to that so-called college on her rivet money, Crystal would be happily married to Roger Lee Combs today, and that's the truth. She would have babies and maids. If somebody hadn't let on to Crystal that she was smart—which was a real mistake, in Agnes's opinion, because Crystal never had a grain of common sense in her life, not a grain of it, and that's the only kind that does you any good in the long run.

In college Crystal majored in English and started looking like some kind of a beatnik. She never came home if she could help it—just like her brother Jules, all over again. It's funny how things will repeat. Lorene clearly didn't like the way things were going, but there wasn't much she could do about it after she had sent Crystal up there. Whenever anybody asked Lorene if Crystal was in a sorority where she was, Lorene just glazed over and said something about the weather. By that time, Crystal wouldn't have touched a sorority or a beauty contest either with a ten-foot pole. She always had to be one way or the other. She never knew about in-between. When she did come home, she dated Roger Lee Combs, who was out of business graduate school by then and held an advanced degree, but she wouldn't go out with him much even though Lorene was really pushing it and he was still crazy about her.

Roger Lee had come into the hardware store several

times to talk to Agnes about it. "I just can't understand that girl!" he said, shaking his head. "She's the damnedest thing I ever saw." But he was smiling about it. Roger Lee was the best catch in town until Crystal ruined him. You would have thought he would have known better by then. He wouldn't look at anybody else, and she treated him so mean! Agnes used to bake him some gingerbread and take it by every now and then to try and pep him up. Because Crystal was *morally loose,* that was the plain truth about it, and everybody knew it. It killed Roger Lee. That's how she wrapped him around her little finger, and that's why she got those long-distance person-to-person calls all the time when she was home. To talk to her, though, you wouldn't have known it: she tried to pull the wool over everybody's eyes by acting so sweet. Agnes asked her straight out one time if she was ever going to marry Roger Lee or just keep stringing him along, and she laughed and said she was going back to school to get a master's degree, so she couldn't very well marry anybody right now, could she? She had let her hair grow out and it was hanging all the way down her back by then. Of course she didn't need any more education. She just wanted to hang around with those weird people you find in places like that, and sure enough she got tangled up with one of them and started living with him in New York City without the benefit of clergy. That's the "we" of "We're in Key West," Agnes is sure of it. A wild-eyed hippie agitator of some sort, like the ones you see on TV. Go around burning things down.

Agnes gets up, takes her cake layers out of the oven, and sets them on the counter to cool. They look fine. She'll get at that icing later; you have to concentrate on icing. Agnes pulls up her sweater sleeves and goes at the mess in the sink. She can handle him, whatever he's like. She's probably getting herself all worked up over nothing, anyway. Crystal saying she'll come is no guarantee that she will. But it *is* Thursday, and there's not much of Thursday left. At least Agnes was farsighted enough to spare her mama all of this. Her mama is up at Cousin Junior's and won't be back until Agnes goes to get her. Mama never did learn how to drive. And Daddy will sleep until she wakes him up. Agnes wipes the counters, wondering what Crystal will be like *this* time, and won-

dering about her friend. Her *lover*—now, that's more like
it! You might as well call a spade a spade.

Roger Lee was the one who told her about it. He went
up there to try to talk some sense into Crystal and there
they were in one room, he said, with a bare light bulb
hanging down from the ceiling, eating off of two portable
burners. Roger Lee said it was a terrible neighborhood
with trash piled up all over the street. You can just imagine. But Crystal sent him back, and Roger Lee just about
died. Then he married Judy Bond, who had always liked
him anyway, and they had little baby twin girls right
away and moved out of town.

Agnes looks over next door. Lorene's new car is there,
but that doesn't mean anything. Now that they are mining
the old Dry Fork property again, Lorene has put herself
on the payroll and she is gone a good bit of the time, off
with that Odell Peacock, and even Agnes has to hand it
to *his*. Odell saw this energy crisis coming a mile off. A
lot of people, over a barrel with a lawyer like Odell was,
would have just sold outright when they made the first
offer. But Odell kept his cool, as Pauletta used to say.
Strike while the iron is hot, Agnes thinks, but she's absentminded, looking out the window at Lorene's house.

Agnes wonders if Lorene got one of those postcards,
too. Of course she wouldn't ask her, and Lorene would
never say. Lorene has not mentioned Crystal one time in
three years, not voluntarily, not ever since the Thanksgiving when Crystal came home and said all those things
about the United States Government to Sykes at the
dinner table and to his poor little Vietnamese wife who
didn't, thank God, speak enough English at the time to
know what was going on. To poor old Sykes, who got a
Purple Heart and is now a deputy sheriff and a good one,
too. Agnes wonders if Crystal has become a Communist.
It's something she has turned over in her mind for a long
time. Roger Lee assured Agnes she wasn't, but then that
was back before Roger Lee married Judy Bond, and who
knows *what* Crystal might be now?

Oh, Agnes would give her eye teeth to know if Lorene
got one of those cards! If you come right out and ask
Lorene a *question*, like if Crystal is still in New York,
she'll answer you, but she will never bring the topic of
Crystal up on her own. It's her own fault partly, as Agnes

sees it. Lorene set too much store by Crystal, always did. Maybe she couldn't help it, but that's the way it was. So that now she has been too deeply hurt.

Agnes admires the way Lorene handles it, though. If a truck ran over Lorene, she wouldn't bleed unless she felt like it, that's the way she is. Lorene just goes on about her business, and if people talk about her and Odell she never seems to notice it or care. Everything is all right along that line anyway, as far as Agnes can tell, and if there was anything else to know about what goes on next door, she'd know it. There's nothing wrong with a business partner, Agnes thinks, although she wouldn't have one herself.

Agnes likes to run her own show, and, thinking about the Laundromat she just bought down at Harmon Junction, she smiles. Nobody, not even Mama, knows about that yet! It's her little secret, her very own, until she decides to tell it. Agnes knows it won't be very gratifying to tell it to Mama. Mama will just smile and say, "That's nice, dear," no matter what you do. Lorene, on the other hand, will wrinkle up the corners of her eyes appreciatively—Agnes can just see her—the sharp upturned wrinkles cutting into the skin. Lorene is holding up. She goes right on singing in the choir, getting older, taking care of the Sykeses and treating Sykes's wife better than anybody else would, treating her in fact like she is *white*, which Agnes feels she is not. Lorene goes right on giving everybody these little Mason jars of green tomato pickle every year for Christmas, acting like she never had any daughter who ever raised such a commotion at all.

Agnes is setting out all the ingredients for the icing when the doorbell rings. At once her whole heart jumps into her stomach and she feels like she's getting diarrhea, which is ridiculous. She takes her time removing her apron, buttoning up the jacket of her light-blue polyester pantsuit, smoothing it down over her hips. She takes off her house shoes and puts on her heels, and by then the doorbell has rung again. Well, let them wait. It won't hurt Crystal Spangler to wait for something for once in her life. Agnes walks slowly along the plastic runner through the dining room into the front room, putting her feet down firmly with great precision, hearing the plastic crackle with every step.

So Agnes is ready, or thinks she's ready, by the time she gets to the door and opens it, but when she sees them really there on her own front porch she knows she wasn't ready at all. The wind is cold. It whips Crystal's long blond hair all around her face, and Crystal is hunched up, obviously cold in her thin raincoat, a dirty old belted raincoat like a detective might wear in a movie. Crystal looks just awful, not even clean. Skinny as a rail with that coat all bunched up around her. As for her friend, he doesn't look like the weather or anything else could bother him. He doesn't look like he would let it. He has wild black hair that stands out from his head in a big bush all around, so kinky that not one hair of it moves in the wind. He has thick eyebrows that grow almost all the way across his face, a messy black mustache that half covers his mouth, and he wears no jacket, just stands in the wind like he owns it with his shirt open so Agnes can see the curly black hair on his chest. He is one of the hairiest men Agnes has ever seen. He probably has it growing in clumps on his back. He wears faded old blue jeans like any common day laborer, and sandals (imagine a man wearing sandals!) with his toes showing long and brown. The sight of these strong brown toes offends Agnes more than anything else, for some reason. Bare feet in February! This hairy man, who has his foreign-looking face half turned from Agnes as he looks up at Black Mountain, turns back now, no hurry, and stares at her there in the door. His stare gives Agnes quite a jolt. His eyes are black and liquid in the manner of Omar Sharif. They stare down into Agnes's own small pale-blue ones, down, down, until Agnes jerks her eyes away and feels herself turning brick red.

"Well, look who's here!" she says with a high silly giggle, but she makes no move away from the door.

They look so funny, Crystal Spangler and this man, deeply tanned and ragged, on her own front porch. They look like something the cat dragged in. No, stranger than that—like people from some other planet.

"Agnes," Crystal says. "Aren't you going to let us in?" she asks.

Agnes stands back from the door. She says, "Come on in," but she knows that Crystal can tell how she feels.

"This is Jerold Kukafka," Crystal says, but Agnes

can't bring herself to look straight at him again. Agnes would say something to him, though, if she could think of something to say. He doesn't look like any kind of a brainy writer, that's for sure, even though Agnes knows that's what he's supposed to be. Only of course he hasn't published any books, probably too busy getting a tan.

Crystal sits on the sofa wrinkling up Agnes's mama's antimacassars. She keeps pulling at them with her long fingers, and her fingernails are all bitten off. No wedding ring, Agnes notices. Crystal seems lost in her coat.

As for this Jerold Kukafka, he keeps walking around and around the room like some kind of skinny hairy jungle cat in a cage at the zoo. Agnes has one whole wall full of shelves where she keeps her teacup collection and he keeps picking up the teacups and looking at them. Then he walks away and then he comes back and does it again. It makes Agnes so nervous. Finally she reaches out and turns on a light, not to give Jerold Kukafka any light to see by, but to give herself some purchase on her own living room, which looks so unfamiliar with these brown windblown people taking it over.

"You're still collecting your teacups, I see," says Crystal. Her voice is low and musical. Her face is still beautiful too, Agnes thinks, if you go for that half-starved look.

"Yes, I am," says Agnes.

"You haven't changed a bit," Crystal says. "You still look the same, only now you look sort of, I don't know, *imposing*."

It's a typical Crystal remark, and Agnes lets it pass.

"We're on our way back from Florida," Crystal goes on. "From the Keys. Jerold has been doing some research for his novel."

"Well, why don't *you* write a novel?" Agnes asks her point-blank. "Looks to me like you'd have plenty of material."

"Oh, I couldn't do that," Crystal answers lightly, her blue eyes roving around the room, finding Jerold, jumping away, finding him again. Not that he's paying Crystal any mind, with his kinky head bent down over the cups.

"I don't see why not," Agnes tells her, remembering then the way Crystal always thought she had to have a man to do anything. "I don't see why not," she repeats. "You

149

know I'm running the hardware store now." Agnes begins to relax.

"I heard that," Crystal says. "Is your daddy still sick?"

"Terminal," Agnes says.

"Oh, I'm so sorry!" Crystal *seems* sorry, too, but you can't ever tell about her, Agnes reminds herself. "How awful, Agnes," Crystal goes on. "I didn't realize. What's the matter with him?"

"He's got the big C," Agnes says, enjoying the look on Crystal's face.

"What?" Jerold Kukafka barks out, clashing a cup back into its saucer, and Agnes almost jumps out of her skin. It is the first word he's said in her house. He cat-foots around to stand behind the sofa where Crystal is sitting and he puts his hands on her shoulders, staring right straight at Agnes.

"What did you say?" he asks, almost interrogating her, but Agnes refuses to be intimidated by the likes of Jerold Kukafka, so she stares stubbornly down at the coffee table.

"Cancer," she says briefly. "It's only a matter of time."

"Shit," says Jerold Kukafka.

"Oh, I'm sorry," Crystal says again, drawing her long brown legs up under her on the sofa like she thinks she might catch it, too, and Jerold Kukafka resumes his stalking.

"This room is the same, too," Crystal goes on finally. "You haven't changed anything except added those shelves. Do you remember sitting over there at the table and making paper dolls out of magazines? Do you remember how we used to play gin rummy and Babe would get so mad?"

"I have to go get Mama in a minute," Agnes says abruptly. "She's up at Junior's right now."

"Oh," Crystal says.

Out of the corner of her eye, Agnes sees Jerold Kukafka looking at her cup from Limoges, France.

"How is Lorene?" Crystal asks.

"Why, she's all right," Agnes says carefully. "I'd go over there if I was you."

"We went over there," Crystal says, "but nobody came to the door."

"She might not be home," Agnes says.

"There's a car in the driveway," Crystal says.

"What kind is it?"

"A blue car," Crystal says. "It looks new."

"That's hers all right," Agnes tells her. "Buick Skylark, she bought it about three months ago. But that's still no guarantee that she's home. She works part time now, you know, and lately she's been helping Sykes's wife pick out everything for that house he's building up at Slate Creek." Imagine, Agnes thinks, not knowing what kind of car your own mother drives!

"Sykes is building a *house?*" Crystal says.

"Ranch style," says Agnes.

"Well, how *is* Lorene?" Crystal asks again, sort of pitiful, as if she wants more information or possibly some other answer; Agnes can't figure it out. Agnes sits big and respectable in the light by her solid chair, and Crystal's face is dim to her now over there on the couch. Crystal's cheekbones stick out and her eyes look way too big and they keep shifting, shifting everywhere. She keeps running her tongue along the bottom of her upper lip and it puts her jaw at an angle. She's still wearing her raincoat. God only knows what she's got on underneath *that*, Agnes thinks. Probably some Indian thing. Outside it is starting to rain.

"Your mother is just as well as you can expect," Agnes says, "considering. In fact, I would say she is doing just fine. Maybe she was taking a nap."

Jerold Kukafka is looking at Agnes's cup from the Brussels World's Fair. "Let's get out of here," he says.

Agnes jumps. Crystal stands right up and goes over to him like she is pulled by a magnet. She looks up at him and he leans down and kisses her on the mouth. When Crystal turns back to Agnes, she is holding his hand, and her eyes look exactly like they did that time when she had the religious vision at Girls' State. Exactly like that, all starry and wild and blue.

"Tell Lorene I asked about her," Crystal says. "And tell her I'm real happy." She is happy, too; Agnes can see that. Some people thrive on sin.

Crystal leaves with Jerold Kukafka in the pouring rain not ten minutes before Junior brings Mama home on his way to town; he thought he'd save Agnes a trip. Not ten minutes! It's a close call. Agnes does not mention Crystal's visit to Mama, who comes in large and old and steamy out of the rain, shedding layers of clothing, turning on lights, taking over the icing for the cake. Agnes spreads her legs straight out in front of her and leans back in the chair, closing her eyes.

She doesn't want to, but behind her eyes Agnes can see suddenly and clearly the two of them, Jerold Kukafka and Crystal, brown and naked on a sandy beach kissing each other, and bright-blue water as shiny as glass behind them. Palm trees, and in slow motion he gets on top; she can see the hair on his back. Agnes grinds her teeth without knowing it, without ever opening her eyes. It's disgusting, isn't it, what they have all come to, all those girls she used to know. Agnes is always running into them downtown, Sue Mustard Matney, Lynette Lukes Ratliff, Susie Belcher Rife who is still as tacky as she ever was, all the girls who used to be in the 4-H Club—heavier, married, with scabby little children that pull down the displays which Agnes has so carefully arranged in the hardware store. Still she smiles at them, keeping her voice even as she hands them back their change. It wouldn't do to offend a customer. Agnes grows full of unfocused fury, of a sudden nameless loss. An unaccustomed, perverse little trickle of tears comes out the corners of her eyes and leaks down into her hair. She sits up with a start and why here is Mama with the cake iced already, the icing perfect for cortisone-puffy Hassell who will have some after dinner. Age sixty-one and half dead, no candles. Agnes's mama can really make seven-minute icing, but she could never, never manage a hardware store. Agnes smiles as she remembers her little secret, and her mama smiles back, thinking that smile was for her. Agnes takes off her heels and slips into her house shoes again.

Agnes thinks about Crystal a lot during the months that follow her visit. In particular, she remembers Crystal saying to tell her mother how happy she was. As if Agnes would have ever told Lorene any such thing! Agnes thinks about Crystal even more after she hears the news, and she guesses Crystal wasn't so happy the day Jerold Kukafka hung himself dead from an exposed pipe in the bathroom in that place where they lived, and Crystal found him with his tongue hanging out and all black in the face. But the death is so awful that Agnes can't bring herself to think "Serves you right," even though she has always known that the wages of sin is death. It's one thing to *know* that, and another to have it come up and slap you in the face. Agnes looks at her teacups, remembering the way Jerold Kukafka picked them up and handled them, and shivers. She wonders what will come next.

But Agnes has her own hands full that summer. Her daddy dies, and even though she has gotten everything in order long before, still there is lots to do. Hassell's death falls right in the middle of June, and it is well into July before Agnes can catch her breath. Lorene hasn't mentioned Crystal all this time, except for telling Agnes about Jerold Kukafka's death, and of course nobody has asked. So when Lorene invites Agnes and her mama over that August evening after supper, the thought of Crystal doesn't even cross Agnes's mind.

It's a hot night. Agnes sits with her legs well apart in the darkness because she has been troubled lately with prickly heat. She sips at her iced tea with mint, looking out at the fireflies beyond the screen and listening in every now and then to her mama and Lorene, who discuss casseroles in a desultory fashion. It's real pleasant on Lorene's new screen porch. Everybody admires the Spanish-style Solarian floor covering which looks like real Spanish tiles, the curved white iron outdoor furniture ornamented by little white wrought-iron roses, the little iron cart full of blooming red geranium plants in their pots.

"Odell bought those in a greenhouse in Roanoke," Lorene is telling them. "I like to have had a fit when I saw them! All that money, I said, for just one summer's worth of flowers and half of it already gone! I could have gotten some artificial ones down at the Ben Franklin just as well." Lorene's tone is scornful and lilting, and in her snort of laughter Agnes can tell how pleased she is. Well, let her be pleased. Let her. Why not? Through the window into the house, Agnes can see Odell himself, or at least the back of his head. He's sitting in the rocker in Lorene's conversation area watching television, and every now and then they hear him laugh out loud. Odell has changed a lot in the past three or four years, ever since Lorene got ahold of him. Agnes cranes her head back to see him through the glass, and he's wearing a gold-colored polyester jumpsuit. Imagine, Odell Pe~ ~ck in a jumpsuit! Agnes wonders if Lorene will marry ~ ~ when she gets him like she wants him. It would be hard to say. She cooks supper for him every night. Sometimes they have a glass of cold duck with their dinner. Agnes can see them right from her own kitchen window. Agnes wonders what's holding Lorene up. Sykes wouldn't care; he and Odell go hunting and fishing together all the time. Jules is out of the picture. It must be Crystal. Lorene has always had this unnatural attachment, God knows why. But Crystal is as old as Agnes: she ought to be able to take care of herself.

Then Lorene says something which gives Agnes the creeps, just like Lorene has been reading her mind. "I got a letter from Crystal today," Lorene says easily. In the flickering light of the Bug-Off candle, Agnes cannot see her face, but her voice is as chirpy as ever. You'd think she mentioned Crystal every day.

"Well, how is she doing?" Agnes's mama loves news.

"To tell you the truth, Louise, she hasn't been well at all. I've been real concerned about her, in fact, ever since her friend passed away," Lorene says calmly and confidentially, leaning forward.

Agnes almost dies. Friend, my foot! But she keeps quiet and Lorene goes on.

"She's been in the hospital," Lorene says. "But she got out last week and she's coming home Friday for a nice long rest. Odell is going to pick her up at Tri-Cities Airport at three."

"He *is!*" Agnes's mama exclaims. "Well, it sure will be good to see her. How long is she coming for?"

"I don't know exactly," Lorene says. "She might just stay for good. When she's strong enough, she wants to look for a job."

"Well, my goodness!" This is Agnes's mama's strongest expletive.

"Do you need any help getting ready?" Agnes asks, even though she knows Lorene's got a cleaning girl now.

"Oh no!" Lorene brushes off this suggestion with a tinkly laugh. "Oh no, we'll take care of everything. I'm just so pleased that she's coming home. You'll have to come over, Agnes," she adds. "You girls used to be such good friends. I kn v you'll have a lot to talk about."

Agnes since doubts it. "I'm sure we will," she says, getting up from her chair. "Come on, Mama, time to go."

Odell comes to stand brilliantly in the door and tell them goodbye. He has grown himself some sideburns, Agnes sees. Real mod.

"It's so nice Crystal's coming home," Agnes's mama's voice trails back over the yards.

"It sure is!" Lorene cries out into the night, but Agnes wonders if that's what she really thinks. It could upset Lorene's little apple cart, that's for sure.

"Mama," Agnes says carefully when they're back in their own house again and her mama has exhausted the subject of Lorene's beautiful porch floor. "Mama, did you notice she never did say exactly what Crystal's been in the hospital *for?*"

"Well, now, that's a fact," Agnes's mama says. "She never did say, did she?"

"No, she sure didn't," Agnes answers with a special emphasis, and pauses to let that sink in, but no light dawns in her mama's calm face. Agnes gets a little exasperated. It's not like talking to Millie Shortridge, her good friend at the bank, who catches on to everything right away.

"Don't you think it's kind of *strange*," she pursues, "that Lorene didn't say what Crystal has?"

"Now, doctors don't know everything," Agnes's mama points out. "Don't you remember that time when Marvelle spent three whole months at Charlottesville and they never did know what she had? Or when Mrs. Belcher, Fay's mother-in-law, got those raisings on the head? Why, they sent her to Duke Hospital for that one and finally she just came home."

"*Mama,*" Agnes says. "I know all that. What I think about Crystal, though, is that it's mental. If it wasn't mental, she would have said."

"You mean like a nervous breakdown?"

"Yep," Agnes says. "That's exactly what I mean."

"Well, I think you ought to be ashamed of yourself! That's not very nice, Agnes," her mama says with a quiver in her voice, and they finish turning out the lights and go to bed. Agnes is so mad, going up the stairs. Her mama has no right to talk to her like that. Where would Mama be right now, if Agnes hadn't come home from VPI to take care of them all? Never even learned to drive a car! Still, Agnes grins when she gets to the bend in the stairs: Mama does have a point, and anyway it's the most spunk she has shown for years.

Odell is all spruced up and fifteen minutes early at the Tri-Cities Airport to pick up Crystal. The runways are so hot that heat rises and crests in little shimmery waves at the end of each concrete strip. Standing inside the air-conditioned terminal, chewing on a mint-flavored toothpick, Odell squints through the glass at the runways and watches the big plane land. A jet plane, taking off or land-ing either one, is one of the prettiest things he can think of. The jet wind whirls trash around and blows a woman's hair forward and into her eyes. Odell waits patiently. He's good at waiting. He didn't mind driving over here to get Crystal either. Anyway, it gave him a chance to go through Bristol and order a car he's been thinking about, white Cadillac Coupe de Ville, a little surprise for Lorene. Odell does not move forward to wait outside by the rope. He stays where he is, squinting from behind the glass, and watches the passengers get off the plane. An old woman in a straw hat, greeted by grandchildren. Two Bristol busi-nessmen with briefcases, some students in blue jeans, a bald-headed black man—they go everywhere now. Sud-denly Odell leans forward, opens his mouth, and spits out the toothpick. You don't think that's *Crystal,* now? But it has to be. There's no other girl—or woman, Crystal is a woman now—no other woman that age getting off the plane. Odell watches her walk across the concrete and down the roped-off sidewalk. Son of a gun.

Crystal's hair is short, parted on the side so that a piece of it falls across her sunglasses and down her cheek and she keeps brushing it back with one hand. She wears high-heeled sandals, a white sleeveless dress, gold jewelry that flashes in the sun as she walks. The sunglasses are big and round, hiding half her face.

I'll be damned, Odell thinks. Lorene will be tickled to death.

He looks again to be sure it's Crystal before he goes over to the door where she'll come in. It's Crystal all right, but a new Crystal like a picture straight out of a magazine, still thin but not bony, all white and golden, yellow short straight hair. Only in the way she moves, in the way she hesitates and draws back a little from the automatic door, can Odell find any trace of that other Crystal he knew best, Grant's little girl sitting so still under a bush or in the corner of a room that seeing her made you jump.

"Over here, honey!" Odell hollers.

"Why, *Odell!*" she says, coming right up to him and hugging him, something she never used to do. "Let me look at you," she cries. "I just can't believe how much you've changed!" Odell kisses her on the cheek and smells perfume. He would not have done this in the past, but during the last couple of years he has picked up a lot about what you do and don't do in airports. "You look so *good!*" Crystal says. She takes off her glasses to get a better look at him, and Odell sees that her eyes are still that same dark blue, that they have little wrinkles at the corners of them now and light circles, like bruises, beneath.

"You don't look half bad yourself," he says, and Crystal laughs. She has a new way of laughing, throwing her head back a little.

On the way to get her luggage, Odell keeps glancing sideways at her. Not that he'd thought much about it— you take care of your own, that's what you *do,* you don't even have to consider it—not that he's given it much mind, but he'd sort of figured from what Lorene said that Crystal would be sickly-looking, washed out, puny. But she looks like a million bucks.

Crystal watches the bags go around on the revolving belt. She hesitates and then reaches out and grabs off a medium-sized navy leather bag with her initials on it in red, CRS. She had them put on at extra cost out of Lorene's generous check.

Odell continues to wait patiently, watching the bags revolve.

Crystal pokes him in the ribs. "Let's go," she says.

"What?" Odell turns and takes her bag. "You mean that's all you've got?" he asks.

"I travel light." Crystal grins at him.

Women. Odell shakes his head. Now, if it was Lorene,

she'd have half a dozen bags, plus some more suit bags and then some packages tied up with string. Odell remembers picking Lorene and Neva up here after they went to the cosmetology convention in Hawaii. You never saw so much stuff in your life! Well, you can't tell a thing about women. Crystal walks ahead of him out into the glare and across the parking lot toward where he points. Odell can't help watching the sway of her hips, the way she steps along. He can remember when Crystal was not as big as a minute. Now she's more like Lorene, and Odell smiles when he thinks of Lorene. Lorene is all plump and easy, a woman like a big soft chair. You don't have to talk too much with Lorene. Everything is simple and straightforward with her; she's a woman like a man in many ways. Odell just plain likes her. He likes her age, the way the flesh is soft and freckled and loose on her back between her shoulders and he can bunch it up in his hand. He likes the way she says, "Git *on!*" when she wants him to hurry up and do something, mock annoyance hiding a real annoyance, severe pretending. If Lorene decides they ought to get married, fine. If she doesn't, fine. There's no rush. Odell has lived a lot of years without getting married. The thought of Grant doesn't bother him, either. They never mention Grant. When Grant bothers Odell it's not in connection with Lorene at all: it's just sometimes if he happens to remember something they used to do as kids, fishing down at Harmon or shooting craps behind the American Legion Hall with old man Mose Drew. Odell has been known to show up at church with Lorene upon occasion, but he doesn't hold much with heaven or hell. The dead, including Grant, are under the ground, that's how he feels about it. Odell knows the ground and what's down there; anything else is made up.

Crystal gets into the car and crosses her legs. "Some car." She smiles at him. She lights a Salem from the lighter in the dash; Odell can't remember her smoking before.

Now that they're in the car, air-conditioned and doing seventy down Interstate 81, Odell finds he doesn't have a thing to say to her. But he's comfortable being quiet, and after Crystal points out a couple of things along the road, new motels and such as that, she grows quiet, too, and smokes and looks out the window.

"Tell me something, Odell," she says abruptly.

"What is it?" He's instantly wary, ducking his head in the old way.

"Do you think this is really all right, me coming home, I mean? Do you think it's all right with everybody?" *With you*, she means, *with Mama, with Sykes, with Agnes, with whatever way you are living now. Because here I am.*

"Well, shoot." Odell grins. "Now, how the hell would I know, Crystal? It's all right with me."

Crystal laughs and stretches back in the seat. "I forgot how far it is from the airport," she says.

"There's plenty of people's got private helicopters now, Crystal. Fly right from Tri-Cities up to the top of Black Mountain. It's just us poor folks got to drive." But Odell is grinning his dark animal grin; he knows he isn't poor folks anymore.

"Aren't you going to stop for a drink and a Slim Jim?" Crystal asks suddenly. "Don't you remember when I was little, every time you took me someplace in the truck we used to stop at a store and you'd get us both a Slim Jim and me an RC and you'd get a beer. Don't you remember that? I thought you couldn't even go on a trip without a drink and a Slim Jim."

Odell had forgotten. "Road beer." He grins. "Well, your mother has got me counting the calories now."

"Let's get some road beer," Crystal says. Maybe it will help her stomach, help her head; the top of her head feels like it's going to fly off and disappear. Anxiety, of course, and she knows it. But still . . .

"Your mother would have a fit."

"She would not. This is a celebration. Pull in there, Odell. No, we've missed it now. Pull in the next one."

When Crystal gets her Slim Jim she gulps it down, barely chewing. She hasn't had a Slim Jim or a pickled hard-boiled egg in years. She drains about half of her beer and makes a face at Odell. "Schlitz! I thought you drank Pabst all the time."

"I'll be honest with you, honey, I don't remember."

"It was Pabst," Crystal insists.

"Well, I'll tell you," Odell says. "That might be so. But things change, and you have to just kind of go with it, if you know what I mean."

Odell drives fast through Swords Creek, whipping around the curves.

"Now tell me a story," Crystal says after a while, and her voice is so high and so peculiar that Odell looks away from the road for a minute to stare at her. But she just smiles back at him, all open and golden, and he goes back to driving without a word. It's funny about Crystal. Trying to figure her out. There was one time, years back up on Dry Fork, when she had that sick spell or something, and now he can't remember it. Peculiar, though. Trouble with Crystal is, sometimes she almost makes you think something, but then she makes you stop and you never know what it was. You never get it thought through.

"I don't know no stories, now," Odell says. "Grant was the one with the stories."

"Tell me something true, then," Crystal said. "Let's see —tell me about Goldie Coe."

"Goldie Coe? What you want to hear about *her* for?" Odell hasn't thought of her in years.

"Grace used to tell me about Granddaddy," Crystal says. "But she never would tell about Goldie Coe."

"Hah!" Odell laughs. "That Grace is really a case, now. You just wait till you see old Grace."

"Please tell about Goldie Coe. Nobody ever would."

"Well, there's actually not much to tell, Crystal. She was just a girl from up on Hurley, worked at the Ben Franklin, and Iradell took a fancy to her, that's all. She used to work the popcorn machine."

"Then what?"

"Then, hell, I don't know. Iradell got to buying popcorn, he'd take me with him, then he got to bringing her up to the house, then the first thing I knowed, we was all in the car going to Charlottesville to get Goldie some new teeth." Odell's own gold tooth flashes in the sun as he tells it. "It was a long trip in those days, two days it took us. We put up at Natural Bridge. But she was about to bust to get those teeth."

Crystal sips her beer, letting it slide slowly down her throat. The beer—or perhaps it's the story—is helping. "Who went?" she asks.

"Well, let's see. There was me driving, and Iradell and Goldie in the front seat. Iradell used to sit over by the window with a paper bag full of apples and a pint of bourbon. He'd take a bite of the apple and then a drink of bourbon and chew it all up together, glub it around in his mouth a long time before he swallowed. He used to pinch Goldie every now and then and she'd holler at him."

"What did Goldie look like?"

"Well, I don't know how to tell you exactly, honey. It's been a long time. Styles have changed. She had a whole lot of hair, all this yellow curly hair that she got her name from. Her real name used to be something else, but nobody knew what it was. She used to comb her hair all the time with this little tortoiseshell comb. She was sort of fat, I guess, except for her legs. She had big old long legs."

"Was she pretty?"

"She was pretty when she kept her mouth closed."

"Was that all of you who went?" Crystal asks.

"No, Nora was in the back seat and——"

"Nora! I thought she wouldn't go anywhere with Granddaddy."

"Well, she says she didn't, but she did. She used to go, all right. In fact, it was hard to go off anyplace without her. She wanted to go to Charlottesville this time to get your daddy some culture, as I remember it. He was in the back seat, too. Nora used to make him hold a paper bag in case he got carsick."

"Did he?"

"Did he what?"

"Get carsick."

"I don't know, Crystal. I can't remember if he did that time or not. Sometimes he did, though."

"What did he do, riding along?"

"*Do?* Well, hell, there wasn't nothing to do on a trip like that but ride, honey. That's all. Besides, he never talked much when he was little, anyway. He was scared of your granddaddy, I guess."

"Everybody was, right?" Crystal asks.

"Yep. Including me."

"How old were you then, Odell?"

"*Me?* Well, let's see, I guess I was sixteen maybe, something like that. I started driving your granddaddy when I was fourteen years old." Odell seems inclined to stop talking, but Crystal keeps asking him questions.

"Then what? What happened on the trip?"

"Let's see. The main thing I remember is I had to keep putting the window up and down. If it was up, Nora would holler that the smoke was killing her. Then I'd put it down, then Goldie would start in about how the wind was messing up her hairdo, then I'd put it up. I put it up and down for two days. Neither one of them ever rolled their own window up or down for theirself."

Crystal is laughing. It reminds her of going to the Miss Virginia Contest with Neva and Lorene.

"The other thing is, every time we stopped for gas, your granddaddy used to make everybody get out and go to the bathroom. *Make* 'em, he didn't care whether they had to go or not. He'd stand over there by the gas pump and holler.

"We went in a restaurant," Odell continues, pleased and somewhat surprised that Crystal is laughing so hard. "I tell you, it was the first time I was ever in a restaurant like that, silver and all. Goldie said she wanted something with a cream sauce, anything with a cream sauce, she didn't care what. We had this pop-eyed nigger in a red suit waiting on us. Then Nora, she'd eat up everything left on everybody's plate when you were through."

"Then what? Then did Goldie get her teeth?"

"Hell, yes, she got 'em all right. See, this was the second time we went up there. The first time they got her fitted. This time, Goldie kept saying, 'Do you reckon it's going to hurt?' and your granddaddy would take out his bottom teeth and let her look at them. Then Nora got to looking for this special wall, once we got up there, and I had to drive her around to find it."

"Serpentine," Crystal supplies.

"Yes, well, we got there, and Nora took Grant off to look at tombstones or something, and I had to sit with your granddaddy in the waiting room while they put in Goldie's teeth."

"What did he do in the waiting room?"

"Went to sleep," Odell says. "Snored."

"What did you do?"

"I just sat there, I guess."

"Then what?"

"Well, then, around four o'clock this nurse came out and told me they were almost finished with Miss Coe and I had to wake your granddaddy up. I used to hate to have to wake him up, he never knew where he was. I tell you what he said," Odell adds suddenly.

"What?"

"I kept saying to get up, that they were just about through with Goldie, and he kept saying for me to go on and leave him alone. See, the bourbon used to get to him, is what it was."

"Then what did he say?"

"He said just as plain as anything, "Well, that's that,' and I said, 'What, sir?' and he said, 'You get a girl a set of new teeth and she'll leave you every time. She won't even stop to pack her clothes.' He told me to remember that."

Crystal is silent, sipping.

"I always thought that was funny, him knowing it and then going on and buying her the teeth anyway."

"You're right," Crystal said. "It *is* funny." She lights another Salem and leans back against the seat to smoke it. The only thing real now is Odell beside her driving this big car, the road climbing and twisting out in front of them. *Not real* includes the city, includes Jerold. She and Jerold in the city seem like characters in a novel she read so long ago that she has trouble remembering the plot. Jerold, of course, is dead. It was funny when his sisters showed up from New Jersey, big hefty women with frizzy black hair. "He had it coming!" one of them kept insisting, while the others kept shutting her up. They were Catholic and so there was some question about the funeral, which in any case Crystal did not attend. Of her stay in the hospital, she remembers little. She had been tired, anemic, and everyone kept saying she needed a rest. Then they were annoyed when she rested more than they thought she should. Later after they got her up they encouraged her to talk, but there just wasn't anything to say. Then one day she said, "This is a waste of time. I ought to get up and go home," and she did. The doctor she was talking to had seemed surprised, and he had called in another doctor and they argued about her right in front of her while she got out of bed and packed. Crystal didn't even bother to listen. In the end they had released her.

Crystal took the last of her money out of the bank and went straight to the airport and flew to Richmond, where she checked into a Holiday Inn, bought some clothes and a bathing suit at Montaldo's, called Lorene, got Lorene's check and cashed it, threw all her old clothes into a dumpster in the motel parking lot, bought more clothes and a suitcase in Miller and Rhoads. For three days she lay by the motel pool and got a suntan, burning the last traces of her hospital whiteness away, making jokes with the boy who cleaned the pool. On the fourth day she had her hair frosted and cut and spent the night with an International Harvester salesman who picked her up in the motel's Jolly Roger Pirate Club. Then she made her plane reservation, packed her new clothes in her new bag, and flew home. Jerold was wrong, wrong. She had proved him wrong. He used to tell her over and over that she was doomed— Jerold was into doom—but she wasn't doomed. She was saved. Crystal grins, remembering the time Agnes told Jubal Thacker she didn't need to go to his revival, thanks anyway, she had been saved for years. Well, so has Crystal.

At the door, Lorene hugs her so hard that Crystal thinks she'll suffocate, be drawn entirely into Lorene's big soft body and absorbed. "Honey, honey," Lorene says. "I'm just so glad you're home! Look here—I even fixed you some three-bean salad for dinner."

Odell grins, chewing on a toothpick: he keeps toothpicks, cigarettes, and a lot of his clothes at Lorene's these days.

Crystal wanders the house before dinner, picking up objects and putting them down. She has some trouble, not much, in telling how far anything is from her hand. The objects seem to recede and then flow back to her. It's very strange. There are some things she remembers and some things she does not, and then other things are completely new, like the back sun porch with all the plants. She doesn't realize that she's looking for Grant's poetry books until she finally finds them, upstairs in a pile on the bottom shelf of the bookcase by the phone, next to two stacks of old *Reader's Digests*. Lorene follows Crystal around, giving her all the news. One thing is that Neva is considering leaving Charlie, who has had something going on the side for the past eight years. Neva never even suspected, if you can imagine that! Lorene says *she* wasn't surprised, though; she felt it coming, and Charlie has always had a screw loose someplace.

Then Lorene goes into the kitchen to set the table, and Crystal sits on the sun porch and looks at the Bluefield paper while Odell talks on the phone to a man about some roofing.

"Come and get it," Lorene calls. "I'm taking the cornbread out of the oven right now, and the bean salad is already out on the table."

Crystal bursts into tears.

Lorene and Odell go ahead and eat, leaving her alone in her room upstairs, and Crystal sits by the window and looks out at the lightning bugs rising. On the bureau sits a gold-framed picture of her at sixteen, wearing a tiara and a long white gown. Crystal gets up and looks at it for a while and then she puts it back and turns off the light and sits in the dark, looking out her window. The phone rings two times, and after a while Lorene comes up the stairs. Crystal can hear her heels clicking down on the wood. Lorene switches on the light and Crystal blinks.

"Crystal Renée, that was Sykes on the phone. He and Bunny are coming over here to see you in a minute," Lorene says. "You'd better go put on your face."

Being back home in Black Rock is not as difficult as Crystal thought it might be, and it isn't as boring either. Black Rock itself has changed a great deal during those years she has been away. With the climbing price of coal, millions and millions of dollars have poured into the county. Odell and Lorene have grown rich, for instance, not that you could tell it from the way they live. But the new prosperity has touched everyone. Some people have more money than they know what to do with. Other people know exactly what to do with it: they've bought Cadillacs, diamonds, boats. The Jurgensens flew to Colorado to ski. Another time they flew to Venezuela. There are people who go to Duke Hospital for three weeks at a hundred dollars a day to lose weight on the Rice Diet. Mrs. Cartwright saw Elvis Presley there; he was on the Rice Diet, too. The Lord Brothers have recently bought a whole island off the coast of South Carolina. A whole island! The Lord Brothers go everywhere in private planes, and their wives fly up to New York to shop. The Lord Brothers opened a new bank downtown a few weeks before Crystal came home, and the first day they took in over a million dollars in deposits.

Royal Looney, who owned nothing but a sidetrack ten

years ago, now owns eight mines—a good percent of the coal in this county—and a lot of neighboring Wise County, too, where he has built a house with an aquarium wall separating the kitchen from the dining room. When the Looneys entertain, big old fish swim back and forth to watch everyone eat. In an interview with Charles Kuralt on CBS, Royal revealed that he first got into industry back when he was a poor little mountain boy of ten, when he found a sheep stuck in a ditch and carried it home and saved its life and started a flock. Odell claims that this is a lot of shit. It amuses people around Black Rock so much that they have taken to calling Royal "Little Bo Peep."

Lulu and Green Belcher received their share of comment, too, when they built a house up on Yellow Branch which is nothing but cubes of glass and some little wooden runways stringing them together. Martha and Johnny Reno have a car wash built into their garage.

So Crystal is nothing to talk about, in comparison. Nobody bothers her at all. Only Agnes seems unable to recover from the sheer gall of her just coming home. But people don't like Agnes much anyway, and after a while even Millie Shortridge at the bank gets tired of hearing Agnes go on about it. So Agnes shuts up and gives in. She grows friendly. She can tell which way the wind is blowing, after all.

Crystal is grateful that Black Rock has turned into a boom town, that it is full of money and eccentricity. For she has changed, too. She has a lot to think about. All she wants is rest, quiet, time. Odell and Lorene give her plenty of room. She can hear them downstairs every night when she goes to bed, playing gin rummy and drinking Scotch and laughing and fussing over the score, but they do not insist that she join them. She lies upstairs on her old bed watching the changing shadows in her room made by the lights of the passing cars on 460 out in front, and listens to the sound of the tree frogs coming in through her open window. She hears the train whistle out in the night, mournful and far away.

Sometimes it's hard for her to believe that she ever left Black Rock at all, that she went off to school and grew up and moved away. Sometimes it's hard to remember that Grant is not down there right now, in that front room. But Crystal likes Odell, she has to admit it, both for himself and also because he doesn't try to take Grant's place in any way. Her mother deserves some happiness, a measure of gaiety, after all. And Odell helps out: he takes care of people, that's what he does, and right now he is helping to take care of Crystal. Gradually, Crystal begins to relax. One Sunday she goes to Garnett's church with Lorene, wearing a seersucker suit and white shoes. She smiles at herself in the mirror, thinking of what Jerold or Lane would have said about her appearance. But Crystal likes the way she looks. She goes over to the Breaks Interstate Park, just across the line in Kentucky, with Lorene and Odell for Sunday-night supper. Finally one day she drives to the post office by herself to mail a letter for Lorene. Finally she goes to the Rexall.

At the Rexall she runs into Sue Mustard Matney, who in the end married Russell after all. "Hi, Crystal," Sue says nonchalantly with that same old flip of the head, and again Crystal has the sense that none of these intervening years ever happened. But Sue has had two children and gained twenty pounds. She's in the Rexall buying birth-control pills and Valium, she tells Crystal, grinning. Then she invites Crystal to a baby shower she's having for a girl who is going to marry Russell's branch manager. Crystal goes straight into the Ben Franklin and buys pink and blue felt, glue, and sequins. When she gets back home, she makes a mobile to take to the shower, with little pink and blue sequined fish swinging from it. Lorene admires it profusely. Crystal can't figure out exactly how she knew what to buy for the mobile, or how she knew how to make it. It's as if the mobile has leaped fully made from some reservoir deep in her mind—and who knows what else might be lurking down there, unrecognized all these years? Recipes, Tupperware, polyester plaid. Crystal laughs at herself. But she is absurdly pleased with the mobile, which really did turn out well. "Oh, *Crystal!*" Sue exclaims at the shower. "How beautiful! You always were so creative." Was she creative? Crystal laughs at Sue; she can't remember. Never mind. She joins the Junior Women's Club, and then they ask her to be head of the ornament committee for the annual Christmas bazaar. Crystal spends hours and hours making little red felt birds to sell. She is very proud of these little birds.

In late October, at the bazaar, she sells them. The bazaar is held in the cafeteria of the high school where once Neva adjusted her beehive between rounds in the Miss Black Rock High pageant. When she reminds Sue of this, Sue throws back her head and laughs. "I'll never see size ten again, that's for sure! Do you remember that blue chiffon dress I had?" Sue seems perfectly comfortable with herself.

"I didn't have any choice about whether to win that beauty contest or not, you know," Crystal says suddenly to Sue. "Mack Stiltner didn't save me a seat. He was supposed to, but he didn't, so I had to win. Then I was so upset about all that, I didn't even enjoy winning the contest."

"Typical," Sue says as she prices the red felt birds. "Just typical. *Men*," she adds in a significant way, around the straight pins in her mouth where she keeps them while she prices the birds.

Crystal buys a Coke for herself and one for Sue. Then the doors of the cafeteria are opened to the public, and a flood of women come chattering in, ready to buy at the bazaar. Crystal hurries back to the table she shares with Sue. Sue and Crystal and all the other young women in the Junior Women's Club wear red-and-white striped ruffled aprons, so that they can be easily identified by customers. Crystal likes her apron; she likes being a part of this group of women, making things, talking about men in the deprecatory, resigned tone which all the women adopt whenever they talk about men.

"Can I show you something?" Crystal asks an old, old lady who has come up to their table and is peering near-sightedly at the candles.

"What? Why, Crystal Spangler!" The woman turns and looks at Crystal closely, still holding a Santa-shaped candle in one clawed hand.

It's Mrs. Muncy, who was old already when she was Crystal's teacher, all those years ago. She must be ninety now.

"How are you, Mrs. Muncy?" Crystal asks. "Just look who this is, Sue!"

But Sue Mustard was never one of Mrs. Muncy's favorites, and now Mrs. Muncy won't even look at her. "*Crystal Spangler!*" she says again. "What in the world are you doing here?" Her voice is small and cracked, like a radio with static, and she's bent nearly double with arthritis or plain old age, but her eyes behind the gold-rimmed glasses are still as alert and unclouded as ever.

"I've come back home to stay with Mama for a while," Crystal explains, conscious that Sue—who has carefully avoided asking her that same question—is listening intently. "So I'm just helping these girls out while I'm here. I think they do so much good, don't you?"

"Good!" Mrs. Muncy snorts, exactly the way she used to do whenever someone said something stupid in class. "You were the most talented student I ever had," she says to Crystal, putting her lips in a severe, straight line. She sets the Santa candle back down decisively on the table and turns and leaves, clutching her old-fashioned jet-beaded bag close to her as she heads for the door. She looks like a little black crow, Crystal thinks. Mrs. Muncy makes her bleak way through the brightly dressed, busy women and leaves.

"Well!" Crystal says to Sue.

"Old bitch," Sue says, and Crystal laughs. But she isn't so sure. It occurs to her that she should find a job—that she *could* find a job. Maybe a teaching job. The jobs she had before were exactly that: just jobs, none of them having anything at all to do with her education or with all this ability which some people thought she had. She had taken whatever jobs she could get, depending upon whatever man she was with. Face it. But it was also true that she used to be good at certain things. She might be able to get a teaching job right here, for instance. Of course she doesn't have a degree in education—she isn't certified—but probably they won't be as picky here in Black Rock as they might be somewhere else. Crystal grins, remembering Mr. Roach: his plump white hands, his quiche Lorraine. She might just go by the Board of Education tomorrow and ask. It wouldn't hurt anything just to ask, even if school has already started.

"Crystal!" Sue is practically yelling at her. "This lady wants to buy a paperweight."

"Sorry," Crystal says. She adjusts the ruffles on her striped apron and takes the woman's money, smiling.

The next day she goes by the Board of Education—just to inquire about the possibilities—and to her surprise they say that in fact they will have an opening in two weeks at the ninth-grade level, since a Mrs. Marcum has gotten pregnant.

"I'll take it," Crystal says.

But that first day, Crystal is awake for hours before it's time to get up, going over her lesson plan in her mind. Mrs. Marcum has said she ought to have a lesson plan every day, so she will. She will do everything she's supposed to. In fact, she has Mrs. Marcum's own lesson plans for the first week and a half, since Mrs. Marcum did them so far in advance. Mrs. Marcum learned to make these lesson plans as an education major at Longwood, a teachers college in Farmville, Virginia, where she also studied adolescent and child psychology and philosophies of testing, among other things. She knows the ropes, and she has made it quite clear to Crystal that Crystal does not. Mrs. Marcum is one of those early-aging women with a saggy, doughy face but a surprisingly trim body aside from the pregnancy, no hips at all and skinny legs. "Don't let a thing get by you," she advised Crystal. "The harder you are, the more they'll learn. If you start off too easy, they'll walk all over you, believe me. You'll never get it back." Crystal is not sure what "it" is. She's not sure why she's doing this at all, and as she lies in bed it seems that the most sensible thing to do would be to go back to sleep. But she knows she can't do it. She slept so much in the hospital, for days and days and days. Remembering those days—or *not* remembering them, that's more accurate—she shudders. This time, she really cannot. *Must* not: there. She hears Lorene getting up and then she can smell the bacon frying. OK.

Crystal gets out of bed and puts on a black pleated skirt and a black-and-white striped blouse. She looks in the mirror for a long time, putting her makeup on. Does she look like a teacher? Does she? What will her students think? Crystal has a headache right behind her eyes. It's raining, too, outside; beyond the window, fog covers the top of the mountain.

"You look nice, honey," Lorene tells her when she goes downstairs, and this helps some, but Crystal can't eat much breakfast and she still has the headache, even later, after three Bufferins, when she faces her first class.

They come in after the first bell and go right to their seats, which seem to be predetermined—probably by Mrs. Marcum, Crystal realizes. In alphabetical order, no doubt. Her hands are sweating as they fill up the desks and she opens Mrs. Marcum's grade book and her lesson plan book on her desk, smoothing the pages again and again. The tardy bell rings. The ninth-graders look at her with cold little narrowed eyes. Crystal stands up.

"Hello," she says in a voice which rings in her ears. "I'm Miss Spangler, your new ninth-grade English teacher. Mrs. Marcum's replacement."

The ninth-graders continue to stare, and a radiator hisses in the corner.

"Here," Crystal says. "I'll write my name on the board." She takes the chalk from the desk where Mrs. Marcum has urged her to keep it locked away so it won't be stolen, turns to the blackboard and writes MISS SPANGLER across it in large block letters.

"Can't you do cursive?" somebody asks.

"What?" Crystal turns.

"*Cursive*," repeats the black-haired girl in the second row. "You know, *cursive*. Where you link your letters together. Mrs. Marcum won't take anything if it's not in cursive. She gives you an F if you print."

"Oh." Crystal can't think of what to say next. They used to call it longhand when she was in school. She flushes, fiddling with the chalk and looking at them ("Maintain eye contact at all times," Mrs. Marcum said), as a low rolling contagious giggle starts somewhere in the back of the room and crawls forward across the desks. They're laughing at her. Or are they? Better not press it. She'll write on the board some more. Crystal turns and prints: WORK FOR TODAY, followed by the page number and the exercise numbers from the grammar book, but while she's putting up the exercise numbers there's a commotion at the back of the room, and a door slams as loud as a shot. She turns to see a boy come slouching into the room and take a seat in the back row, slamming his books down hard on the desk. Just then a blond girl in the front row passes a note across the aisle right in front of her, and Crystal for a minute is caught up in trying to decide if she should take it away or not. She could: all she'd have to do is reach right out and grab it. But on the other hand . . .

"Good morning, Miss Spangler." The boy in the back has a nasal, insolent voice. "How are you today?"

"I'm fine," Crystal snaps. "But you're late for class." Amusement ripples across the classroom again at this exchange, and Crystal feels she's scored her first point, or maybe half a point.

Which she loses right away when another student says, "Aren't you going to mark him tardy?" and before she can answer, the little blonde right under her nose says, "Of course she's not, stupid. She doesn't even know his name. She doesn't know any of our names. She hasn't even called the roll."

Crystal sits down, pulls the roll book closer, and starts: "Abbott, Janice. Blackman, Eugenia. Claris, Susie Louise. Clapp, Pamela. Dark, Ross Junior . . ." She has twenty-six ninth-graders in this class. Sure enough, they're seated in alphabetical order except for the boy in the back row, who apparently sits where he wants. He looks like he's twenty if he's a day, although of course he couldn't be. His name, surprisingly, turns out to be Lee Fontaine Hallahan. "Everybody calls me Bull," he says.

"Lee Fontaine *Bull* Hallahan," Crystal says, and he says, "Yo." Most of the girls say, "Present," and most of the boys say, "Here," but some of the boys try funny voices which Crystal ignores.

"OK," she says when she's called the roll. "Since I'm new at this, it will probably take me a little while to learn all these names. Please open your books and get out your pencils and paper. The exercise on page eighty-eight has to do with punctuation, semicolons and periods and commas, which I understand you've been studying for some time. So get busy on that right now, and then we'll check them together in class."

The black-haired girl in the second row raises her hand, speaking out over the noise of rustling papers and shifting books. "Don't you want to hear us recite first?" She has a prim little lisp because of her braces.

Crystal stares at her. "Recite what?"

"Every time we do a new unit in the grammar book, we have to memorize the rules before class. Then we have to come up to the front and say them in class and if we can't do it we have to write them a hundred times for homework."

"There's nothing in the lesson plan about that," Crystal says.

"Well, we do it. We do it every time. Like for today one of the rules is 'The semicolon divides elements of equal importance, such as independent clauses'."

"Show-off," Ross Junior says.

"It would take all period for everybody to say that," Crystal says.

"It *does* take all period." The black-haired girl, whose name in the grade book is Clara Sparrow, purses her lips smugly.

"Well, then, when would you do this?" Crystal points to the exercise number she's listed on the board.

"Probably for homework," Clara Sparrow tells her airily. "It takes a real long time for us to recite."

"OK," Crystal says. "OK." She stands up and comes around the desk and sits on top of it. The ninth-graders watch every move. Crystal sits on the desk swinging her foot and looks at them and then suddenly they seem so small. They're hardly more than children, most of them, with braces or pimples or uncooperative hair. She remembers, too, that this is the room where she had health class and also maybe the room where she had American history, and nothing has changed since then. The same green paint is still on the wall, and even the desks look the same. Printed heads of the Presidents parade across the top of the blackboard, and a large chart of French verb endings hangs at the back of the room. Maybe she had French here, too. No matter. Crystal smiles.

"Listen," she says. "I don't ever want to hear you recite rules. Never. I don't care so much about this exercise either. In fact, this is how much I care about this exercise." Crystal leans back on the top of the desk and erases the directions she wrote on the board behind her. Clara Sparrow's mouth opens and then shrinks to a perfect little pink O. "Now," Crystal says. "Let's start over. One thing I don't seem to have written down anyplace is what you've been reading—besides library books, I mean. Don't you have a literature book?"

Ross Junior raises his hand. "No, ma'am. We didn't get

it yet. We've been doing grammar first because it's the most important. Later on we can read."

"What about writing? How many writing assignments have you done?"

"How many what?"

"Writing assignments. You know, *papers*. Or whatever Mrs. Marcum called them," Crystal says, very conscious again that she never went to Longwood, but not caring suddenly at all.

"Ross Junior *told* you," Clara Sparrow says. "He told you. We have to do grammar first."

"Well, not anymore." Crystal draws a deep breath. "I'm going to find those literature books and you'll have them tomorrow morning. If I have to order them, you'll have them as soon as they come. In any case, as soon as we get them, you will read them along with grammar, or spelling, or whatever else we may be doing. Got that?" The class is nodding like so many puppets; heads bob all over the room. "Now," Crystal goes on. "We don't have very much time, so hurry. Get a blank sheet of paper and a pencil. Close those grammar books. Or something. Get them out of your way. Now, *concentrate*, or you'll run out of time. What I want you to do is write a good long paragraph about yourself, using—now listen—at least two semi-colons, two commas, one colon, and plenty of periods correctly. Got that?"

They don't get it. Crystal repeats the directions and then writes them out on the board.

"That's too hard," says Clara Sparrow, who has never made a grade below ninety-three in her whole life. Her bottom lip trembles; she chews on the end of her pencil.

"What do you want us to say about ourselves?" Ross Junior asks. "Do we have to have a topic sentence?"

"Oh, for God's sake." Crystal causes a collective gasp in the room. "Look. Say something interesting. Say anything you've got on your mind. Now start."

They start, heads bent over the desks, and Crystal stretches out her arms and then rubs her neck. She's as tired as if she's been running. Then, looking around the room, she comes to Bull Hallahan, down low in the desk he is ludicrously too big for, staring at her in a way she can't quite figure out He's not even pretending to work.

"Bull," Crystal says sharply. "Get on it."

Bull Hallahan mumbles something she's glad she can't hear, and bends his head down over his desk. OK.

When the bell rings Crystal takes up the papers, but Clara Sparrow doesn't want to turn hers in. "It's not neat enough," she says. "I can copy it over in study hall."

"That wouldn't be fair to the others," Crystal points out. "Give it here. Come on, Clara."

"But it's not neat." Clara is wailing.

"I don't care if it's neat or not." Crystal loses patience. "I care if it's interesting and if it's right. I don't care a thing about neat."

"You don't?"

Crystal grins. "No, honey. You don't even have to write in cursive unless you just want to. You can print all you want, for all I care. This is not going to be a handwriting class."

"We're too old to print!" Clara screeches, finally relinquishing her paper to Crystal as she runs out of the room, and Crystal laughs.

"Lord," she says, and the whole 9 A.M. class leaves laughing.

The 10 A.M. class goes more easily because she is more relaxed, and the 11 A.M. class is fine, too, except that she is beginning to feel like a broken record by then and except for a little boy named Norman Little, who falls like a stone from his desk right onto the floor a few minutes before the bell rings for lunch. Crystal leaps forward, but the class laughs. "That's just Norman," they tell her. "He does that sometimes."

"Why?" Crystal asks. "What's the matter with him?"

Norman Little lies curled on his side, one hand under his cheek.

"He's always done that," they say. "He's got some kind of fits."

"Fits," Crystal repeats, and later, smoking a cigarette in the teachers' room during her free period, she asks Mrs. Mooney about it. Crystal's glad she has the free period along with Mrs. Mooney, an older woman with black lace-up shoes and a certain amount of sense. Mrs. Mooney has taught history for twenty-five years. When Crystal was in school, Mrs. Mooney was teaching up on Council in the one-room school building at Fletcher's Ridge. Now that building has been torn down and the

Council kids are bused here, and Mrs. Mooney with them. Although she looks like she still teaches on Fletcher's Ridge, Crystal thinks, with her rough red face and her long gray hair pulled back any old way.

"His brother had fits too, as I recall," Mrs. Mooney says, grading quizzes with her red pen while they talk. She seems to be giving everybody either an A or an F. "Little Arvon. But I don't think he has them anymore. He works for the Appalachian Power Company now, you know. You wouldn't think they'd hire him if he still had fits. You wouldn't think he'd be safe in those little baskets they run up so high from those trucks."

"No," Crystal says.

"No, what?" Mrs. Mooney lifts her hooded old eyes from her grading.

"No, you wouldn't think so," Crystal says. But she resolves to take Norman Little over to see somebody at the County Health Department all the same, and this is the first note she writes in the little blank notebook she bought which says "Memos" at the top. Mrs. Mooney sniffs at the smoke from Crystal's cigarette, but she doesn't say anything, and Crystal opens the folder of papers from her nine-o'clock class and starts to read. "I was born in the middle of the night on Valentine's Day; which is why mama says I am so sweet," the first paper says. "I have two dogs, they make Daddy sneeze, I plan to become a Lawyer," Ross Junior writes. Crystal reads on, folded up in the close hot coffee-smelling stale air of the teachers' room, sitting on a curious purple stain on the tattered yellow sofa. When she gets to Fontaine Hallahan's paper, she stops. There's nothing on it but his name written in big straggling letters like Crystal imagines a second-grader might make.

"Mrs. Mooney," she says. "Mrs. Mooney."

The older woman looks up at Crystal, but her mouth twists down in annoyance. "What?" she says.

"This boy, Fontaine Hallahan." Crystal holds up his paper. "He can't even write. Look at this."

"Of course he can't write," Mrs. Mooney snorts.

"But what's he doing in ninth-grade English?"

"Well, look at him."

"What do you mean, look at him?"

"Just look at him," Mrs. Mooney explains patiently.

"He's so big, where else do you think they're going to put him? There's nothing wrong with him, he just never learned to read, that's all. Or write. Some of them don't. Besides, he's on the football team. This will be his last year, anyway. He'll be sixteen come August."

"Oh," Crystal says. "But what am I supposed to do with him in the meantime?"

"Do whatever you want to with him." Mrs. Mooney takes out a package of Roll-Aids and eats three. "You can ask him his questions out loud if you've got the time to. Or you can just let him sit there. You might as well," she adds.

Crystal goes back to reading papers. "If I could have anything in the world I wanted, it is ESP," Eugenia Blackman writes in a neat little back-slanted hand. "I would like to look into the dark heart of man. I would like to know what is real and what is made up. I would like to know if granddaddy thinks at all or just sits there. I would like to know what is going to happen in the future so that if I didn't like it, I could just stay home that day. But I would not be stingy; and use my gift for peace in the world."

Strangely enough these papers remind Crystal suddenly of Jerold, and she wonders what he was like at this age. She cannot imagine. Nor can she imagine him ever teaching school, although he did once; it's one of the few facts she ever knew about him. Psychology, she thinks it was. It's odd how little she really knows. He had been into photography and sculpture and Zen; he had had one or more fellowships and wives. These blank spots used to give her a thrill: all the dark unknowns about Jerold, but sometimes she used to wish he had a real past, anything to put your finger on. There had been no future with Jerold either, and even then she knew it. Jerold had insisted on the present, the present only, created new each day like a gift and made so intensely that it was a long time before she could smile to herself at some of the things he said. This was what Jerold created: today. Not literature. "I hate art," he liked to say. "Art sucks." Other days he said he was probably doing the most significant work in contemporary literature. Crystal never saw his novel. She typed one story for him, "The Puppy." Now she smiles, thinking that the puppy was not nearly as interesting as

Eugenia Blackman's desire for ESP. As she remembers it, the only character in "The Puppy" was the puppy himself, left alone on a four-lane highway to die. The puppy tried to cross the highway and was run down, eventually, by a milk truck. "The Puppy" was symbolic, Jerold had explained, an existential parable about a lost soul in modern America, killed in the end by that which seems to nourish. It's the bitch/mother image, he said. But apparently no one could understand it; it was rejected again and again. Editors called for plot and narrative, conventions which Jerold had outgrown.

Jerold burned like a dark meteor, "exploring new space," as he said, in his work. It was fine to be a part of this excitement, for a while, especially in the night when Jerold came sweating out of sleep to her, swimming upward out of the dark strong current of his dreams. When he was on top of her, then all the old intensity came back and the way he made her feel was wonderful again, was like it used to be back at the beginning in the room on Rivington Street when she never felt so much alive. She understood him, Jerold used to tell her over and over at the end, because she was also doomed. But this was wrong, and he was crazy; even at the beginning, he was crazy. She did not then nor had she ever believed she was doomed. *"Become."* That was another thing Jerold used to like to say. "You are just *becoming*, baby. Don't worry about it. Don't worry abut anything. You'll get there. Don't think. Live. Breathe. Get high. That's all you've got to do." He used to tell everyone that.

"Miss Spangler?" It's Eugenia Blackman herself, beet red with her diamond-patterned knee socks falling down. Students aren't allowed in the teachers' room, Crystal knows, unless they have a special message.

"Yes, Eugenia," she says.

"Well . . ." Eugenia twists her foot around and picks at little balls on her sweater. Mrs. Mooney does not look up from her grading.

"We were wondering, I mean, I'm on the cotillion committee, and we were wondering if maybe you could chaperone the sweetheart dance next week." Eugenia's words come out in a rush.

"I'd love to," Crystal says, and Mrs. Mooney says, "Ha," enigmatically. She thinks girls like Crystal are a dime a dozen with all their smart ideas. But they burn out fast enough. Get married or pregnant or both, or take to crying in the bathroom and then decide to get their license in real estate. Mrs. Mooney has seen plenty of them come and mostly go. Eugenia blushes, closing the door, and Crystal writes the date of the sweetheart dance in her memo book. She used to have a sweetheart, but he died. *Becoming,* she thinks, as she writes "Very Interesting" on Johnny Malone's paper about how he hopes to go to trade school if he can ever pass ninth-grade English. Becoming: maybe so.

Crystal falls into the rhythm of teaching school so easily that it's as if she has never done anything else. It's like there's a part of her which knows how to do it already, like the part which was up on the baby mobile. She chaperones the sweetheart dance; she serves on a curriculum review committee for the eighth and ninth grades; she serves two weeks of lunch duty in the cafeteria. She attends bake sales and talent shows. After thinking about Jerold a great deal when she first began work and found that she *could* think of him, she thinks of him less and less. She's very busy.

This is a coup of sorts, but another coup concerns Bull Hallahan. One spring day when she asks him to come back for a few minutes during lunch period so that she can find out whether he was or was not listening while she read the poems aloud to them that morning, she gets really exasperated because he won't pay attention to her at all. He keeps looking out the window, where all the noise is coming from. Finally Crystal says, "Bull! Will you pay attention or not? I'm trying to ask you something."

Bull turns his big head slowly in her direction. "What, Mrs. Spangler?"

"*Miss,*" Crystal says for the fifth or sixth time.

"What?"

"*Miss* Spangler, not Mrs."

"Oh," Bull says. He's only fifteen, but he has lines in his face already, and all of them run down. He has, Crystal thinks, *jowls.*

"I'm trying to ask you something. It's my lunch hour,

179

too, remember," she starts in again, but then because Bull Hallahan continues to look so woebegone she attempts to get him into a better humor. "What are you looking at, anyway, out that window?"

Bull Hallahan gives a long profound sigh. "Martha Bell Rice," he says.

"Is that your girl friend?"

"No, ma'am." Bull Hallahan shakes his head. "I ain't got no girl friend."

"Well, that surprises me," Crystal says. "A big old boy like you."

Bull continues to look out the window. "I can't get one neither," he tells her. "Lessen I can get my driver's license."

Crystal just looks at him for a while, and he looks at Martha Bell Rice out the window where she is practicing with the other majorettes: she throws her baton up in long slow circles, and her curly hair blows in the wind.

"I tell you what," Crystal says to Bull Hallahan. "You quit coming to my nine-o'clock class and use that period for your study hall. Then you come in here every day at lunchtime, and I'm going to teach you something. I'm going to teach you how to read."

But Bull Hallahan shakes his big head. "I don't know about that," he says.

"What we're going to use for our textbook is the driver's manual," Crystal tells him. "And we'll study it until you can pass that test."

Which takes a full two months of lunchtimes, as it turns out. And it works, even though Lorene swore up and down you can't teach a Hallahan anything. But when they finish, Bull Hallahan passes his driving test, even though Martha Bell Rice has gotten herself, in the meantime, pinned to a Deke at East Tennessee State. Bull Hallahan may have a broken heart, but at least he can read; not anything hard, but signs, newspapers, labels—enough to get by in the world. Crystal feels really good about Bull Hallahan, about this whole year, in fact. She's already signed her contract for the next year too; Mrs. Marcum had a seven-pound boy in April and a postpartum depression after that, and she won't be back for a couple of years. Summer has crept up slowly and now school is nearly over and Crystal can't believe it. Her students pile up her desk with presents: a loaf of homemade bread; Estée Lauder powder from the Rexall; a paper bag of string beans, picked that morning in somebody's mama's garden. When the last class leaves on the last day, she sits at her desk surrounded by presents as the final bell rings in her ears, and the silence after its ringing lasts and lasts. But Crystal feels fine, ordering books for next year.

Lorene buys a charter membership in the country club being built at the Breaks. After the courts are finished, Crystal takes lessons from the imported pro and soon has a little tennis group, two of the Lord wives plus Sue Mustard Matney. They try to play twice a week all summer whenever the weather is good and the Lords are in town. Lorene's new car arrives, a big surprise. Crystal takes bridge lessons. She goes to Myrtle Beach for a week with Lorene and Odell. Agnes buys another Laundromat, this time up on Slate Creek, and Bobbi Lord gets an *au pair* girl. That September, Roger Lee Combs gives up a lucrative insurance agency in Alexandria and moves back to Black Rock with his wife Judy Bond Combs and their little twin girls, coming home to go into the coal business with his first cousin Lewis Dean Wright. Everyone feels that Roger Lee and Judy are a big addition to the community. Judy Bond Combs joins the Junior Women's Club and she and Crystal are very friendly, but Judy never asks her over, of course. Speculation rises and dies. Crystal is working very hard at the junior high school; sometimes the comments she writes on her students' papers are longer than the papers themselves. Everybody is delighted with her teaching: such a nice, quiet young woman, and all that education to boot. Neva divorces Charlie, who promptly declares bankruptcy and leaves town with his girl friend. Crystal teaches *Silas Marner*, and her uncle Garnett suffers a slight stroke.

One time, in the middle of the night, Jules calls up. "Crystal?" He slurs the word into the phone. "Crystal?"

"This *is* Crystal." She has been up late grading spelling tests. "Who is this?" Crystal tries to keep her voice down so she won't wake up Lorene.

"Want to speak to Crystal."

"This is Crystal. Who is this—Jules?"

"What are you doing, Crystal?"

"Well, I was asleep, if you really want to know." Crystal gropes for a cigarette, putting as much ice into her voice as she can manage. It's just like Jules to call up in the middle of the night when she hasn't heard from him for two years.

"I mean at home. What you doing at home, Crystal." It's not a question but a statement, trailing off at the end.

"What? I can't hear you," Crystal says.

"At home. What you doing at home." Jules's voice is faint across miles and miles, almost the whole continent.

"I'm teaching ninth-grade English at the junior high school," Crystal says. "I love it. Next year I'm going to put in applications for a teaching job in Richmond." Or Atlanta, she thinks. Or Charlotte, or maybe even Washington.

"There's something sad, Crystal. I thought I would tell you about it, thought you might like to know. The only kind of man I like is the kind you can't live with, the kind you pick up in a bar."

"What?" Crystal burns a hole in her yellow robe.

"The kind I'm attracted to," Jules says softly across the whole country, "is the kind I could never love."

"What?"

"Isn't that tragic, Crystal? Don't you find that tragic, too?"

"Do you want anything special or are you just drunk or what?" Crystal is annoyed to hear her own voice shaking so much.

"Go away," Jules says. "Go away, go away."

"Well, you're somebody to talk," Crystal starts out, not knowing what she'll say next, but there's a click on the other end of the line and Jules has hung up. She holds the buzzing receiver for a long time in her hand. Isn't she doing well now? Isn't she? Yes. *Isn't she finally happy?* Why does Jules have to call up out of the blue like this? Crystal remembers when she was little and Jules tore the heads off all her paper dolls. She used to keep them in a Stride-Rite shoe box and he got hold of it and decapitated every one. She understands more about that now than she did then, of course. Since he couldn't have them, he didn't want her to have them, either. Probably. She is sure it was something like that. Well, he still can't have them, Crystal thinks now. *But I can.* Yet Jules's call upsets her and she never tells anybody about it. She loves Jules, after all. The trouble is that she still loves everybody. It's as though Jules has reached down inside her and plucked one note on an antique musical instrument, and the echo goes on and on, a high painful keening note. The next day, trying to teach her third-period class what a metaphor is, Crystal feels ill suddenly and has to go back to the faculty lounge and throw up. She cancels her classes, goes home, and sleeps for the rest of the day. The next day she feels fine.

Now, Sykes, on the other hand, is around all the time. He is still a deputy sheriff, with two dogs trained to kill on command penned up behind his new brick house. Sykes and his wife have three small children, slightly slant-eyed and roly-poly, who get into everything. Lorene won't keep them unless she has to; they wear her out, she says. Crystal gets a kick out of Sykes's wild kids and his wife. She is small and plump like her children, but her arms and hands are slim. Sykes gets drunk at the new country club and tells everybody that Bunny can do acupuncture. But she can't. Bunny is always in a good humor, always giggling "Hee-hee-hee" behind her hands. Crystal likes Bunny especially because Bunny appears so delighted all the time, so happy with whatever you say to her. "Yes?" Bunny squeals in delight, making it a happy question. "Yes?" she always answers.

Everybody keeps trying to get Crystal a date. She is still so attractive, after all. But Crystal won't have a date with anybody, so tragic rumors grow up around her in the junior high school, propagated by her students, who are too young to know anything real about her past. The old fiancé-who-died-in-a-car-wreck-on-the-way-to-the-wedding rumor starts. Crystal is amused. She refuses to go out with Bobbi Lord's recently divorced brother or with Babe's director from the Barter Theater in Abingdon. Once Sykes and Bunny try to get Crystal a date with an old Army buddy of Sykes's who is passing through town.

"We will be going to the Hukilau Room in Bristol for some dinner, yes?" Bunny lilts into the phone. "Maybe we dance some."

"I'm sorry, Bunny, but I've got a whole set of term papers to grade."

"You cannot come, yes?" Bunny seems transported by delight.

Tired at last of waiting around for Crystal to get married, Lorene gets married herself. She and Odell tie the knot in a brief ceremony in the Spanglers' front room on Valentine's Day. Garnett officiates, leaning on his cane. Garnett looks old and sick. Lorene wears a white pantsuit and Crystal wears a light-green jersey dress. Babe McClanahan comes over from Abingdon at Lorene's request to read aloud from *The Prophet* by Kahlil Gibran. Odell grins and grins during the ceremony, and his gold tooth winks in the light. Later, he and Lorene will drive off in Lorene's new car for two weeks in Hilton Head, South Carolina.

During the ceremony, Crystal stares out the window into the front yard, where Lorene's forsythia blooms riotously, illogically, amid the last gray tatters of snow.

It's awkward talking to Babe. Babe is the one who is awkward, perhaps because she used to idolize Crystal so much. Babe's red hair is long and curly, and makeup rings her eyes. She wears violet stockings beneath her long black skirt.

"Are you happy with your career?" Crystal asks, trying to make conversation. They don't seem to have much in common anymore. "Do you like working with the Barter?" She gives Babe a cup of punch.

"It's what I always wanted to do," Babe answers, staring at Crystal curiously, but Crystal goes on giving out little cut-glass cups of punch. Crystal is happy that her mother has finally married Odell. She is happy to give out punch. In fact, she made the punch herself from a recipe in *Southern Living:* two parts ginger ale, one part cranberry juice, a lot of raspberry sherbet. Unspiked because of Garnett. Later Babe leaves, too, in her little blue sports car, and Crystal watches her go, trying to remember what *she* had always wanted to do. Teach English? Surely not. On the other hand, she's good at it. She's successful. Babe is successful. Agnes is successful. Jubal Thacker is certainly successful, with his TV show *The Divine Ministry* now shown over sixteen stations in the Southwest. Crystal watched it once, saw little Jubal heal a fifty-six-year-old man who had never walked in his life. Crystal watched the man throw his wheelchair into the wings.

But probably the most successful of them all is Mack Stiltner, whose second album has just been released by Columbia. He has had two gold singles already. Sometimes, idly, Crystal thinks of calling him up. But she knows she will never do it. He's married, for one thing. To a starlet. She saw their pictures together on the cover of a movie magazine in the Piggly Wiggly while she waited in line at the checkout. "Collies Brought Them Together," the headline read. Thinking about it, Crystal smiles. Some people she knew are not successful, though: Pearl Deskins was arrested recently for shoplifting in the Ben Franklin—Sykes told her about it. Other people are dead. Crystal turns from the window with a shiver and helps them throw rice on Lorene.

Giggling like a girl, Lorene runs out through the rice and vanishes into Valentine's Day. Lorene and Odell seem like a perfect match to Crystal, who could never have conceived of such a marriage years ago. If anybody had predicted it then, she would have laughed and laughed. Agnes and her mama and the cleaning girl help Crystal clean up, and then that's done and they leave, too, and suddenly the house seems so large and empty that Crystal gets into the car and drives up to Dry Fork.

Agnes, next door, removes her girdle first and then goes in to talk to her mama, who is watching ABC's *Wide World of Sports.*

"Well, *that's* over with," Agnes says, sitting down.

"It was real nice," her mama comments dreamily, watching TV. "It'd be nice if Crystal would get married now, too."

"Well, she won't," Agnes says.

"Now, Agnes, how do you know? She might. You never can tell. Why, Babe might even marry again, too, one of these days. She said she's got a new part, did you hear? Going to play a crazy woman."

"She won't even have to act for that one," Agnes snaps. She can't for the life of her see why her mama is so fascinated with Babe's acting, with her "career." After all, Agnes has a career, too. But every time Babe gets a part in something new, Agnes has to drive her mama all the way over to Abingdon to look at it. Her mama is star-struck, that's what. Second childhood coming on. But Agnes herself is not as interested in what Babe does as in what Crystal does. It was clear from the word *go* how Babe would turn out, and once she got out of high school she knew what she wanted to do and she did it and never looked back. It was never so clear what Crystal would do; that's the difference. And Agnes is all mixed up with Crystal some way. For instance, nobody can make her so mad.

Her mama turns sideways from the television long enough to say, "You know what I think? I think Crystal is doing just fine now. I think she's turned over a new leaf."

A new leaf! Maybe so.

"Now looky there," Agnes's mama goes on. "Look at that little old Rumanian!"

Agnes settles back in her favorite chair to watch.

Crystal drives furiously up Dry Fork, whipping around the curves she knows by heart. Odell's big car jerks and shudders over the potholes in the road; the highway department has not kept pace with the mines. Crystal feels a little sick, ill at ease between places. When she reaches the old entrance she slows down. Little Emma Mining Co. Granite. But things have changed up here so much: big machines, new buildings everywhere. The exposed raw earth is wet and red, still sogged with snow. Some snow, left on the shady banks here and there, is gray with coal dust. The old house still stands, an anomaly among the huge bright pieces of earth-moving equipment, anachronistic with its little patch of yard, Devere's dog pen in back. Odell and Lorene have been after Grace and Nora to tear it down, to put Devere into the hospital in Radford where he belongs and move into town, so they can be closer to doctors. Nora and Grace have plenty of money by now, from their interest in this land, but they haven't changed a thing. You'd never guess they had money at all. Crystal parks in the mud. The huge forsythia by the mailbox is blooming profusely just like Lorene's, gay and foolish in the cold wind.

Grace, a little frail eggshell of a person now, all muffled up in an ancient blue coat with a shiny fur collar, is poking about at the side of the yard. Crystal goes over to her.

"Hello, Grace," she says. "Isn't it a little bit cold for you out here?"

"Daffodils," Grace says. "Look." She thrusts a whole handful of them at Crystal, smiling simply.

"The wedding was real nice," Crystal says.

"Weddings are lovely," Grace announces in her sing-song voice. "Is Nora there? Is it time for dinner now?"

"No," Crystal says. "It's still afternoon right now. I just drove up to see how you all are doing." And to get out of the house, she thinks. But Grace has forgotten all about the wedding, humming as she picks more daffodils. It's probably just as well. Crystal goes into the house, where Nora wants to hear all the details. She just can't get over it—Odell Peacock and Lorene!

"Why didn't you come?" Crystal asks when she finishes telling it. "Odell would have been glad to come up here and get you, you know that."

"What do I want to come to a wedding for?" Nora laughs hard like a man, and Crystal can't answer that one. Why indeed? Nora wipes flour on her apron and Grace comes in with the daffodils, sliding in sideways quietly, but Nora catches her after all.

"Feet!" she hollers. "Look at your feet. Wet clear through. You'll catch your death of cold."

Grace obediently sneezes and Crystal leaves them arguing in the kitchen and goes upstairs. It's like a different world. There are four big bedrooms, each with its high ceiling and dark woodwork, its dark wood floor, its big windows with the wavy glass. At the end of the hall, one window looks out on Devere's workshop, where he probably is right now, taking things apart and putting them back together, out past the workshop and the pen with the yapping dogs, on up the holler where the mountain lies undisturbed on one side, all rutted and cut up on the other. Bright February sunshine falls in a solid block all around Crystal as she stands, the sunlight alive with teeming, whirling bits of dust that spiral downward to the worn patterned rug at her feet. Crystal looks out for a while and then goes blinking out of the sun and back along the hallway, searching. But she isn't sure what she's looking for. The beds are made up in each room—Nora does that— and in each room Crystal finds a curious peace, a stillness, as if they are exhibits in some museum. Crystal goes into Devere's room, which is the least cluttered, and opens his closet. There are Devere's plaid flannel shirts, all of them almost alike. He wears a clean one every day; Crystal knows he has one on now, in fact, up the holler wherever he is and whatever he's doing, helping somebody fix something, probably. Devere always smells just like these shirts. Nora has washed them so many times that they are as soft to the touch as baby clothes. Crystal fingers them awhile, her mind whirling.

She goes into Nora's room, with its big solid oak bed made by hand in this county, the stacks of magazines and clothes and boxes piled high along the walls. Neither Nora nor Grace can stand to throw anything away. A beautiful quilt covers Nora's bed, fan pattern like the one downstairs; she made it herself. Another quilt is in progress. Crystal picks up the little squares of fabric and fingers them curiously. It's hard to imagine that they will ever add up to anything as finished as a quilt.

In Grace's room, the brass bed has been shined to a deep dull sheen and the bed itself covered by an extraordinary bedspread, a peacock strutting along haughtily yet daintily, picking up his feet. His multicolored feathers curl in all directions to fill the bed. It's a cheap chenille spread like the kind you see hung out for sale on clotheslines up and down the Shenandoah Valley, tacky and awful and beautiful all at once. Crystal knows how mad it makes Nora for Grace to insist on keeping this spread on her bed. But Grace has a painting of a rose on black velvet, too. Maybe she bought them at the same time. Crystal wonders when Grace might have bought them, what trip she might have taken and when. Every available surface in Grace's room is covered with little china figurines, knickknacks, pictures in frames. Crystal looks at them one by one. She sees poor little Emma with a parasol, Nora and Grace and Emma in long dark dresses with big white collars staring solemnly into the camera with a painted backdrop of a lake, swans, behind them. She sees herself, her senior picture, smiling, wearing an initialed silver barrette in her hair. That barrette has been lost for years. She sees an Olan Mills photograph of her whole family, Grant and Lorene and Jules and Sykes and herself, grouped on a sofa, Grant looking slightly off to one side. She sees an old official picture of her grandfather, eyes stern and dark above his mustache and the awful jut of his nose, dressed up in a high collar with his hair parted right in the middle of his head. He stares straight out ahead through all the years, and Crystal wonders what he is thinking now. There's a photograph in a little oval frame on the candlestand table right next to the bed and she knows it must be Mr. Hibbitts, the long-dead rheumatic sewing-machine salesman. Mr. Hibbitts looks like a rabbit, scared of the camera, but his bulging eyes are sort of sweet. Crystal looks at all the pictures.

She opens a little heart-shaped filigree trinket box she finds on the top of the chest, empties it and studies the contents: a ticket to a concert in Baltimore fifty years ago, mellowed and soft with age; a spool of white thread; a cheap gaudy bracelet of square red rhinestones; an un-signed Christmas card picturing a deer in the snow; a green felt ribbon; a place card saying "Grace" in ornate script; an old picture of some fat solemn baby, maybe Grant; a buckle with fake gray pearls; some plastic but-tons. Crystal stares at the small pile of clutter, then re-places the objects one by one in their box.

Crystal goes downstairs soundlessly, skirting Nora and Grace still arguing in the kitchen, having a big time, and goes down the basement stairs. Here it is very cold, damp, and the hanging light bulb gives little light. Off to the left is the furnace, old and dirty and huge. To the right is the storeroom, and Crystal opens this door and snaps on the light. More boxes, more junk. She begins poking through it all systematically, stopping once to light a ciga-rette and admire the lovely rows of canned vegetables in Mason jars which line the shelves. Every summer, Nora and Grace can for days, the old way, boiling the jars in a kettle on the stove. Seeing these vegetables now, dim and preserved behind their stickers, it's hard to remember how Nora's garden runs riot with them during July and August. There seems no relation between the bright ripe tomatoes or corn and these dusty jars. Poking again, Crystal comes across an old leather-covered journal in a box of molding *Upper Rooms*, Methodist home devotionals from years and years ago. She takes it out, opens it, sees "Emma Turlington Field, Accomac" written in spidery letters on the flyleaf. She turns the page and reads:

* * *

Moonlight nights Will and the little Negro children would play marbles in the path near the door steps and I would sit and watch them. While I was always ready for play, I cared nothing for marbles except to throw them up or catch them on the back of my hand. When tired of play we would take a seat, one on either side of Mama, put our heads on her lap and sleep until bedtime. In summer she would spread us a lodge on the floor, but in winter she took us in with her.

The women sniffed snuff and one day I tried it too, they had to put me to bed, I was so sick.

Mama used to often visit sick folks so one Sunday she took me with her to see a sick woman, Mrs. Fluheart. She took a basket of nice things for her to eat. Just before we started home we all went out to look at the garden and get a drink of water from a sweet spring back of the house. Around the corner a big dog rushed out from under the house, and standing on his hind legs, put his front feet on top of my head. I was frightened so that I screamed and fell. The others drove off the dog and quieted me, but from that day to this, I've been afraid of dogs.

Crystal rubs her eyes with her hand in this dim light. This journal—or something like it—is what she has been looking for. Something to establish the past, continuity, now that Lorene has left. Which is so silly when you analyze it. After all, they'll be back in two weeks. But just right now, today, she needs something to hold on to, so this might as well be it. Crystal leaves the storeroom, closing the door behind her, still holding the dusty journal, and climbs back up the steps.

"Well, look who's been down in the cellar!" Grace booms. "We couldn't for the life of us figure out where you'd got to. Look at what you did to that pretty dress, now. Turn around."

Crystal turns around in the hall. "Nora," she starts, but Nora is brushing her vigorously, swatting her pale-green skirt.

"Lord, that's awful!" Nora declares. "You'll have to send that to the cleaners."

"I will," Crystal says. "Listen, Nora. Look what I found

190

down there. Somebody's diary. Who was Emma Turlington Field?"

"Lemme see that," Nora barks. She takes the journal, grabs at the glasses on her chain and fits them grimly to her nose, ignoring Grace, who twitters to see, like a bird, at her elbow.

"I never saw this before," Nora says finally. "Must be some of our people from around Baltimore, must be something Emma had. Where'd you find it, anyway?"

"Down in the storeroom in a box."

"Shoot!" Nora says. "Look how she wrote. Looks like bird tracks to me."

Grace grabs the journal, retreats a step or two and fingers it, turning it over and over in her hands. "I think I remember seeing this," she says finally. "I think it's been here a long time."

"Oh, go on!" Nora snorts. "We never set eyes on it before."

"Well, can I borrow it?" Crystal asks. "I want to read some more in it."

"Oh sure, take it and keep it as long as you want," Nora offers, losing interest in the whole thing. "I don't see what you want with it, though." Nora's tone is scornful, as if she herself reads better books and can't be bothered with anything dull. But Crystal knows that Grace is the only reader in the house—historical romance after romance—while Nora sticks to the newspaper.

"Well, I guess I'd better be getting along," Crystal says, and stands up to their pleas that she stay at least for supper. "I have to grade papers," she explains. She has three stacks of book reports waiting for her at home, and she looks forward to seeing if they have learned anything, if all that talk about paragraph development and transitional sentences ever sank in. Crystal smiles at her aunts. "Now you all tell Devere I said hello."

It's late afternoon by then, and the mailbox sends a long slanted purple shadow over Odell's shiny car. Crystal puts the keys into the ignition, then opens the journal again and reads:

At times my brothers would dress me up in some of their clothes and one day they dressed me and put me up in a little plum tree in the yard. Someone hollered out, "Master Jack's coming," and they flew into the house, forgetting me entirely. I do not remember if Papa whipped us for it or not.

Soon after that I had a gathering in my head which left me deaf in one ear. One day Papa wanted to give me a dose of Castor oil and he had to bribe me to take it with the promise of a nice silver thimble. I got my thimble and was very proud of it.

Crystal shuts the journal and starts the car. She can see it all as if it's happening right now: somewhere on the Eastern Shore, a little girl deaf in one ear wearing her thimble, playing marbles, afraid of dogs, all so long ago. These peculiarities delight her; this ancient, ancient Emma.

Crystal has already parked in the driveway when she notices the other car there, parked in Lorene's regular spot. But this is not Lorene, Lorene being of course on her honeymoon. Crystal is so used to seeing a car there that she didn't even notice it at first. This is a Volvo station wagon, forest green. Crystal remembers seeing it somewhere before, but she can't remember whose it is. Not Neva's car, not Bobbi's or Sue's or Garnett's or Sykes's or Bunny's, not anybody who usually comes by. Slowly, wondering, Crystal gathers up the journal and her purse and the jacket to her dress and walks around to the back of the house. She remembers that she has locked all the doors. She's careful about that. Well, maybe it's somebody visiting the McClanahans. Still, a premonition raises the hair on her arms and she walks slowly past the budding daffodils and the japonica and up the steps and opens the screen porch door.

Roger Lee Combs sits waiting for her in one of the white wrought-iron chairs, wearing a plaid sports coat, his hat on Lorene's glass table. He looks like he's been waiting for a while.

"Hello, Crystal," he says.

Like a sleepwalker, Crystal walks right past him and unlocks the kitchen door, then hesitates and turns back on the step. "Roger, what do you want?" she asks. Her head it light and very far away. She has papers to grade, things to do. But suddenly she's conscious of the dirt on the back of her dress, and she halfway turns in the door to hide it.

"I just want to talk to you," Roger says, standing up. Crystal has forgotten how big he is. "Aren't you going to let me come in?"

"Come on in, then," she says, and goes in and leaves the door open behind her. Roger sits down in the arm-chair in Lorene's conversation area and Crystal goes over to the sink and washes her hands.

Roger appears calm, watching her, but Crystal almost doesn't know what she's doing. She drops the towel on the floor.

"Come over and sit down," Roger says.

Crystal sits on the edge of the love seat. "Roger, what are you *doing* here?" she blurts. "You know you haven't got any business coming over here like this."

But Roger leans back in the chair. "I've waited a long time to come," he says. "I waited as long as I could. I just want to see you," he says.

"But I've *seen* you!" Crystal finds herself suddenly and embarrassingly near to tears. "I've seen you all over the place for months, Roger. I see you at the country club, I see Judy at the book group, I saw you just the other day at Agnes's store. I was downtown buying some nails for Odell. Don't you remember that? I was buying some nails." Crystal's voice goes up higher and higher and she knows she can't control it.

"I remember that," Roger says calmly. He crosses his legs like he has all the time in the world.

Crystal bites her lip and sits back on the love seat, pulling her skirt down as far as it will go. "Well, I've seen you," she says again. "God knows, I've seen enough of you to last me for the rest of my life. *Before*, I mean," she adds. Now she's really angry and for the first time she looks at Roger directly, her eyes losing for once their deep limpidity, flashing. Roger looks straight back. His eyes are calm. His whole face is calm. She sees that Roger has aged well. When he was younger, his face looked silly to her sometimes, so grave and so thoughtful and conscientious stuck up there on a teenage body, like one of those cardboard cutouts you step behind to get your picture taken at carnivals. When she was a girl, she used to do things on purpose to try to shake up Roger's face, to disarrange those careful features. Once when he had sprained his back playing football he had to wear a back brace for two months, and somehow Crystal has kept this image of him, sitting up ramrod straight in any chair with that giant Ace bandage around his ribs beneath the shirt.

She sees that this image is no longer accurate—if, in fact, it ever was. He doesn't look braced any longer. He still sits up straight, but he is relaxed like that, and his body has filled in and changed to fit his face. Now Roger is handsome in a dependable way, twenty pounds overweight, gray streaking his brown hair, a deep line already there between his eyebrows. Strangest of all, he has a mustache, mostly gray. Suddenly self-conscious, Crystal drops her eyes to the floor and sees his dark-brown lace-up shoes, the kind of shoes Jerold used to make fun of. Size twelve and a half, she remembers. It's surprising how much she already knows about Roger. He's like a big aberration, filling up this whole room. Only that's not right, either. He's not aberrant, she's wrong—she is the aberrant one. She was the one who left. Roger has always belonged in this house; just look at him. But Crystal doesn't know what to do with him there. He is watching her so closely, so kindly. He has such trustworthy light-brown eyes. No wonder he's making a fortune. Anybody would buy anything from him; anybody would trust Roger Lee.

He smiles at her, warm and slow. "I wish you'd relax, Crystal," he says. "I'm not going to rape you."

"Why did you say that?" she snaps. "Don't be ridiculous." She lights a cigarette. "Well, what do you want?" Now she's not mad or frightened so much as curious.

"This is going to take me awhile," Roger Lee says. "I ought to feel like a fool, I guess, but I don't. I am a fool. I know it. I've thought it all out, but I don't care. I don't *care*, Crystal." Roger Lee says this almost violently, slamming his hand down hard on the TV.

"I don't know what you're talking about," Crystal says.

"Oh, I think you do." Roger Lee speaks with such patience, with such gentleness and conviction, that Crystal grows alarmed.

But he goes on that way. "I don't care if you think I'm a fool. I'd have to agree with you. But like I said, I'm past that now. I've been waiting to talk to you, Crystal. I've been waiting a long time—months, years. I know Lorene and Odell are gone right now. I waited for that too. I don't want any interruptions. This is what I came to say, Crystal. I love you. I still love you. I guess I never stopped. I guess I never got over you in the first place."

"You're kidding," Crystal interrupts weakly, but something clicks in the back of her mind, and she knows she has always known it.

Roger Lee doesn't seem to hear her. He leans forward intently, going on, apparently determined to say it all. "I know you didn't love me back when we were kids," he says. "You were too young when we started. You were into too many things. You were just a kid, and then later I pressed you too hard. I pushed you. I should have given you time to grow up. I realize I have only myself to blame, and I do blame myself, in many ways, for all the things you've gone through."

"That's not even true," Crystal says. "None of it was your fault. It didn't have anything to do with you. Besides, I treated you terribly. Don't you remember that?"

"Anyway, it doesn't matter," Roger says. "It should, but it doesn't. I don't care. I don't care about that weirdo you lived with in New York, I don't care how many men you've slept with, I don't care about anything you ever did to me in the past. What I'm talking about is right now. I love you right now, Crystal. I can't help it. I wish to God I didn't, but I do. Sure, I married Judy. Sure, I love my girls. And I was doing all right with that, I guess, until we moved back here, and here you were. I didn't have any idea. Nobody told me you were here, nobody mentioned your name. Do you know the first time I saw you again, Crystal? I can tell you exactly. I was standing on the street with Lewis Dean after work, at five-thirty, and you drove by in that car of Lorene's, looking straight ahead. You didn't even see me. You had a red scarf in your hair."

"A scarf," Crystal repeats. Part of her mind is frozen.

"I said to Lewis Dean, 'I've got to go, I'll see you tomorrow,' and I just turned around and left. I guess he thought I was crazy." Roger Lee grins. "Then you know what I did? I went back up in the office and locked the door and cried. I couldn't stand it, you see. As soon as I saw you, I knew I still loved you, I knew I had never stopped. I probably knew it before then, even—I just wouldn't admit it to myself. I thought you were unattainable, you see, all those years. But then I came home and you were here, and I could see that you needed me."

"You're crazy, Roger," Crystal says. "I don't need you at all. I wish you'd go home. I wish you'd quit telling me this."

"I can't," Roger says. He grins again. "I've got to tell it, you've got to listen. I need you, too. At first I thought, I won't say anything, I'll get over it. I threw myself into my work. But the harder I worked, the worse it got. I took Judy to Mexico—big vacation, just the two of us. Judy had the time of her life. I felt like shit. We came back, I kept on working. I had entered politics in a small way, as you probably know. People tell me I've got a brilliant future. I don't care. I don't want it. I used to wait and see if I could catch a glimpse of you anywhere. But I wasn't going to say anything."

"Obviously you changed your mind," Crystal says. She smiles at Roger, and Roger laughs.

"Well, this part sounds dumb, too. It sounds almost as dumb as the rest of it, but I swear to God it's the truth. We were watching TV one night and I saw that beer commercial, you know the one I mean. Well, I must have seen it a million times before, but all of a sudden something clicked. It was that one about 'You only go around once in life,' you know the one I mean. Schlitz. And I thought, Hell yes, Roger! That's right. Once is it. That's the ball game. That's all she wrote. So here I am."

"I see."

"Now," Roger continues. "That's what brought me here. All of that is what brought me. I haven't had a fight with Judy, nothing like that. I waited to come and I came here to say exactly what I'm saying. That's all. I want you, Crystal," he says suddenly, more intense than ever. His brown eyes glitter as he leans forward.

"Oh no." Crystal draws back. "No, Roger."

"It's not like you think," Roger says. "I want you to go away with me. I want to marry you. I don't care about Judy, I don't care about the girls, I don't care about anything but you. I've got the money to do anything I want —you know that, Crystal. It's really quite simple. I want to make you happy."

"I am happy," Crystal says quickly.

"No you're not," Roger says with absolute conviction.
"I am so. I am happy!" Crystal screams.

Roger grins at her. "Crystal," he says gently. *"Baby.*
I've known you all your life, remember? I know you,
sweetheart, I know everything you've been and everything
you've done. I've watched you go through all these
changes, one right after another. You might *think* you're
happy now, Crystal, but you're not. Living with your
mother and a stepfather, what kind of a life is that for
you? What kind of life is it for your mother either—to be
blunt. Don't you suppose she wants some privacy? What
are you going to do, Crystal? Teach junior high school for
the rest of your life? Dry up and be an old maid?"

Crystal shakes her head to clear it, but she can't. Roger
goes on.

"This is not any kind of life for a woman like you,
Crystal. This is crazy. A woman like you needs a man.
You need your own home, children, a position in the
community. You need love. I want to make you happy,
Crystal. I can do it if you'll give me a chance. It's all I've
ever wanted, all my life."

"My God," Crystal says with no expression at all in her
voice.

"I want you, Crystal," Roger Lee says, standing up.
Crystal stands, too. Roger kicks Lorene's hassock out of
the way, grabs hold of her and kisses her. A deep shock of
feeling runs all through Crystal when they kiss; it's almost
painful. It's been so long. It was there with Mack, then
Jerold, some other times maybe, but it was never there
with Roger before. "I want you," Roger says again.

Crystal reaches behind her and unzips her dress and
for once the zipper doesn't stick and the dress falls evenly,
soundlessly, around her feet onto the floor. Crystal stands
in her pantyhose and slip. Very gently, Roger pulls the
straps down over her shoulders.

"I always wanted to see your breasts," he says. "I never
saw your breasts before." He leans over, kissing them,
sucking on her nipples. Crystal moans. A feeling she has
almost forgotten sweeps over her, closing her in.

"Come on," she says, pulling him toward the stairs.

But Roger won't come. "No," he says, and by his voice
she knows he means it and she stops. Roger picks her
dress up from the floor and slips it back over her head.

"Turn around," he says and she does, and he zips it up, lifting her hair, and kisses the back of her neck. "Not like that," he says. "Not now. I want us to do this right, Crystal."

"For God's sake," Crystal says. "There's no way to do this right. There's nothing right about it."

"No, it's right," Roger says. "It's exactly right. I'll need about two weeks to get everything in order, that's all. Then we're leaving."

"Where are we going?" Crystal asks. "Where will we live?" She is almost chanting.

"We'll probably live in Bluefield eventually," Roger Lee says in a matter-of-fact tone. "He's got it all figured out. "I've got more interests there than I have here, actually. It's a pretty nice town. But before that we'll take a trip. A long trip. How would you like that?"

"Whatever you think," Crystal says. Some part of her is screaming, or almost screaming, and then it breaks off and is still.

Roger puts his hands on her shoulders and turns her to face him. "I'll let you know," he says. "I won't see you again before we leave. I don't want any messiness, any intrigue. I want to make a clean break, do you understand?"

"Yes," Crystal says. Roger is the only man in the world who would do it this way. "But what about Judy?" she asks.

"I'll feel some guilt," Roger says slowly. "Of course. It will be difficult for Judy at first. But I'll take care of that. You are not to worry about Judy," he adds forcefully. "You are not to worry about anything."

"All right," Crystal says.

He continues to hold on to her shoulders and to stare at her face like he's memorizing it. Now that things are settled, he seems dazed. "The craziest thing is that I don't even care if you don't love me," he says slowly. "You will love me," he adds.

"I have to tell you something," Crystal says.

"What is it?"

"It's just that I don't know. I don't know if I can do it or not."

"Do what?" he asks.

"All of it. Any of it. Marry you, be your wife. I don't

know if I'll be good at it," Crystal says. "Can't we wait? a little while, anyway? At least until the end of the school year? I'll never be able to get another job if I quit now."

"But you'll never have to work," Roger says. "Don't worry, baby, I'll take good care of you." Roger pulls her to him and kisses her again. "I've got to go," he says. "I'll call you. Oh, one more thing," he adds, and puts his hand into his pocket and gets out a little square box and gives it to her.

"What's this?"

"A Valentine present for you. Go ahead, open it. Well, go *on*," he urges when she hesitates, and she does, and it's a square-cut dark-red ruby with a wide gold band.

Of course.

"It's just beautiful!" Crystal says.

Roger slips it on her finger. "I bought this two weeks ago in Washington. It just kind of reminded me of you," he says.

They cling together in shadow now. Roger snaps on a light, and Crystal looks at the ring. "It's so beautiful," she says.

Roger kisses her hard and Crystal says, wanting him, "Oh, just come on, Roger. Come on now. Nobody will ever know."

"*No,*" Roger says. "I think I can wrap it up in a week, OK? I'll let you know." He kisses Crystal again and puts on his hat and leaves by the screen-porch door.

Crystal goes into the bathroom and turns on the light. She looks at herself in the mirror: messy hair, no makeup, filthy wrinkled dress. The *femme fatale.* She holds up her hand, and the ruby flashes red in the mirror, red as blood in the mirror, holding secrets. But what about her classes? Darryl Whiteside has done better this year than he ever has before. Ellen Livingston just wrote a sonnet for her, last week. But of course they can find somebody else to take over her classes. It won't be hard at all to find somebody else. Roger is inevitable. He has always been inevitable, but she hasn't always known it. She washes her face, plucks her eyebrows, brushes her hair until her scalp is tingling. The idea of Roger slides all over like body lotion, covering her, working in. It's so comforting, really, to have somebody again to tell her what to do. She goes through all the clothes in her closet, deciding what to leave and what to take. She goes through all her shoes. She does her nails. Then she turns out the light and lies down on her bed and cries and cries as if her heart might break.

The first Agnes hears about it is in the Rexall, where she is having her lunch, when Brenda Looney comes bursting in at the door. Brenda Looney, a teller at the Levisa Bank and Trust, sees everybody and knows what's going on all over town. She wears these harlequin glasses. Agnes has never cared for her and she never stands in Brenda's line when she goes to make deposits at the bank. But here comes Brenda, slamming into the Rexall on her break, can't wait to tell it.

"Did you hear about Roger Lee? Roger Lee Combs?" she asks, talking to Mrs. Ritten, who works at the cosmetics counter and is a big friend of hers, but her shrill voice carries all over the store. *"Well,"* she goes on, and although two counters are in between Agnes and Brenda Looney, Agnes can imagine how she looks, how she would draw up her mouth, "Roger Lee Combs and Crystal Spangler have *run off!* Eloped! They say he left a note for his wife."

"Why, Lord, they can't elope!" Mrs. Ritten cries. "He's married! You can't elope if you're married."

"Well, run off, then," Brenda Looney says in her loud voice. "It's the gospel and I'll swear it."

"Oh, and those poor little twin girls!" cries Mrs. Ritten. "That's just awful! I can't imagine Roger doing a thing like that. He's just too nice of a person. Or Crystal Spangler either one, to tell you the truth. I'd gotten real fond of Crystal."

"Well, that's what they did all right," Brenda Looney says. "I didn't know if you'd heard it or not."

"That beats everything," Mrs. Ritten says.

"What does?" asks old Mrs. Tyler Rockbridge, coming up, and they tell her and they tell everybody who comes their way. They say that Judy Bond Combs is under heavy sedation and her mother is being flown in on a private plane which Roger Lee is paying for.

But you can be sure that everybody shuts up pretty

quick when Agnes gets up out of her booth and goes over to the cash register. They forgot Agnes was in there. Agnes takes her time, too.

"I want two packs of Dentyne," she says, "and put it on the bill, please, Sue." Agnes doesn't have to tell Sue what she had for lunch. She always has the same thing, a tuna salad and a Coke and a small bag of barbeque potato chips. Agnes takes her time leaving—somebody connected to the Spanglers has to show some dignity, after all—and you could hear a pin drop. On her way past the cosmetics counter, Agnes sees the Coppertone ad up over the lotions, that little girl with her hair in pigtails and a dark tan. Agnes could just cry about Roger Lee's poor little twin girls.

Of course, as she reminds herself so many times later, it wouldn't have done any good. Roger Lee has a lot of money by that time, and he gives Judy Bond the most alimony anybody ever heard of. Judy builds herself a new Cape Cod house in Richlands and then marries Dr. John Wheeler two months after the divorce goes through. Dr. John Wheeler is a gynecologist at the Clinch Valley Clinic in Richlands. Crystal and Roger Lee come back from Florida and move fifty miles over to Bluefield where Roger Lee has some mines anyway, and they just lay low for a while. Nobody in Black Rock says a word about them, at least not to Agnes. It's exactly like they have both fallen into one of Roger Lee's mines. They get married eventually, of course—Roger Lee wouldn't live with anybody without marrying them, Agnes reflects, he was always too nice for that—and about a year after this, all of a sudden Crystal comes out of retirement. Lorene and Odell have kept in touch with Crystal anyway, going over there to visit, and for all Agnes knows, Sykes and Bunny and Neva and anybody else might have been over there, too. Agnes herself hasn't been invited. Of course, it isn't any of Agnes's business and she isn't about to ask. Besides, every time she thinks about Crystal Spangler, it makes her want to either cry or else throw up.

But then Crystal comes out of retirement, so to speak, and everybody in Black Rock sees what she's up to. The first thing Agnes knows, Crystal is all over the *Southwest Virginia Messenger,* smiling out of the society page every Sunday like she deserves to. Mr. and Mrs. Roger Lee

Combs return from Jamaica! Mrs. Roger Lee Combs has an intimate luncheon! Mrs. Roger Lee Combs heads the Heart Fund! That one really cracks Agnes up. She shows it to her mama, who says, "Well, I think that's real nice." Another day her mama says, "Well, they always were *in love*," right in the middle of nothing, but Agnes knows exactly who she's talking about. Her mama thinks it is romantic.

And Lorene is beside herself. As she tells Odell one night after supper, while they are cleaning up the dishes, it makes her feel really good to know how things will work out for the best in the end. She takes her rose-flowered plates up out of the soapy water one by one and runs hot water over them, putting them in a wet straight glistening line in the plastic drainer, and it seems to her right then that her whole life has gotten to be that way, as clean and orderly as those hot round dripping plates.

"Things work out for the best in the end, huh?" Odell says, goosing her, but she slaps his hand away from her hip.

"No, I mean it," she says. "I'm serious." She wrings out the dishrag and lets the water out of the sink.

"I'm serious, too." Odell is behind her, reaching around her waist to grab at a breast. Odell smells like onions and Marlboros and work, a hot male smell, breathing right into her neck.

"*Honey*," she says, stepping sideways away from his hand to wipe off the counter top, "listen to me a minute. You know what I mean. You know how it used to be around here. I guess you get the bitter with the sweet, as they say, but that's all we got for a while and you know it. And now look! I never thought Sykes would amount to a hill of beans, for instance. Nobody else thought he would, either. And I never could tell what Crystal was going to do next. You know how she changed. But I guess it's all over with now. That's what I'm saying. I used to tell myself, 'Now, Lorene, all you can do is keep on doing,' and that was true, of course, but you still don't know how it'll all come out. You never know a thing about something when you're in the middle of it, and that's the Lord's truth. But just look at Crystal now!" Lorene takes off her apron and rubs cold cream into her hands. "Look at Sykes!"

"Don't look at Jules," Odell says, grinning at her. He likes to get a rise out of Lorene now and then. She slaps him—playfully, he thinks, with her sweet-smelling cold-cream hand, but then she slaps him again.

"Whoa there." Odell grabs both her hands. "I'm just kidding you. I swear. Why, Jules is all right. He just turned out different from what you thought, not a thing in the world you can do about it. He's probably just as happy as he can be, out there in L.A."

"You reckon?" Lorene perks up.

"Sure," Odell says. "Why, California is the best place in the world for Jules."

"I guess so," Lorene agrees. "Anyway, he's got a good job."

"See what I'm telling you?" Odell grins and Lorene smiles back and shuts up about it. Odell squeezes her hand and then goes on into the front room to watch TV, her own man, now so big he fills up the whole door when he goes through. What she ought to do is put Odell on a diet, and put herself on it, too. Lorene thinks she'll start the diet on Monday, after she makes that German choco- late cake she bought all the ingredients for today. Odell just loves German chocolate cake. But he's right, about Jules: let sleeping dogs lie, leave well enough alone. Still, he can't have any idea of what it's like to bear a child, wash his clothes and feed him and tend to him for sixteen years—Lorene remembers turning on the shower, hot, and standing in there with Jules screaming, when he was little and he had those asthma attacks—doing all of that, and then have him just disappear from the face of the earth. Because California might as well be the moon, as far as Lorene is concerned. Oh, it happens all the time and she knows it; it's not all that unusual. Look at poor old Belle Varney: one of her boys, Horn, killed in Viet- nam, Daris off working on the Alaska pipeline, Belle get- ting old all alone in that house down the road, not even bothering to grow tomatoes anymore. Plus she and Odell have a big time, they've still got their health, knock on wood, and three normal grandchildren to boot. I better count my blessings, Lorene thinks, and stop standing here

in the middle of the kitchen like a fool. Odell laughs out
loud and Lorene smooths her hair and then heads for the
front room, where she will sit on the couch with him and
watch Carol Burnett.

When Crystal comes over for a visit that summer, this
is all Agnes hears from Lorene and her mama and everybody else in town for two weeks running: how attractive
Crystal is, how Crystal hasn't aged a day, how she has a
diamond wedding band that will knock your eyes out.
Agnes is down at the hardware store and misses the big
visit herself, and even though Crystal calls her up from
Lorene's she's just too busy to come to the phone. Then
Roger Lee enters the Democratic primary for congress
and, further, *wins* it, so Mrs. Roger Lee Combs has her
picture on the *front* page of the Bluefield paper, just like
she's Jackie Kennedy or Betty Ford. And even Agnes has
to admit she looks good.

Crystal sits in the white quilted armchair in her living
room and watches the caterers swarm through the dining
room and the kitchen like so many bees. One of them
seems to be singing in Spanish and she likes this, likes the
way the sound comes out foreign and strange from her
own kitchen, out past the rest of them setting things on
the dining-room table, out into the living room itself,
where it is finally lost in the high ceilings and turning
motes of dust in the last of the sun which comes in across
the Oriental carpets from all the windows. The caterer's
song rings high and sweet, barely audible, just like a song
in her mind. Maybe it is. She really ought to go get
dressed. The living room is spotless: Mary came today
and brought her little cousin to help her clean for the
party, a tiny black teenage girl who turned out to be, of
all things, hugely pregnant, so that Crystal had to resist
the urge to *help* her, all day. ("Baby," Roger would have
said, she can hear him saying it right now, "remember
who the help is.") So she did not. Now Crystal fluffs up
the quilted pillow by her side in the white armchair, aim-

lessly, then smooths it out on her lap. Fan pattern: yellow and red, picking up the warm dusty-rose shade of the walls. This is a beautiful room. Everybody says so. This pillow reminds her of Mary's cousin's stomach, black and full of baby, and her not much more than a baby herself. Sixteen, maybe. Barely. Roger has said she can have a baby nurse any time she wants to have a baby, but she won't. Not now, she says, and Roger says don't worry the nurse will do everything. But she won't, not now, not yet. There are some things she knows a baby nurse can't do, but she doesn't think she can do them, either, and she hasn't told Roger this. Later, she thinks, and the caterer's song goes on in the back of her mind. There will be shrimp, crepes, asparagus rolled up in toast. Crystal is sleepy. There will be chicken livers on toothpicks. Mary comes into the living room still straightening here and there and putting out extra ashtrays, her face so severe and abstract that Crystal goes upstairs. Mary takes a party like the second coming, and Crystal is not even dressed.

She runs a bath and gets into it, sinking down to her chin. When they used to have parties it was so hard: she had to do it all. Now it's easy, but it's not fun anymore, not like it used to be when she stayed up the night before, baking bread. Or was that fun? At least it took hours, filled time.

She comes out of the bathroom in a cloud of steam with the lavender towel wrapped around her, all pink-faced from the heat; and Roger, reading a newspaper in the armchair, smiles. He's dressed. He's been dressed for an hour, downstairs on the sun porch supervising the bar.

"You'd better hurry up," he says. In truth Roger loves her lassitude, the way she trails in and out of rooms and leaves her cigarettes burning in ashtrays. He likes to find her car keys, to pick up the clothes she took to the cleaners four months before.

Crystal crosses the carpet to her dressing table and unpins her hair. It falls just short of her shoulders, waving damply, and she brushes it with the absolute concentration she always assumes in front of a mirror, like a glaze has come over her face. Roger is charmed, watching from the chair. Right now Crystal looks to him exactly as she did in high school, when they were so young and he loved her so much. Her still face, the huge blue eyes so open they broke your heart. Roger remembers a coat she had in high school, red-and-black plaid with a missing button, third one from the top. Roger remembers everything.

Crystal puts on her makeup and then she puts on her slip. "Is anybody I don't know coming to this?" she asks, and Roger starts naming the names and then breaks off.

"Lawrence Wright is not coming, if that's what you mean," he says. Roger does not mention that he knew about Lawrence Wright and Crystal all along, when it began and when it ended; he does not mention that he was instrumental in Wright's losing his job at the bank—that in fact Lawrence Wright has left town.

"That's not what I meant." Crystal lights a cigarette, standing in her slip.

"Look, it's OK." Roger puts the newspaper down. "He's not coming, he's not invited, OK?"

"Why did you have to say that? I wasn't asking that, Roger."

"I know you weren't. I'm sorry."

"You're trying to—you're trying to—"

"*Crystal.*" Roger stands up and goes over to her. "Come on. I'm not trying to do anything, OK, except maybe save us all some embarrassment. That's all."

"Shit." Crystal puts the cigarette out and turns from him, but he comes closer and puts his arms around her and kisses her.

"Roger—"

"Hush. It doesn't matter. Hush."

"Roger."

"Hush. Here." Roger snaps off the light by the chair and takes her over to the bed and then takes off his clothes. Crystal watches, feeling that she has known his body so long, so well, that it's her body, in fact. Hers too. She starts crying. Roger comes down on top of her, kissing her, and at the end of it she lies with her legs wrapped around him and his face pressed into her hair. The doorbell starts ringing downstairs: once, twice, more. People are coming to their party.

"Baby. Don't cry."

"I'm not crying. I won't cry. I'm not."

"I'm sorry," Roger says.

"No, I'm sorry, I am. I really am. It was stupid, the whole thing, I was stupid. I'm sorry."

"You're not stupid," Roger says. "Forget it. It doesn't matter." Roger means this. Nothing matters about Crystal except Crystal herself. For almost his whole life, she has been as inevitable for him as business and death and taxes, as the sun coming up across those mountains he grew up in.

"Roger." Crystal struggles to sit up. "Listen. I love you."

"Hey," Roger says. "It's OK." Crystal lies back on the pillow and Roger kisses her all over, her face, her throat, her breasts, her stomach, the sticky trail of semen on the inside of her thigh, as the level of voices at the party rises, floating up the winding stairs and under their closed door. Crystal smiles, rubbing her hand in his hair.

"It sounds like a good party," she says, and Roger laughs.

But as the campaign picks up, there are too many mornings like this one when Crystal lies curled up against Roger in their king-size bed and waits for light to come, for dawn to seep in finally through her Levolor blinds, for soft edges to appear and then harden all over the room. But she dreads the coming of day. Like this, in darkness, nothing is finite, nothing is ever over, nothing is resolved, everything is possible. Daylight puts an edge on things. Roger's back moves up and down in sleep. Once he sighs and murmurs something. Crystal leans forward, trying to make it out, but he turns slightly from her, moves his leg, quits talking. Probably it's something about business or the campaign anyway. Something straightforward, like Roger himself. Crystal sighs. It is true that she loves him, as he had said she would. In fact, she loves him more than she knew was possible, so much that she can't have that baby or do anything else that might change things, change the way they are. Because things are not exactly as Roger thinks, anyway. Things are more precarious. They have edges now. Crystal props herself up on one elbow, watching Roger sleep. Ever since the beginning— ever since that day when he came to her mother's house —she has been conscious of the end.

Crystal watches him sleep as the light grows in the

room and the wallpaper changes from black to gray to blue. Sleep has become the greatest mystery of all, since she isn't sleeping anymore. She can't even remember sleeping the whole night through. Roger sleeps like a baby. Crystal smiles. But she never sleeps, never really sleeps. Only sometimes her mind wanders and she dreams. Crystal traces a pattern, long and complicated, on Roger's broad back. Roger sleeps just like a baby. But she sleeps the sleep of the damned. Which is so dramatic she almost laughs out loud. Doomed, maybe. Jerold has been coming into her mind a lot lately with all his talk of doom, the way the hair curled down low on his neck. It was ridiculous, everything he said. Jerold was a madman. But still.

The light comes in full at last, silky and golden, and Crystal watches the pattern flower in her rug. Sometimes she thinks of other things to do. She makes up other selves. For instance she might be a businesswoman, like Agnes, getting up now in this rosy light, checking over a straight column of neat black figures somewhere, going down to her little shop in the early-morning light when there is no traffic at all in some impossibly charming town with the trees planted in holes in all the sidewalks. She might be dressing mannequins in the window of her shop. She might be dressing children. She might be plaiting pigtails, tying strings of saddle oxfords or whatever it is they wear now, frying bacon, wiping tears. She might be cooking bacon in a yellow housedress, buttering six pieces of toast. Or she could be going over lesson plans with her hair pulled back in a bun. Or she could be lying in bed beside Roger and thinking realistically about the day ahead, which is what she ought to do, since Marion Fitts has that hospital tour scheduled for her. But Crystal remembers yesterday, the Kiwanis luncheon, when her eyes did that funny thing so she could see only one thing at a time—one person, no crowds. It was as though her eyes had become a closeup lens. A zoom lens. It was disconcerting. It made her see more than she wanted to, of everybody. It was like she could see into their souls.

Crystal thinks about, and rejects, the idea of telling Roger how she feels. "Roger," she would say, "I feel like a person in a play." But then, of course, he would be too considerate. He would have Marion Fitts cancel the hospital tour. And if she tells him anything at all, then she might tell him everything—about her not sleeping, about the way she is conscious of endings and edges—and then he won't love her anymore. But she doesn't *know* that, of course. She doesn't know he wouldn't love her anymore. It isn't worth taking a chance on, though, not after Lawrence Wright, or. Or. Crystal resolves to wear her dark glasses on the hospital tour and see if Leonard can get her some sleeping pills.

She gets up quietly and crosses the flowered carpet to the armchair. She switches on the light, settles herself, and picks up the diary of Emma Turlington Field, which lies in a jumble of books on the round table beside her. Most of these are Roger's books. Some of them are Crystal's, but she can't really read anymore. She can't keep her mind on the page—another thing not to tell Roger. Crystal pushes back a piece of her hair and opens the diary:

> Every Sunday morning Major, the family coachman, took some of the family to Drummond Presbyterian Church, and after dinner, to Sunday school. One Sunday he took only Mary and me. On our way home, Mary was sitting on the front seat with her back to the horses. I had the back seat facing them when I noticed something that looked like a big fire. I told Mary and she called to Major and asked where the fire was. By that time I was so embarrassed because we all saw it was the moon rising!

Crystal smiles and closes the diary. It reminds her of nights back in her old neighborhood, a whole procession of nights all exactly the same, a whole parade of moons rising like a string of Chinese lanterns. She wishes she could remember the song Jubal's daddy used to pick on his guitar. He used to play it every night and then they knew it was time to go in and sure enough, their mothers would come to the screen doors and call them.

Crystal thinks of calling Agnes to ask her about the song, but it is still too early, so she takes a shower instead, hot hot water to wash away the way she thinks she smells, sour and old, like a washcloth left for too long in the sink. She sprays herself all over with cologne and when she comes out of the bathroom Roger is already up and dressing. He gives her a great big hug that folds around her like a tent, and if she could stay right there she thinks she would be all right. If she didn't have to *do* anything. Roger gives her a kiss too, but she can't get him to go back to bed with her because he has to show up at an Episcopal prayer breakfast in twenty minutes. "Tonight," he says, kissing the back of her neck before he leaves.

Later that morning, Crystal calls Agnes after all. She hasn't talked to her in months, not since last August when she and Roger went over to Black Rock for the opening of the new library. Now Agnes has become a real businesswoman, hardware store and three Laundromats. No sense trying to get Agnes at home, in fact. Might as well try the hardware store.

"Hello. Could I please speak to Agnes McClanahan?" Crystal asks the girl who answers.

"Who's calling, please?"

Crystal can hear people talking in the background, something clanking.

"Mrs. Roger Lee Combs." Crystal lights a cigarette; she never smokes in the morning if Roger is home.

After a pause, the girl says, "Can you hold for a moment? Miss McClanahan will be right with you."

"Sure." Crystal waits. She hears a car in the driveway —Roger leaving. Then she hears the maid come in the front door.

"Hello," Agnes finally says.

"Hi, Agnes. This is me, Crystal." Crystal tries to make her voice right. "I just wondered how you're getting along."

"Well, fine, Crystal, just fine. It's funny you called. Odell was in here not five minutes ago."

"Are you busy?" Crystal asks. "I mean, can you talk for a minute?"

"Well, actually," Agnes says in her old nasal, guarded tone, "I was just on my way out the door. I've got some salesmen from Roanoke here to see me."

"Oh. Well, I'll let you go, then. But wait—this won't take but a minute. I was wondering if you could remember which song it was that Jubal's daddy used to play on his guitar every night when it was time to go in. Do you remember?"

"Lord, Crystal. I couldn't tell you." Agnes sounds like she wouldn't want to, even if she knew. She sounds like somebody who has some salesmen waiting right outside the door.

"Well. Well, thanks anyway. Well, I'll see you the next time I come over. You be sure and vote for Roger, you hear?"

Agnes laughs. "I'll do it," she says. "You tell Roger that, too, now."

"OK." Then there is a long pause and Crystal can imagine Agnes on the other end of the line, looking at the watch on her freckled arm.

"What is it, Crystal?" Agnes asks suddenly. "Is anything wrong?"

"No, no, nothing like that. Listen, you go ahead, I'll see you the next time I come over. We might come next weekend, in fact."

"You sure?"

"No, it's not anything really. I was just wondering about that song. It was silly. Tell everybody to vote for Roger."

"Oh, he's got this town locked up." Agnes is obviously relieved. "I'll see you, hear?"

"Great," says Crystal. "I'll be looking forward to it." Click. Click. Two very extremely loud clicks. Crystal winces. Then she sits looking at the phone for a long time, winding the cord to make black rings around all her fingers. This makes her hands look very interesting in a perverted way. It would probably sell, in fact, in that shop she doesn't own: telephone jewelry. Crystal gets up and takes another shower before she dresses.

She puts on a dark-green wool suit and a yellow blouse and she's brushing her hair when Marion Fitts, one of Roger's administrative aides, comes to stand in the doorway. Marion Fitts is in charge of Crystal's schedule; she plots out all the meetings, the tours, the speeches, the appearances, on a hardbound calendar which she keeps in her briefcase all the time and takes everywhere as she accompanies Crystal during the campaign. Marion Fitts does everything. She even plans the seating and the menus for official dinners. Marion Fitts has been with them for three months now, ever since Roger hired her away from the *Richmond News Leader* to work full time on his cam-

paign. Marion Fitts also writes news releases and keeps
a gold ballpoint pen on a chain around her neck and
has proved herself, as Roger often remarks to Crystal, in-
valuable. Because this is so obviously true, Crystal likes
to keep her waiting, as she is waiting now, in the hall just
outside the bedroom.

Marion Fitts clears her throat.

Crystal smiles, then drops the brush into her purse and
shuts it with a click.

"OK," she says to Marion Fitts, leaving the bedroom
just as it is—clothes all over the unmade bed, cosmetics
scattered on the dressing table, lights on—because Mary
will be in right away.

She follows Marion Fitts out to the car pulled up in the
wide curving driveway in front of her house. Leonard
Halsey, another aide, sits in the driver's seat reading a paperback. Leonard's blond hair curls in ringlets all over his
head, and his brown eyes look huge behind his thick
glasses. Crystal likes him.

"Pretty as a picture," he tells her when she gets in. He
puts the paperback up on the dashboard and puts the car
in gear.

"Thanks." Crystal gets in beside him, and Marion Fitts
gets in back, unfolding several newspapers.

"What are you reading?" Crystal asks Leonard.

"Trash." He grins at her, his eyes as huge as a cow's
eyes behind the glasses. Crystal's big house grows smaller
and smaller as he drives away down the street, and then it
is gone.

"I used to read," Crystal says.

Leonard looks over at her, and Marion Fitts rattles all
her papers in back.

"Actually, I used to be an English teacher," Crystal
says.

"I know it," Leonard says. "You told me."

"Oh." Crystal smiles at him. It's an old joke between
them, her forgetfulness.

"Everybody in this state ought to know that by now,"
Marion Fitts says in a loud voice from the back seat. In
her news releases she has emphasized Crystal's interest in
public education and mental health. Marion takes some
scissors from her briefcase and begins to clip items from
the newspapers.

212

Crystal sighs. Of course she is interested in public education and mental health—or she was—but today she's just so tired. She fishes in her purse for her dark glasses and puts them on.

"La-dee-dah," Leonard says.

"Dr. Ripley is the psychiatrist in charge here," Marion Fitts tells them. "John Ripley. He'll probably take us around himself. What he wants is a new recreation facility, so he'll harp on that, of course."

"Psychiatrist," Crystal says. Somehow she had thought this was a pediatric facility. She thought Marion had said pediatric.

"Of course, psychiatrist," Marion says. "But I'm sure the tour will be pleasant enough. You don't have to worry about that. He'll be trying to make a good impression, just like everybody else."

"Dr. John Ripley," Crystal repeats. It's awfully important to get their names right.

Lenora Gardner Hospital turns out to be a low rambling building, or cluster of buildings, surrounded by a gray stone wall, high and crenellated, with its iron gate standing wide open. A smiling guard waves them past the gatehouse. Patients—or Crystal supposes they are patients—move around the grounds through falling leaves in the soft autumn air, sometimes two or three of them together, sometimes by themselves. They seem to be enjoying it.

"Nice place," Leonard comments.

"Isn't it," Marion Fitts says in that way she has, with no inflection in her voice at all.

Crystal looks straight ahead. Then she puts on some more lipstick, which turns out to be a good thing, since three photographers are waiting for them by the door. Marion Fitts writes something down in her notebook before she gets out of the car. Leonard helps Crystal out, holding her elbow.

Dr. John Ripley is a big tall man with a silver crew cut and piercing blue eyes which stare right at you until you have to look away. He speaks in a clipped Northern accent. Dr. Ripley walks in a rush, showing them everything, with his white coattails trailing a wake through the halls behind him. The insane are not so different from the sane, he tells them. There is a very thin line here. In fact, we have a great deal to learn from the insane. Insanity,

Dr. Ripley feels, is largely societal. Or perhaps *situational* is the better word. What we are trying to do is change the situation, break the pattern, teach different behaviors. This is where the new recreational building comes in, he adds. How can we help people learn to react to society in a new way if we have no model of society for them to practice with?

"Fascinating," Marion Fitts says.

Dr. Ripley goes on and on. He speaks in a rush, words flying out behind him as he leads them through polished halls, opening first this door, then that. A group of women playing cards looks up, momentarily, at their entrance, a wide crazy social smile lighting up some of their faces. Crystal sees a dance group, an exercise group, a craft group, a children's classroom in progress behind a two-way mirror. The children can't see them, Dr. Ripley explains. All they see is the mirror in their classroom. Crystal stands listening to Dr. Ripley explain about normal and abnormal, that thin line, and about the advantages of the one-to-one learning situation and the extent to which learning and especially language problems can influence behavior, while a child who has been described as both hyperactive and retarded cavorts before the mirror not a foot away from her face. Leonard holds on to her elbow. Marion Fitts takes notes. It is a relief when they finally leave the shadowy little observation booth, the dancing child.

But then sunlight coming in through the picture windows along the hall dazzles her, the way it bounces up from the floor. Even with the sunglasses, it hurts her eyes. Dr. Ripley is making some analogy and Marion Fitts is writing it down. "We must remember," Dr. Ripley is saying, "that darkness is only the absence of light." So what? Dr. Ripley says he is in the business of letting in light. Crystal's eyes hurt. She excuses herself and goes to find the ladies' room, down the hall on her right, they tell her, but after that she is drawn back the way they have come. She wants to see. She wants to look behind some of those brightly painted closed doors, or else she has to. She doesn't believe Dr. Ripley and his theories of light, for one thing. Just one door, perhaps this orange one, and she will rejoin the group.

Crystal pushes the orange door, half expecting it to be

locked, and it gives inward with a sigh. This room is gray and shadowed, its curtain drawn. Four white iron beds nearly fill the whole room, shining out from the shadows all geometric and ghostly, or are they beds at all? Actually they look more like giant cribs. Crystal approaches one and looks down at the woman, straggle-haired and skinny, curled in a tight little ball inside it. Crystal sucks in her breath. She knows she should go back, but something has her now and holds her, pulling toward the next bed, where an old man lies on his back, breathing noisily, staring straight up at the ceiling with open blue eyes that appear to see nothing. Crystal puts her hand in front of his face, but nothing registers. What is wrong with them—cerebral palsy, depression? These are vegetables, then. They'll have a big time in that recreational building, won't they? Live it up.

"Unnh—" It's not much more than a sigh, yet it seems so loud in that still room that Crystal jumps. "Unnnh." She turns to look behind her. It's another one, a young man, hunched in the corner of his crib. He struggles to hold up his wobbling oversized head. He struggles to control his face. Through the bars of the crib, he holds out a hand to Crystal. She shrinks back, bumping the bed behind her. That hand is awful, shaking and small, but it is his face which holds her. It makes her move forward again. His face is a moonface, white and smooth, a moonface like Devere's. In the soft furry light of the hospital room, he holds out his hand.

He holds the wrench in his hand, a strange gesture, jabbing at the air like an experiment. Still he says nothing.

"Devere," Crystal says, caught in a sudden, knowing fear. "Put that down."

Devere circles, hunched, until he is between her and the door. The only sound in the toolshed is his breathing. Crystal reaches back and grabs the edge of Devere's work table, the smooth-sanded cared-for wood. She is at her grandfather's house, it is the night when the black ghosts come that will swallow you whole without ever a word. They come like clouds, thick black. Crystal holds on to the wood. Devere, still bent over, makes queer crablike motions toward her, awkward, moving in. His face puckers up and twists in something private. In his hand, the wrench catches light.

Crystal thinks of silly things: Agnes's new red winter coat; a picture in the kitchen made of dyed corn glued on cardboard, a brown horse pulling a yellow buggy; Roger Lee learning how to do the twist; *whose woods these are I think I know his house is in the village though.* Bobby Lukes told Mrs. Muncy it was a poem about Santa Claus.

Devere comes very close in his curious crablike fashion. "Put it down," Crystal says softly. "Or give it to me, Devere. I know where it goes."

Devere gives her the wrench and she puts it down softly on the workbench behind her, holding on to the wood all the time with one hand. Devere makes a sound like "unh, unh," a thick moaning sort of noise. He pulls down his pants and his penis sticks out thick and red. Crystal has never seen an erection before. It seems strange that Devere has a body at all, under those clothes that he wears all the time. Devere picks her up carefully and lays her down on the toolshed floor. He's a big man and he picks her up easily; easily puts her down; it's cold and damp down there and Crystal can't touch the wood anymore. Devere pulls down her blue corduroy pants and then her underpants, frowning now slightly in concentration, some ease coming into his face. She smells the sawdust and damp down there. He gets on her. Crystal lies absolutely still. Devere is heavy, heavy. He has a smell like the inside of Roger's jeep. For a minute she can see the bare glowing bulb, the wood beams of the roof. Devere is hurting her. She knows, of course, where the hurt is, but for some reason it seems to be traveling up her whole body into her shoulders and then pinpointing itself somewhere up at the very top of her head, like somebody driving in a nail up there. Her face is pressed into Devere's flannel shirt and she can't breathe much. And the black ghosts will smother you to death, they come on Friday nights, and hasn't she been a good girl? Hasn't she? Clarence B. Oliver, greatest of ghosts, Crystal says in her head. Clarence B. Oliver, come in, over and out, Roger. Looked so funny doing the twist. She would laugh if she could breathe. Clarence B. Oliver fails, of course. She should have known he would. Nothing now but pressure and this nail in the top of her head. *He will not see me standing here to watch his woods fill up with snow.* Crystal never moves and soon it's over. Devere rolls off and gets right up, zips his pants, gets the wrench from the work table and hangs it up in the place on the pegboard where it's supposed to go. Crystal, not moving, thinks her legs and her back are broken. Devere looks down at her, a question, or almost a question, in his face. Still lying there, Crystal pulls up her panties and then the corduroy pants. Now things are in order again and the question leaves his face and he turns to go. His deepset eyes, those Spangler eyes, don't seem to see her at all. Now his face is calm and smooth again, like a wide far field. He doesn't know, she sees. He doesn't know anything about it. *My little horse must thing it queer to stop without a farmhouse near the darkest evening of the year.* Is that right? Something missing. Something missing now.

Crystal moves forward to take the young man's hand. And she is still holding his hand, not moving, although she has forgotten why, what she was ever thinking of, when finally at last they find her, Marion Fitts and Leonard and all the doctors and nurses, with Dr. Ripley leading the way as imperious, as impervious, as the prow of a ship. "Come along now, Mrs. Combs," he says to her several times during the next half hour. But Crystal won't come. She stays put and notices a lot of things: some black hairs, an incipient mustache, on Marion Fitts's upper lip; the repeated pattern of fleur-de-lis on Leonard's brown tie; a dark stain low on the wall near the door. One funny thing she notices is that Dr. Ripley is wearing Adidas. She holds the young man's hand.

The day before Crystal leaves Roger, she's sitting on the sofa in her living room, long legs curled under her, while Roger paces the floor and talks and Marion Fitts sits in a wing chair leaning slightly forward, smoking Trues. Just beyond the glass of the picture window, the wind blows and blows. Each time it blows, a shower of bright-colored leaves comes swirling down through the air and scuds along the front walk or settles into the grass. Crystal wants to watch the leaves come down. She wants to read in her journal. But Roger keeps trying to make her pay attention. He has been at it for three whole days, but as far as she can see there is nothing more to be said and nothing to listen to either. Crystal is sleepy. It's over. A burnt-orange leaf sticks flat for a second to the pane of glass and then is gone. There would be noises out there, wind noises, the crackle of dry, blowing leaves. There are no noises at all in the living room. Not even the gas fire in the big brick fireplace makes much noise. No noise at all except for Roger, and occasionally Marion Fitts.

All of Marion Fitts's remarks are addressed to Roger, however. She hasn't spoken to Crystal directly since they brought her back from the hospital tour.

"She doesn't understand a word you're saying," Marion Fitts tells him again. "This is pointless. You'd be far better off following Dr. Ripley's suggestion and letting him take over." Marion Fitts crosses her legs and lights a cigarette. "It's the most humane thing to do at this point. Later, of course . . ."

"*Marion,*" Roger says, a real edge on his voice. "You didn't have to come over here today. In fact, I asked you specifically *not* to come, if you remember correctly. So please, go on in the kitchen and fix yourself a cup of coffee. Go on, now. You know perfectly well that I refuse to have Crystal put in the hospital unless she wants to be put in the hospital. I hope she'll decide to do that. I've made arrangements with Dr. Ripley, Crystal can have wonderful care, but I refuse to commit her. I think Crystal will decide that this is the best thing for her. I hope this will be her decision." Roger never takes his eyes off Crystal, talking for her benefit; he paces in front of the fireplace. Roger looks terrible. In his shirtsleeves, his large forearms are white and pasty. So is his face. He looks haggard, worn out, with eyes like holes in his head. He has stayed home for three days. He has had to cancel five appearances already. The press doesn't know about the young man or the incident at the hospital—nor will they, Roger has made sure of that—but they have asked for a statement regarding the canceled appearances.

"A little rest is probably all she needs," Marion says.

"If you won't fix yourself a cup of coffee, then for God's sake fix me one," Roger tells her.

Marion Fitts gets up, smooths the jacket of her pantsuit, and leaves the room.

Crystal sighs. She opens her journal to read. She yawns once, stretches. Roger stands by the fireplace and watches her closely. It is very odd, but Crystal has never looked better in her life. Her hair is brushed straight back, secured by a barrette. She wears no makeup and her skin is so clear it looks translucent. Her eyes are placid and dark, dark blue. Roger finds it hard to believe she is thirty; she looks more like sixteen, like the dreamy high-school girl she used to be.

She reads:

Another time, two young girls, Kate and Maggie Curtis of Richmond, were visiting their cousin the Paulson girl. Mrs. Paulson, Maggie, and Sarah went out to a revival meeting at Drummond Town. They took the minister home with them to spend the night. There were two nice rooms in the attic. One had two beds in it, and that night Kate Curtis and Charlotte were in one, Mary and I in the other. It was late when they got home and the preacher made some noise pulling off his shoes in the bedroom directly under ours. It woke the girls and they, forgetting the preacher, thought it was someone trying to get in the house. Kate and Charlotte screamed and crawled under their bed; I rolled out and under ours. My bedfellow knew what it was and she just lay there and shook with laughter. Our screams alarmed the family and preacher, too. They all came running to the attic with anything they could catch up handy—brooms and firetongs. We were still under the beds when they took a light up and you may bet we were a sheepish-looking set of girls when we found out the true sense of it all!

Crystal smiles.

Roger comes over to her, takes the journal from her lap and closes it and puts it in the fire.

"I want that," Crystal says, but she makes no move to get it.

"No," Roger says. She watches the journal burn. It goes quickly; its pages are old and crinkled and dry. Roger says, "Crystal. *Baby*. Look at me."

Crystal looks up at Roger. Roger breaks into dry sobs and sinks down beside her on the couch. He buries his head in her lap. Crystal strokes his graying hair absent-mindedly. It's soft, yet sort of bristling, a pleasant sensation. Out in the kitchen Marion Fitts is talking to someone, maybe Mary, maybe Leonard or somebody else. But nobody comes through the door. Out the window leaves are falling. The wind blows. Roger sobs into her skirt.

Then he sits up. "I still don't understand why you did it, Crystal. I just don't understand." This is the hardest part for Roger, who has made it his business to understand things, to accept things. "If you could just tell me, Crystal. Just tell me *why*, baby. I want to understand. I want to help you, that's all. I love you, Crystal."

"I love you too," Crystal says. She looks at him.

"Then tell me. Come on, tell old Roger. I don't *blame* you for anything, Crystal. I'm certainly not holding you responsible. It's all right. Everything is all right. I just want to help you, I just want to know. Did you think you were helping him in some way?"

"No." There is no emotion in her voice. Crystal stares at Roger's face. She thinks suddenly of a short-answer section she gave to her high-school students on their midterm exam, so long ago. "In the following work," she had directed, "identify the hero." Well, Roger is the hero, always was. But she is out of the book. Crystal sighs.

"I need to go home." It's almost the only thing she has said since they found her.

"Think about me," Roger says. "What about me?"

"Believe me, you'll be a whole lot better off," Crystal says flatly. *"You will,"* she adds with more force than she has shown before. "You will, Roger. Believe me. It's all for the best."

"I don't want you to go home!" Roger nearly yells, standing up. "Goddammit, Crystal, you've been there! It's *not home* anymore, don't you understand that? This is home, here, with me. All you need is some medical attention, some rest, and—"

"No, I'm going home."

"Well, by God, if you do, I'll tell you one thing!" Roger is all worked up. He lights one of Marion Fitts's cigarettes; normally, he doesn't smoke. But he has a right to get worked up, by God. He gave up everything for her, everything for this silent girl here on the sofa. He gave it all up and was glad to and then he built it all back, a new life for him and Crystal. For their children, for the family he had hoped they would raise. A house anybody would be proud of, a life anybody would want. "I'll tell you one thing, Crystal. If you go, you're not coming back. I'm not coming to get you. If you go that's it, that's the end of it, it's over. A man has to draw the line somewhere. Now, do you understand that? If you go, you stay."

"I know it," Crystal says. "I will."

"Well," Roger says. He sits back down in the wing chair. "Well, well," he says. He shakes his head, reorienting all his strong features again. "I guess that's that," he says. In three days, Roger has aged years. Still he gets up and comes over to her and kisses her, a long hard kiss. Their dry lips grind together. She is kissing him back, but nothing is left and even Roger knows it.

"OK," he says automatically. "Leonard!" he yells. Leonard appears in the kitchen door, almost as drawn as Roger himself. "I want a drink," Roger says. "Tell Marion I'm changing that coffee to bourbon, all right? Then tell her to go home."

"All right," Leonard says. His big eyes go back and forth between Crystal and Roger.

"Get Al on the phone," Roger says. "Tell him I want him to drive Crystal over to Black Rock in the morning."

Leonard wets his lips. "In terms of the total picture," he says, "I think you're making a big mistake. She's just overtired. She'll be OK."

"I want Crystal to do whatever she wants to do. She's never done that, I think," Roger says, and both men stare at her for a second until they have to look away.

"Right," Leonard says. "I'll get him."

"I want to drive," Crystal says.

"Tell him I want to follow Crystal's car, just to make sure she gets there."

"Right," Leonard says again.

Crystal sits on the sofa until it disappears out from under her and there is nothing there at all and Leonard and Roger are talking and every now and then a leaf blows into the picture window while the wind blows in gusts outside, but she doesn't hear them. She isn't even listening, thinking back to the way the river was when she was little and the way it was even before she was born, the way her daddy said it was, remembering the lightning bugs in summer and the faded floral pattern, red and blue roses, on the rug in the hall upstairs in Nora and Grace's house on

221

Dry Fork. *I will laugh I will sing and my heart will be gay.*
He liked to play blackjack so much. The yellow ghosts
have long thin fingers just like wire, they don't want to
hurt you, though, nobody does. Stop, please. It was because of Iradell they put that stop light there. They will
not see me stopping here, and in summer, in summer how
the sun comes up so late it never hits the flowers
until nearly noon. Crystal yawns.

Agnes can't get over Crystal just coming home, smack
in the middle of the campaign! It goes around and around
in Agnes's head. One day Crystal wasn't there, the next
day she was. This time she came home to stay. Roger Lee
called and called, even though he told Lorene every time
that it was the last time he was calling, but Crystal won't
go back to him. Roger Lee told Lorene that Crystal left
all her diamond rings on the kitchen sink. Roger came
over to Black Rock two times in his Lincoln Continental,
but Crystal locked herself in the bathroom and wouldn't
talk to him, and the last time Odell went out and told
Roger Lee please not to come back. There was a lot of
publicity about it in the paper. Perfect strangers started
calling up on the telephone, until Lorene got a new un-
listed number and put an end to that. Finally it's gotten so
bad that Lorene is having nervous palpitations of the heart
and Odell is worried sick, so Agnes walks over there herself to see what she can do.

Crystal is lying back on the love seat in Lorene's conversation area wearing a frilly old robe of her mother's.
She smokes and looks at the ceiling.

"Well, hello there," Agnes says. Agnes sits down in the
rocker.

"Hello, Agnes," Crystal says. She doesn't seem at all
surprised to see her.

Agnes rocks for a while.

"Don't you think you'd better go on home now and help
Roger Lee run for Congress?" Agnes speaks up after she
thinks she's waited long enough.

"He'll do just fine," Crystal says. Her voice is as flat as
a pancake, Agnes notices.

"What made you come home?" Agnes asks. Sure, she's

222

dying to know, but she thinks she might get at the trouble that way, too. Already Agnes is excited—she knows for a fact that Crystal has talked to her more so far than she has talked to anybody else since she came home. "What made you come?" Agnes asks again.

Crystal raises her head and stares at Agnes, a dark stare which causes Agnes to shift nervously in the rocker.

"Well, it's hard to say, Agnes," Crystal says in her strange flat voice. "I mean, there was this boy in the hospital. He was crazy, I guess, or something, and it turned out that he knew me." Crystal's words come rushing out at first, then slowly die and stop.

"Huh!" Agnes snorts, unbelieving. "That's not much of a reason, if you ask me. Besides, what if he did know you, that's no big deal. He probably saw your picture in the paper, that's all. It's been in there enough."

But Crystal won't talk anymore after that, so Agnes gives up and goes back home. Agnes can't figure out why it upset Crystal so much, whether somebody knew her or whether they didn't. Agnes bets she made the whole thing up in her head. It would be just like her to do that. Agnes's mama is waiting right behind the screen door for the news, but Agnes walks past her without a word.

"Well?" her mama asks, following Agnes into the living room. "Did you see her? What did she say?"

"Nothing, Mama," Agnes answers wearily. "Just a bunch of foolishness, that's all."

The next day is when Crystal paralyzes herself. She just stops moving. She stops talking, stops doing everything. They take her in an ambulance to Charlottesville, and then they send her up to Johns Hopkins in a private plane, and then after a while they bring her back. The doctors can't find any medical reason for it. They say it's all in her mind. Lorene can't see anything that the hospitals have to offer, either, that she can't set up right at home.

So Lorene puts Crystal upstairs in her old room and then she hires two practical nurses, Mrs. Dee and Mrs. Dixon. Mrs. Dee does the day shift and Mrs. Dixon does the night shift. This gives Mrs. Dixon some time in the day to work in her garden. Agnes opens a pizza parlor next door to her hardware store. Sykes's wife Bunny has another baby and names him Odell, which tickles Odell to death. Neva has a hysterectomy. The river comes up again right next to the bottom of the bridge, and the U.S. Army Corps of Engineers says that next time it might cover the courthouse steps and flood the whole town. Odell laughs at the engineers, along with everybody else, the he goes out and buys some flood insurance anyway, the maximum allowed by law. So does Agnes. Better safe than sorry, Agnes says. Babe moves to New York City, marries a stockbroker, and begins appearing regularly in a shampoo commercial on TV. Grace is in the hospital for two months with bronchial pneumonia, and after that they are able to convince Nora and Grace to sell out and take a small apartment downtown over the furniture store, where Grace starts failing fast. Devere is put into the home in Radford. Their old house is razed immediately, and a deep-shaft mine goes down right where it stood.

And Roger Lee? Everybody felt so sorry for Roger Lee that he won that election hands down. Now he's sponsoring a strip-mine bill. When ecology came in, Roger was right on top of it. He divorced Crystal quietly but continues to send a check every month to Lorene, who tears them up one by one. Lorene has turned against him finally, because she has no one else to blame.

"I can take care of my own," Lorene says. "I've always done it and I'll keep on doing it, no thanks to Mr. Big Shot."

"Now, now," Odell says.

But Lorene won't have a thing to do with Roger Lee.

Crystal just lies up there in that room every day, with her bed turned catty-corner so she could look out the window and see Lorene's climbing rambler rose in full bloom on the trellis and the mountain all green beyond the railroad track if she would turn her head. But she won't. She won't lift a finger. She just lies there. Everybody in town takes a fancy to it. Crystal's old uncle Garnett comes and sits with her, resting at each step on the way up the stairs. Garnett reads the Bible to her, although there is no telling if she can hear it or not. Agnes's mama goes up and sits with her, and Susie and Neva, and other ladies in town. People often bring congealed salads to Lorene because once Neva told somebody in the beauty shop that Crystal seems to like them. Crystal can eat, but she has to be fed. The only one she won't eat for is Mrs. Dixon. Some people say why don't they put her in a nursing home, but of course they won't hear of it. "We make out just fine, thank you," Lorene snaps. And truthfully there's not a lot to do, provided Crystal is turned often enough so she doesn't get bed sores. She's no trouble lying there. After a while Lorene and Odell grow accustomed to it and they take a short cruise to the Bahamas. When they come back, everything is just the same as it was when they left. They begin planning a week in Spain.

Agnes goes over there often and sometimes she thinks about how they used to play gin rummy and how they used to sit on the porch, and it strikes her as so sad. It's pitiful how she just lies there. It's a funny thing, but Crystal looks prettier than she ever did. Her hair is growing out and Neva keeps it fixed nice, and Agnes combs it, too, nearly every day. Agnes remembers how Crystal looked so pretty the night she won Miss Black Rock High. She helps Lorene put some of her trophies up where Crystal can see them. Agnes often thinks that if Crystal had married Roger Lee the first time he asked her, if she hadn't gotten all that education and fallen in with hippies, she could be having intimate luncheons for people in Washington right now.

But Agnes is glad she came home. Agnes talks to her a lot, and privately she thinks that Crystal can understand everything she says, even if she won't make a sign. Every day when Agnes comes home from the store she goes over there and sits for a long time. It rests Agnes, sitting in that room, it's so peaceful there. It's always real clean and cool, and Lorene has gotten it fixed up so nice. Agnes tries to keep Crystal up to date: she tells her all about the Burger-O franchise she just bought, and she reads the newspaper to her and the *Reader's Digest*. Agnes never reads her anything about Roger Lee, though. One day Agnes reads her "I Am Joe's Nervous System" out of the *Reader's Digest*, but Crystal's eyelids don't even flicker. A lot of times Agnes just sits and holds her hands, and sometimes she gives her a back rub.

And who knows what will happen in this world? Agnes reflects. Who knows what the future holds? It is not given to us, as Jubal Thacker said just the other day on TV.

Why, Crystal might jump right up from that bed tomorrow and go off and get her Ph.D. or do something else crazy. She's just thirty-two now. Or Jubal might come and heal her. Or she might stay right here and atrophy to death. What Agnes really thinks, though, is that Crystal is happy, that she likes to have Agnes hold her hand and brush her hair, as outside her window the seasons come and go and the colors change on the mountain.

The
Best Modern Fiction
from
BALLANTINE

Available at your bookstore or use this coupon.

___THE COMPANY OF WOMEN, Mary Gordon   29861   2.95
Felicitas, bright, charming and intelligent...raised by five women and a priest...she trades her sheltered purity for a taste of ordinary happiness.

___FINAL PAYMENTS, Mary Gordon   29554   2.75
A compelling love story about a woman who finds herself with what most of us dream of: a chance to create a new existence, but first she must pay for the past.

___CREATION, Gore Vidal   30007   3.95
Set in the Fifth Century B.C., a panoramic view of ancient Persia, India, China and Greece set in the time of Confucius and Socrates.

___THE BLEEDING HEART, Marilyn French   28896   3.50
Tells of the difficulties of achieving true intimacy and understanding between a man and a woman in this day and age.

___ORDINARY PEOPLE, Judith Guest   29132   2.75
The remarkable story about an ordinary family coming together—and apart.

BB   **BALLANTINE MAIL SALES**
Dept. TA, 201 E. 50th St., New York, N.Y. 10022

Please send me the BALLANTINE or DEL REY BOOKS I have checked above. I am enclosing $.......... (add 50¢ per copy to cover postage and handling). Send check or money order — no cash or C.O.D.'s please. Prices and numbers are subject to change without notice.

Name_____

Address_____

City_____State_____Zip Code_____

Allow at least 4 weeks for delivery.